A ROYAL VOW

Abbie stared at Davis' lips, then felt his strong hands on her shoulders, drawing her to him. She didn't resist. She couldn't have resisted even if she wanted to. Their lips touched and Abbie felt the sparks almost before she felt the full contact of his lips on hers. She didn't breathe when his tongue briefly touched her bottom lip, tracing the full line.

Abbie moaned and couldn't wait any longer for him to take her mouth. She turned fully into him and fully pressed her lips against his. She traced the line between his lips with her tongue, silently demanding entrance. Davis opened his mouth and Abbie stuck her tongue inside, tasting the richness and fullness that was Davis. Not the prince or the handyman, but the man who had taken care of her and cared for her for the past three days.

BOOK YOUR PLACE ON OUR WEBSITE
AND MAKE THE ARABESQUE
ROMANCE CONNECTION!

We've created a customized website just for our very special Arabesque readers, where you can get the inside scoop on everything that's going on with Arabesque romance novels.

When you come online, you'll have the exciting opportunity to:

- View covers of upcoming books

- Learn about our future publishing schedule (listed by publication month and author)

- Find out when your favorite authors will be visiting a city near you

- Search for and order backlist books

- Check out author bios and background information

- Send e-mail to your favorite authors

- Join us in weekly chats with authors, readers and other guests

- Get writing guidelines

- AND MUCH MORE!

Visit our website at
http://www.arabesquebooks.com

A ROYAL VOW

TAMARA SNEED

BET Publications, LLC
WWW.BET.COM
WWW.ARABESQUEBOOKS.COM

ARABESQUE BOOKS are published by

BET Publications, LLC
c/o BET BOOKS
One BET Plaza
1900 W Place NE
Washington, D.C. 20018-1211

Copyright © 2001 by Tamara Sneed

All Kensington Titles, Imprints, and Distributed Lines are available at special quantity discounts for bulk purchases for sales promotions, premiums, fund-raising, and educational or institutional use. Special book excerpts or customized printings can also be created to fit specific needs. For details, write or phone the office of the Kensington special sales manager: Kensington Publishing Corp., 850 Third Avenue, New York, NY 10022, attn: Special Sales Department, Phone: 1-800-221-2647.

First Printing: April 2001
10 9 8 7 6 5 4 3 2 1

Printed in the United States of America

ONE

Abbie Barnes closed the door to her apartment unit mailbox, then glanced at her watch. The apartment building lobby was empty, and he was late. She stuck the bundle of advertisements and bills into her purse, then twisted the key in the mailbox again. Only a few more minutes, she told herself, then she would go to her apartment and finish her work. She slammed the mailbox closed and rolled her eyes at her immature behavior. She couldn't wait any longer. She was a busy woman. She had a pile of paperwork and not enough hours in the night to finish it all. The last thing she wanted to do was stand around the empty lobby on a Friday evening and wait for a man.

A very beautiful man, Abbie corrected herself as he finally entered the lobby. She hid her smile as she watched him from the corner of her eye. He was Davis, the repairman for the apartment building. She didn't know if Davis was his first name or his last name. He first started working at the apartment building two months ago, and Abbie had seen him in her dreams every night since. He had smooth caramel-brown skin, large brown eyes, full lips, and wavy black hair. He was tall, with distinctly muscular arms and a well-defined chest that she had ogled, much to her embarrassment, on more than one occasion when he had taken off his shirt on hot days.

Despite being twenty-eight years old and assistant editor

at a local Los Angeles fashion magazine, Abbie gawked at him like a teenage girl would the high school basketball star. Of course, whenever he looked in her direction, she would quickly pretend to look over his shoulder or in the distance.

Abbie had no idea why she acted like a teenager over this man. She wasn't desperate for male company. She turned down most offers for dates because she was always at the office or doing work at home. Although she didn't consider herself supermodel material, she never had a problem finding a date when she wanted one. If Davis had been any other man, she would have started a conversation and, maybe, asked him out, if he gave her the right signs.

But, the problem was that Davis wasn't like other men. There was something different about him. It wasn't just his looks or his lean build. There was something in his eyes that drew her to him. That was why, for the last three weeks, Abbie would speed across town from work, run into the lobby, and pretend to check her mail until Davis walked through the employees' entrance to leave work for the day.

Since Abbie had seen Davis, her day was complete, and she turned toward the bank of elevators that led to the apartments. She stopped in her tracks when she realized that Davis was smiling at her. She decided he was smiling to himself, because in the months since he had been there, he had only politely nodded in acknowledgment when he passed her.

"I am sorry that I'm late," he said, still grinning. Abbie barely registered the unrecognizable accent that tinted his deep, smooth voice. He knew. He knew that she waited for him every evening. Her heart suddenly raced in her chest, and she could feel her hands begin to shake.

"Excuse me?" she croaked, feeling humiliation flush her face.

"A job in an apartment on the third floor took longer than I expected," he explained. "I'm sorry I'm late."

Abbie forced herself to meet his gaze. She realized, to her horror, that he wasn't laughing at her or making fun of her. His wide smile and twinkling eyes told her that he was flattered, or at least amused.

She nervously smoothed errant strands of hair to the bun at the nape of her neck and tried to bluff her way out of the most embarrassing moment of her life. "I have no idea what you're talking about, Mr. Davis. What are you late for?"

"It's only Davis." His deep voice seemed to caress her skin, as his gaze penetrated to her soul. She had a feeling that he could read her mind and that her lie was useless.

"What are you late for, Davis? Or have you confused me with someone else? Although, considering that I'm the only black woman under fifty in this building, I don't think that would be possible, or I hope that's not possible. Unless this is a hint that I should be buying anti-wrinkle cream or . . ." Her voice trailed off as she realized that she was babbling. She always babbled when she was nervous. It was one of her worst habits. She thought she had controlled it in college, but then she hadn't been caught practically stalking a man since college. She firmly announced, "Either way, I don't know what you're talking about."

"It must be my mistake," Davis replied, with a hint of a smile that told Abbie he knew he wasn't mistaken.

With a fake smile pasted on her face, she stumbled across the lobby toward the elevators. She had to escape his intense gaze before she blurted out the truth and humiliated herself more. She hated lying. She cursed herself for not confessing when she had the chance. Maybe Davis would have found it cute in a psychotic way.

"No problem, Mr. Davis—Davis. I have to go."

"You look nice," he said, seemingly in no hurry to end

the conversation. Abbie once more came to an abrupt stop and quickly closed her mouth, which had dropped open. He smiled, but Abbie was too shocked to smile in return. He was flirting with her. Davis was flirting with her, and she had no idea how to respond. His smile grew wider, as if he could read her confused thoughts. She tried to form a complete sentence, but all words fled at his smile. She wanted to tell him that she had interacted with a man before, just never a man that could render her speechless with one smile.

"What?" was the only word in her vocabulary when she finally spoke.

"You look nice," he repeated.

"Thank you," she responded, then stared at his paint-splattered jeans and dirt-smeared green T-shirt. She had never seen a man look more beautiful. Before she could stop herself, she said, "So do you."

Davis laughed and sparks shot through her body. He pointedly looked at his clothes, then he said, shrugging, "Thank you."

He continued to stand in the same position and watch her. Abbie would have liked to end the conversation on a good note, so she didn't seem like a gaping fool, but she couldn't move. She had no control over her body, and it wanted to stay and look at Davis.

Davis continued to stare at her, as if waiting for her to continue. Her eyes drifted to his moist, full lips, and she calculated the distance between them. She forced herself to stop staring at his lips. She took another step toward the elevator, willing her body to cooperate.

"Well, I have—"

"Would you like to have dinner tonight?" he suddenly asked, seemingly unaware of the war raging inside of her.

"With you?"

Davis grinned and answered, "Of course, with me."

"You don't even know my name," she blurted out. She cringed at her own half-question, half-statement.

Davis smiled and simply asked, "What is your name?"

"My name?" Abbie paused as she wracked her brain for her own name. She sighed in relief and said firmly, "Abbie Barnes. My name is Abbie Barnes."

"Abbie Barnes, would you like to have dinner with me?"

"No, I'm sorry."

"Why not?"

Abbie nervously tucked strands of hair behind her left ear and tried to think of a good reason, besides the fact that she only could imagine the disaster of eating food around him. She could picture herself walking out the restaurant with more food on her clothes and face then in her stomach.

She suddenly remembered she did have a legitimate reason. With a relieved smile, she said, "I'm having dinner with my friend tonight."

"He's a lucky man," Davis said. Even though he didn't touch her or come any closer to her, Abbie could almost feel his voice caress her skin.

"My friend's a woman," Abbie quickly corrected him. "We have a standing dinner date once a month because our lives are so busy and if we don't have concrete plans, we'd never see each other. She's a model and she's—" Abbie clamped her mouth closed and vowed not to make even more of a fool of herself in front of this man. She would either have to gain control of herself and remember that she was an adult or move to a different apartment building. "I really have to go. Good-bye."

She refused to look back as she practically ran into the elevator, but she could feel his stare until the elevator doors closed.

* * *

Davis Phillipe Andre Beriyia, crown prince of Juhatu, barely noticed the trash littering the streets of the working-class neighborhood of Los Angeles or the homeless man ambling down the opposite street. Davis didn't notice the light drops of rain falling on his already damp shirt or the cool temperature. All he could see or think about was Abbie Barnes' smile. He had wondered for two months how she would smell if he ever got close enough and tonight he discovered his answer: like the aromatic flower gardens outside the palace walls at home.

He noticed Abbie two months ago when he first applied for the job at her apartment building, and he had thought of little else since that moment. She was even more beautiful up-close than in his dreams at night. She had shoulder-length black hair, amber-colored eyes, honey-colored skin, and full lips. Davis thought she was the most beautiful woman he had ever seen. He realized after the first week of obsessing over her that it wasn't just her looks that drew his attention. It was the fire that burned in her eyes, the way she walked down the street as if she wasn't afraid of anything or anyone.

The last few weeks, he noticed that every time he got off work, Abbie was checking her mail. At first he thought their schedules coincided and he used it as an opportunity to take one last look at her to last for the night. He didn't think she noticed him, since she would never acknowledge his existence. Around the second week, Davis knew it wasn't a coincidence. As a prince, he knew the effect he could have over women, but he never imagined Davis the repairman could influence a woman like Abbie to wait for him.

He didn't know what prompted him to speak to her tonight. He knew it would embarrass her, and maybe humiliate him if he were wrong, but judging from her flushed cheeks and awkward reactions, Davis knew she waited for him. Surprisingly, the idea made him happier than he wanted to admit. For once, a woman liked him for who he was, and not because he was a wealthy prince. Davis hoped she recovered from her embarrassment soon, because he planned to ask her out again and again until she agreed. He smiled to himself as he imagined pursuing a woman, instead of being the one pursued.

Davis reached his apartment building and ran up the stairs to his apartment on the seventh floor. The building was old, dirty, and it probably violated every housing code in Los Angeles, but Davis loved it. Spending his whole life with a twenty-person cleaning crew assigned to his quarters alone, he never realized how much he liked to see dirt and dust, how much he enjoyed throwing a shirt on the floor and finding it still there three days later, how much he even enjoyed emptying his own trash.

Davis unlocked the door to his small, one-bedroom apartment and once more thought of his encounter with Abbie. He loved the idea of getting to know her like a normal man would get to know a normal woman.

Davis stopped smiling when he saw Lowell Murae stiffly sitting in the middle of the couch Davis had bought at a flea market three weeks ago. The idea of Lowell Murae, the chief royal administrator, sitting on a five-dollar couch would have made Davis laugh, if he was able to. The fact that Davis had gone to a flea market was one he would have to take to his grave.

Lowell's chocolate-brown face deepened into disapproval at Davis's barely concealed laughter. Like a towering tree, Hiram Inga stood in the corner of the living room, his massive dark arms crossed over his chest. Hiram had been Davis's bodyguard for the last fifteen years. Judging from Hiram's grave expression, Davis knew he couldn't talk his way out of trouble this time.

"Lowell, Hiram," Davis greeted them soberly. Lowell simply stared at him. Hiram silently nodded.

Davis closed the door behind him and walked into the

kitchen. The silence deepened in the room as Lowell watched him. Davis opened the refrigerator door and waited for Lowell to speak. He refused to break the silence first. He had known they would find him, but he hadn't been prepared for the disappointment that overwhelmed him. Their presence meant he would have to return home.

"It took us two months to find you, Your Highness," Lowell spoke in their native French.

"I had hoped it would take a little longer," Davis replied casually.

Lowell sighed, the long-suffering sound of a loyal servant who spent too much time chasing after his twenty-eight-year-old charge. "You are the crown prince of the sovereign province of Juhatu. You have responsibilities and duties, Your Highness. You can't—"

"Lowell—"

Lowell jumped to his feet, his uppercrust breeding making his outrage almost comical. "Your Highness, do you realize the explanations your father has been forced to make to other dignitaries and the press because of your absence? Your mother had to call in favors to friends from her days in America to find you. This has been a complete embarrassment to the royal family and to the nation of Juhatu. Hiram has been dishonored in front of his superiors and fellow members of the Palace Guard for allowing you to escape his surveillance. I know you are not a child anymore and I don't have the right to scold you, but someone should, and you should feel ashamed of yourself."

Davis rubbed the back of his neck and felt the familiar weight of responsibility practically crush his shoulders. He had known that he could not avoid his life in Juhatu forever, but he had hoped to avoid it for a while. As the only child of the king and queen of Juhatu, Davis had no choice.

"I am sorry, Hiram," Davis said, facing his old friend. "I never meant to cause you any dishonor." Hiram smiled in understanding until Lowell looked at him, then Hiram's expression turned into a censuring scowl. "I apologize to you as well, Lowell."

"We were all very worried, Your Highness," Hiram spoke as Lowell's silence weighed down the apartment.

"There was no need."

"Albert Munji was killed three weeks ago," Hiram continued. Davis hid his surprise and regret at the news. Albert was the leader of the small anti-monarchy group in Juhatu. Not many people paid attention to their position because the economy was good and the Beriyias were loved and respected on the island. However much Albert Munji disagreed with their form of government, he had always been a reasonable and intelligent foe, until eight months ago when his wife died in a car accident. Albert Munji and his only son, Kevin, became convinced the Beriyias were behind Maria Munji's death and vowed to make them pay."

"How?"

"There were rumors he planned to buy chemical weapons from a group in Albania. We tracked him to the caverns on the south shore of Juhatu. There was a gun fight and Albert was killed," Hiram answered.

"I am sorry to hear that. Where is Kevin?" Davis asked Hiram.

"Kevin Munji has not been found. There have been threats made against the lives of the royal family. Now is not the time to test your freedom away from the guards and the safety of the Palace," Hiram responded.

"Allow your father to deal with young Munji," Lowell finally spoke. Davis knew Lowell didn't want to accept his apology, but Lowell never could remain angry at Davis for long. Even when Davis was a child, Lowell would lecture him on his royal duties and the need for decorum, then hand him a toy airplane as soon as the king left the room.

"I am forgiven, Lowell?" Davis asked, hiding his smile.

"You are young and allowed lapses in judgment. As we speak, the jet is being refueled. By early tomorrow morning we will be back in Juhatu where you can be properly disinfected from this filthy city and the substandard conditions of this apartment."

Davis didn't respond to Lowell's assessment of his adopted city and asked instead, "Would either of you like something to eat?"

Lowell merely glared at Davis while Hiram walked into the kitchen. The two men settled on last night's Chinese takeout from the refrigerator. With a combination of disgust and interest on his face, Lowell watched them dig into the box of noodles. Davis wordlessly handed Lowell another fork and pushed a box across the table. Lowell wrinkled his nose in disgust and carefully placed the fork back on the counter.

"If you don't mind my asking, Your Highness, why did you come to America?" Hiram asked.

Davis pointedly looked at Lowell as he said, "I checked my calendar and saw there was nothing urgent or pressing that needed my attention for a while and I decided to take a break. I wanted to try and blend in with everyone else for a while. To see what it would be like."

"You're not like everyone else," Lowell said firmly.

"Lady Sophia was hurt you didn't say goodbye to her," Hiram softly chided him. Davis tried not to groan at the mention of his soon-to-be wife. His parents and her parents had arranged for the two children to be married from birth, along with a mutual exchange of assets and wealth. Davis had only met the woman a few months ago and couldn't imagine spending the rest of his life listening to her talk about her latest shopping trip.

"I'm sure she overcame her disappointment with a

shopping trip," Davis muttered, causing Hiram to choke back his laughter under Lowell's disapproving eye.

"I know the weight of the monarch is not for an ordinary man—" Lowell began.

"I've heard this speech, Lowell. From you, from my father, from anyone who could get close enough to me to say it, for the past twenty-eight years." Davis sighed as Lowell bristled from his harsh tone. "I apologize, Lowell, I should not have yelled at you."

"I know you have a lot to deal with, Your Highness, but running away to the United States is not the answer." Lowell studied Davis with a concerned expression. Davis avoided his eyes and scraped the bottom of the now-empty box. "You need a decent meal and a good night's sleep. Fortunately, I had the foresight to bring clothes suitable for a man of your rank and position. We have time for dinner before the jet will be ready for take-off. You will dress and then we will go to dinner at a decent restaurant."

"If you insist, Lowell." Davis walked into the bathroom and closed the door. He thought of Abbie and wondered how it would have felt to touch her. He sighed because he knew he would never find out.

TWO

Abbie tried to concentrate on the mound of paperwork on the table in front of her. She tried to think about fashion articles and models—anything but Davis. All she could see was his sensual smile. She cursed herself for still thinking about the man, two hours after their two-minute conversation. She wasn't in high school with a crush on the star football quarterback. She was a grown woman who shouldn't be daydreaming about a man like she was a teenager.

She knew nothing about him. She didn't even know what country he was from, why he was in Los Angeles, whether he was a nice man or not. Those were all questions that she could have asked him at dinner, but she had a standing dinner date with her best friend, Chris. Although knowing Chris, Abbie was sure that her friend would have canceled the date herself if she had known Abbie had an offer from a man she had panted after for the last two months.

Abbie sighed relieved as the doorbell rang. She needed to stop dreaming about a man who she barely knew. Abbie quickly ran to open the door and smiled as Chris Andrews breezed into the apartment. The two had met at a magazine party three years ago and had become instant friends. Abbie had met many models through the magazine, but she had never met one like Chris. Chris ate what she wanted, dressed how she wanted, and hated the makeup and strange outfits she was forced to wear. But, with uncontrollable brown curls, almond-tinted skin, hazel eyes, and a body with enough curves to make an hourglass feel shame, Chris was in popular demand in the fashion world. She wasn't on the level of Tyra Banks, but Abbie knew her friend was close.

"I'm glad you're ready because I'm starving," Chris announced, with her usual dramatic flair.

"You're always starving," Abbie muttered, as she closed the apartment door. "And even though you eat enough for the both of us, you never gain one pound. Meanwhile, I gain five pounds, just by watching you eat."

"You look great, Abbie," Chris complimented, getting around to their greeting as she hugged Abbie. Abbie smiled as she squeezed Chris in return. One of the reasons she loved Chris was because Chris always thought Abbie was as beautiful as she was. "How is everything going? I feel like I haven't talked to you in ages."

"Work is good, but I have been feeling tired lately."

Chris was instantly concerned. "Tired? Have you been to the doctor?"

"I'm not sick," Abbie dismissed. "I'm just tired of the same routine, tired of going to work and coming home, tired of paying my bills on time, tired of being predictable. Do you know what I mean?"

"I wish I did," Chris muttered, rolling her eyes. "Within the last week, I've been in Paris, England, and New York. I haven't had time to be bored. . . . Are you sure you're not ill?"

"I'm positive," Abbie said, shaking her head. "Since you're starving, we should go to dinner. You can eat, and I'll watch you eat."

Chris grinned then jumped to her feet. "What we both need is a night out. We need a good dinner, a bottle of wine, and maybe we'll find two handsome men to flirt with."

"I don't flirt."

Chris rolled her eyes then said, "I'll flirt. You can sit there and look angry."

"You flirt about as well as I do," Abbie said, laughing.

"I'll admit that flirting is not my strongest point, but I, at least, talk to the men," Chris pointed out. "Every time we go anywhere and men approach us, you look at them as if they're the scum on the bottom of your shoe."

"That's because the first thing most men say usually involves going back to their apartment and taking off all my clothes."

Chris grinned for a second and Abbie laughed as her friend said, "And there's a problem with that?"

"Yes, Chris. I want a man to, at least, talk to me and get to know me first. I want to be able to tell him my dreams, tell him about myself. I want to be able to look at him and know what he's thinking, when no one else can tell."

Chris sighed. "That sounds beautiful, Abbie. Too bad that man doesn't exist. Men only want one thing, and it doesn't involve long, meaningful conversations."

"I refuse to believe that," Abbie said firmly. "Somewhere out there is one guy who'll care more about me as a person than about sex."

Chris rolled her eyes doubtfully. "Is this why you haven't had a date in six months? Because you're waiting for some man that doesn't exist?

Abbie shook her head at Chris's cynicism. then smiled. "Didn't you just offer to buy me dinner?"

Chris rolled her eyes then nodded. "I'm buying."

Abbie grinned and grabbed her keys from the table.

The two women walked into their usual Italian restaurant near Abbie's apartment. As usual, the majority of the men in the room went through a variety of motions to check out Chris discreetly. Abbie, wearing jeans and a cardigan, barely drew a cursory glance walking behind Chris. They had been friends so long that Abbie no longer noticed the stares or felt jealous of them.

Chris gave the waiter a dazzling smile as the young man handed her a menu. The man flushed then stumbled from the table, without giving Abbie the other menu. Chris shrugged innocently at Abbie then shifted in her seat so they both could read the menu.

"Do you enjoy that, Chris?" Abbie asked, ignoring the offered menu.

"What?"

"Making men act like complete fools."

Chris looked over the menu at Abbie with a surprised smile. "What are you talking about?"

"I'm talking about the waiter. You smiled at him and he lost all common sense."

"What should I do? Stop smiling at people?"

Abbie sighed and twirled the cloth napkin on her lap. She uneasily glanced around the dimly lit room. "I've never had power like that over a man. Even my past boyfriends didn't drool over me like that."

"I see guys act like fools over you all the time. What about Harvey Moore, the guy from accounting? He always became flustered when you walked into the room."

"Harvey liked the idea of Abbie Barnes, but not the real Abbie Barnes. As soon as he realized I had my own opinions and that I wouldn't bow to his, I suddenly wasn't his ideal woman any more."

"But, for a while, he thought you were the moon and stars," Chris said, with a triumphant smile.

"I don't think two weeks counts," Abbie muttered, shaking her head.

Chris set the menu on the table and Abbie groaned at the quizzical look in her eyes. She recognized the look in Chris's eyes. Abbie was about to be officially grilled.

"What's wrong, Abbie?" Chris began. "Since when do you care about men and their opinions about you? You're the one always telling me that our careers are the most important thing in our lives right now. I've been listening to you. Don't tell me you've changed your mind. I actually have to go on dates now and shave my legs?" Abbie laughed at Chris's desperate expression.

"You don't have to do anything, Chris, but I'm wondering if maybe I'm missing something. I like my life. I like my job and my friends and family, but there has to be something more."

Chris slammed her fist on the table and declared, "You're absolutely right, Abbie, and I know this photographer who'd be perfect for you—"

"No."

"You haven't even heard what I'm going to say," Chris protested.

"I know what you're going to say. You want to arrange another blind date for me with some photographer who won't leave you alone."

"Nigel Hawthorne is a kind man. He has a small sweat problem but—"

"Sweat problem? What does that mean?" Abbie asked, not bothering to hide her laughter.

"He sweats a lot . . . Buckets of sweat. He has to change shirts during photo shoots. He has to change shirts when he breathes." The two women began laughing, not caring that everyone in the restaurant was staring at them.

"Excuse me." Abbie froze in her chair as a deep baritone voice traveled down her spine with such familiar ease. She would know that voice anywhere. That voice had haunted her mind since that afternoon.

Even if her body hadn't known it was Davis, Chris's wide eyes and sudden seductive smile said it all. Chris pretended not to notice her effect on the opposite sex, but when it suited her, Chris could turn on all her charm and sex appeal. It had always amused Abbie, until now.

Abbie took a deep breath then turned in her seat and almost fell from the chair. Davis stood like an African god in the soft candlelight of the restaurant wearing a dark, tailored suit. Abbie could tell the suit was expensive from the way it enhanced his already admirable physique. She had only seen Davis in jeans and T-shirts or shorts. She had thought he had been born to give other men an idea of how jeans were supposed to be worn—until she saw him in the suit.

"I thought it was you, Abbie," Davis said in a low voice, as if they were alone in the room. She could feel an embarrassed flush crawl over her face at the heat that burned in his eyes as he assessed her. "I almost didn't recognize you without the suit and briefcase."

"Hello, Davis," Abbie murmured in a weak voice she barely recognized.

"Abbie, who's your friend?" Chris pushed for an introduction, sticking out her ample chest.

Abbie glanced at Chris then back at Davis. For the first time in their friendship, Abbie was jealous. She knew as soon as Davis saw Chris's long legs and heard her silky laugh, he would barely remember her name.

"I'm Davis. I do repairs at Abbie's apartment building," he said to cover Abbie's silence. He offered his hand to Chris who shook it while she gave him the full appraisal. Abbie noticed how long the two held hands and couldn't believe she had to clench the napkin in her lap to fight back the anger.

"Nice to meet you, Davis." Chris's voice had immediately lowered an octave or two to the husky tone she used on handsome men. "I'm Chris Andrews, Abbie's good friend. At least, I thought we were friends. She didn't tell me about you."

Davis extracted his hand from her grip, with a friendly

smile that Abbie liked to think didn't quite reach his eyes. Then she imagined he was too busy trying to figure out the quickest way to get Chris back to his apartment to fully smile. To Abbie's surprise, Davis actually turned from Chris's suddenly visible cleavage and gestured to a man standing behind him. "Abbie, I would like you to meet someone. This is my . . . this is Lowell Murae, a friend of my father's, visiting from our country."

Abbie hadn't even noticed the older, dark-skinned man standing behind Davis. He stood like a tall, thin rod, almost guarding Davis from Abbie and Chris. Abbie immediately smiled at Lowell and shook his hand. There was a firmness about him that was betrayed by the gentleness she saw in his eyes.

"It's nice to meet you, Lowell," Abbie managed, avoiding Davis's eyes. "I'm Abbie Barnes."

"It's a pleasure to make your acquaintance," Lowell replied formally, his accent thicker than Davis's.

"Why don't you two join us?" Chris abruptly suggested.

Abbie glared at her. "Chris, we shouldn't intrude—"

"The restaurant is packed, they'll never find a table." Chris dismissed Abbie's words, then sent a blinding grin at Davis. "Please, I insist you join us."

Davis glanced at Abbie, and Abbie shrugged in acceptance. She watched with curiosity as Davis waited for Lowell to gather two chairs from nearby tables. The two men sat down and Abbie uneasily shifted in her chair as Davis's left knee brushed against her thigh. She ignored the uncomfortable stirring sensation in her stomach at the closeness of Davis and smiled at Lowell.

Lowell appeared to be assessing her until she stared at him, then he quickly looked away. Abbie heard Chris ask Davis about his job and she decided to ignore the budding lovers and coax information from Lowell. "Are you from the Los Angeles area?"

Lowell seemed offended by the question. "I'm from Juhatu."

"The same place as Davis?"

Lowell's eyes slightly widened. "Of course."

"Where is Juhatu?"

"We're a tiny island with a population of half a million off the western coast of France, a little farther south than Monaco. Our main export is minerals, but we also export fruits and vegetables. Our national language is French with a unique admixture of Italian and our people comprise a mixture of French, Italian, and native Juhatuans who were originally from North Africa. We have international trade agreements with—"

"Lowell, you're boring her," Davis interrupted. Abbie was surprised to find Davis listening to their conversation instead of responding to Chris's flirtation.

"No, he's not," Abbie said quickly. "I've never heard of your island before."

"What?" Lowell exclaimed. Abbie stared at him confused.

"We like to keep it a secret," Davis quickly interceded before Abbie could question Lowell. "We have a low crime rate, beautiful unpolluted beaches, and a strong local economy. We like to keep tourism to a minimum."

"Sounds lovely," Chris said with a sigh. "A tropical paradise."

"Your—"

Davis interrupted Lowell. "Lowell, would you say our island is a tropical paradise?"

"As close as one could hope for," Lowell responded dryly.

"Abbie and I take a vacation every summer. Maybe this summer we'll go to Juhatu," Chris said excitedly. "That is, if Davis would agree to be our personal tour guide."

"That could be arranged," Davis said. Abbie quickly looked at Lowell as Davis stared at her. There was something about the way Davis looked at her, as if he could read her private thoughts. Even the ones that involved her pulling him across the table and claiming him as hers in front of Chris.

"I won't be taking a vacation for a while," Abbie said to Lowell, since she couldn't look at Davis without making an idiot of herself.

"Why is that?" Lowell asked politely.

"Work," Chris interrupted. "Abbie doesn't know the meaning of the word *vacation*. The few weeks I have gotten her away from that office, she brings her computer, her modem. . . . She doesn't take a vacation, her office just relocates to a hotel room."

"Maybe Abbie hasn't been to the right place," Davis replied softly, still staring at her.

Abbie felt the heat pool in her face and she immediately stared at the menu in front of her. "The veal looks good."

"I agree," Lowell said. Abbie stared at him surprised and almost choked when he winked at her. She didn't think a man like Lowell was capable of something as frivolous as a wink.

"Davis, you work on Abbie's building?" Chris asked, leaning closer to him.

"He worked," Lowell responded. "Unfortunately, the prince—"

"I have to return home," Davis said. "Lowell, may I speak with you outside for a second?"

"Certainly." Lowell stood and Abbie watched the two men walk out of the restaurant and disappear from view. It was almost amusing how she felt the sudden chill in the restaurant without Davis beside her. Abbie hated herself for feeling helpless, for feeling like she needed Davis to notice how softly the candles glowed in the restaurant, to notice the warm scent of fresh bread in the air.

"That man is incredible," Chris exclaimed, squeezing Abbie's arm. "Why did you keep him a secret for so long?"

"He's a handyman, Chris. I thought you never dated any man who made less than sixty thousand," Abbie reminded her, only half teasing.

"Except when they're gorgeous enough to have their own swimsuit calendar," Chris said, with a gleeful scream. "I want him, Abbie. I want that man."

Abbie forced a smile for her friend then, with a trembling hand, reached for her water glass.

Davis tried not to slam the restaurant door as he followed Lowell outside the building. He also didn't want to break Hiram's nose as the guard followed behind them. He welcomed the feel of the fresh night air to calm his anger. Unlike Juhatu's hot, sultry nights, Los Angeles became ten degrees cooler every night regardless of the temperature of the day. Before speaking, Davis took several deep breaths like he had been taught to prevent irrational outbursts, then glared at Lowell.

Hiram cleared his throat, causing both men to look at him. Hiram indicated the cars speeding on the street in front of the restaurant, as he said, "This is not a safe place for a discussion."

Lowell gestured toward the restaurant. "Maybe we should move inside, Your Highness—"

"Don't call me that, Lowell. If you haven't noticed by now, I don't want that woman to know who I am."

"How would you like me to address you, Your Highness?"

"My name is Davis. Call me Davis."

Lowell's mouth dropped open for a spilt second, which was an eternity for someone like Lowell, who usually refused to show emotion. He finally sputtered, "I don't think I can do that. I can't show such disrespect to you, your father, and the House of Beriyia by calling you anything other than your proper rank and designation. As for those two women, while the one with the nice smile is rather pleasant to look at, the other one with the long nails looks at you like a wild lion would look at an unprotected gazelle."

"I think I'm offended, Lowell," Davis said, smiling in spite of his annoyance. "You're comparing me to a gazelle."

"Your Highness, I suggest we leave this place and find another restaurant. We have an early flight tomorrow and once you get home, you have a very busy schedule awaiting you."

"I want to spend my last night in America with Abbie Barnes."

Lowell stared at Davis confused. "The one with the nice smile? She barely even looks at you. You don't need to crawl on your hands and knees to garner the attention of an African-American woman when the perfectly respectable and pleasant Lady Sophia waits to announce your engagement at home."

"Pleasant?" Davis laughed at the description of Sophia then grinned at Hiram. "Didn't you once tell me that a man has to work for anything worthwhile in life."

"Your Highness has been in this country for too long," Hiram responded, his eyes twinkling.

"I cannot allow this charade to continue," Lowell said stiffly.

"Lowell, when I return to Juhatu I will never have the chance to just be Davis again. Please, Lowell, allow me this one night, then I'll return to Juhatu and do what I must do."

Lowell hesitated then glanced at Hiram, who pointedly stared at the street. "As you wish, Your Highness," Lowell finally muttered.

"Please call me Davis, for the remainder of this evening, Lowell. I promise no one at the palace will ever discover the truth."

Lowell appeared to mull over the statement then nodded reluctantly. "Whatever you wish, Your Highness."

Lowell walked into the restaurant and Davis grabbed Hiram's arm before he followed Lowell. Hiram glanced at him surprised.

"Did you want something, Your Highness?" Hiram asked, carefully.

"If Abbie saw you, it could cause questions that I don't want to answer."

"What exactly are you suggesting, Your Highness?"

"Give us some space."

"Your Highness, I'm not allowed—"

"I'm not asking you to turn a blind eye. I just would appreciate it if you acted like a stranger who happened to be heading in the same direction as we are."

Davis saw a smile tug at Hiram's lips, but then he simply nodded and opened the restaurant door for Davis.

Davis nodded then walked into the restaurant, to Abbie. He saw her, fidgeting with the napkin on the table, looking more beautiful than only five minutes ago. Compared to the made-up face of her friend, Abbie looked natural and fresh. She had a dignity and beauty that her friend could not buy with all the makeup in the world. She looked like an American princess.

With the soft candlelight and classical music breezing through the restaurant, Davis thought he had stepped into paradise when he first saw her in the restaurant. A night that began on a low note, with Lowell's constant reminders of his duties at home, was turning into the best night since he had come to America. If he could leave America with one night with Abbie, then his stay would have been successful.

Davis sat next to Abbie, who ignored him, but smiled

at Lowell. Davis couldn't determine if Abbie had no interest in him, disliked him, or couldn't figure him out. Davis knew he couldn't leave America without finding out.

"Is everything okay?" Chris asked, as she leaned closer to him, giving him a healthy view of her full breasts. Davis glanced at what she offered then smiled politely. He had been all over the world and dealt with a lot of women. He could handle a woman like Chris without lifting a finger.

"Everything's fine," Davis answered then turned to Abbie. "What would you recommend for dinner?"

For some reason, Abbie appeared flustered as she met his eyes. "I . . . I usually get the veal."

"Abbie is definitely not one for experimentation. We come here at least once a month and she gets the veal, each and every time," Chris said. Davis didn't bother to dignify Chris with a glance and continued to stare at Abbie.

"There's something to be said about routine," he murmured. Abbie smiled briefly at him then glanced at her hands. Davis felt his manhood harden at the flush that blossomed on her cheeks.

"I think I'll take the veal, as well," Lowell said then added with a slight smirk, "Davis."

Davis grinned, then signaled the waiter.

Abbie wanted to run from the restaurant. She wanted to run all the way to her apartment and escape the hot stares Davis continued to direct at her. No man had ever made her feel the way Davis made her feel. He made her feel beautiful, desirable, wanted. Abbie always thought she'd want a man to look at her like men looked at Chris but now that it had happened, she was too uncertain and frightened. She now realized that all the times when Davis had been watching her, he had been attracted to her. There was no denying the invitation in his eyes this night.

After dinner, the four headed toward the welcoming fresh air outside the restaurant. Abbie glanced over her shoulder as Davis held the door open for Chris. Lowell followed behind them.

"Thanks for paying for dinner, Davis. That was terrific of you," Chris gushed as she clung to his arm.

Davis once more directed his questioning eyes at Abbie. Ashamed for being caught staring at him, Abbie stared at her hands.

"I owed Abbie a dinner. In fact, I think I also owe her a cup of coffee," Davis responded lightly.

"We'd love to," Chris said, as Abbie began to protest.

"Actually, mademoiselle, I would be delighted to escort you home," Lowell said with a slight bow. Chris glanced at Abbie then back at Davis. Abbie groaned as she recognized the hurt and disappointment in Chris's eyes.

"Davis, you don't owe me anything," Abbie said quickly. "Thanks for the dinner, but—"

"You go on, Abbie," Chris said, with a smile Abbie knew wasn't genuine. "I'm sure Davis can give you a ride home."

"Chris—" Davis took Abbie's arm, effectively interrupting her. "Take your hand off me."

Chris walked across the parking lot, to her car. Abbie yanked her arm from Davis's grip and followed her. She heard Davis and Lowell's footsteps behind her.

"Chris, don't go," Abbie pleaded, as her friend unlocked the driver's door of her car. Chris smiled and Abbie wondered if she imagined her friend's disappointment.

"I'll admit I'm a little jealous, but if I can't have him then I'd rather you have him. Have fun for once in your life, Abbie. Call me as soon as you get home, no matter how late, and tell me everything that happened."

Abbie stepped away from the car and watched Chris

drive from the parking lot. She turned to Davis, her anger and confusion making her chest heave.

Lowell delicately cleared his throat and said, "I think I'll retire for the evening. I'll see you early in the morning, Davis. We have a long trip ahead of us." Lowell turned and walked toward a black limousine, idling in front of the restaurant. As soon as he got inside and closed the door, the limousine drove down the street.

Abbie continued to glare at Davis who returned her gaze with an unreadable look in his eyes. Abbie couldn't handle the silence any more and threw up her hands helplessly and said, "That was really rude, Davis."

"What was rude?" he asked, truly surprised.

"The way you . . . you just dismissed my friend."

"I don't like the way that woman treats you. I think she's jealous of you," he retorted, obviously insulted on Abbie's behalf. Abbie sputtered speechless at his characterization of her relationship with her best friend.

"Chris . . . jealous of me? Are you insane? Have you seen her?"

"What do her looks have to do with the fact that she is jealous of you?"

"With all your great knowledge about women, please tell me what Chris is jealous of." Abbie wished she had never asked the question as she noticed the slight change in his expression. His eyes, slowly but thoroughly, traveled from her head to toes, seemingly taking in every curve and valley. His gaze seemed to burn through her clothes, and she unconsciously crossed her arms over her chest.

"Do you really want me to answer that question, Abbie?" he asked softly.

Abbie nervously dragged her tongue over her lips then, glanced at her watch. "I appreciate the dinner and the offer for coffee, but I'm tired and I'm going home."

"This is my last night in America. I would really like to spend it with you."

Abbie was slightly shocked by the sincerity in his voice but her suspicious nature, honed from years of living with two brothers, activated. She smiled as she said, "For a moment, I actually thought you were telling me the truth."

"Why would I lie?"

"Because most men do when they want something."

Davis smiled and Abbie knew that smile had gotten him many things from many women over the years. "What do I want from you, Abbie Barnes?"

Abbie squared her shoulders and met his eyes. She shook her head and said, "I'm not certain and I don't think I want to find out."

"If you won't allow me to treat you to coffee, may I walk you home?"

In spite of herself, Abbie laughed. She also realized that she was alone with him and hadn't done anything to embarrass herself yet. Armed with her new confidence around him, she shrugged then said, "Sure. Why not?"

Abbie prayed her good fortune would hold out, and they began the long walk toward her apartment. No one walked in Los Angeles, but Abbie wasn't going to tell Davis that.

"Have you always lived in Los Angeles?" he asked.

"I'm a rare breed—a native."

"I must admit that I've been pleasantly surprised by this city," Davis said. "I wish I could stay longer."

"Why don't you?" Abbie glanced at his gorgeous profile.

"Circumstances at home don't allow it. I have responsibilities and obligations that I can't walk away from, as much as I would love to."

"At least you were able to stay here for a little while."

"And I was able to meet you," Davis said softly.

Abbie laughed loudly, making Davis smile. "You are a

smooth one, Davis. Do they have mandatory classes on charm in Juhatu?"

Davis smiled and took her hand. Abbie knew she should've pulled away, but the warmth of his hand compared to the coolness of the night made her hesitant or, at least, that's what she told herself.

"A beautiful woman like you causes a man to say and think many things," Davis responded.

Abbie grinned again, enjoying the heat that spread through her body. "If you aren't careful, you may make me actually like you."

"I'll have to remember not to be careful around you."

Abbie laughed once more, enjoying herself for the first time in months. She impulsively linked her arm through his and switched the subject, "Tell me what Lowell does for a living to have a limousine take him to dinner with his friend's son."

"He's a type of consultant. Tell me more about your job. Chris told me that you worked for a fashion magazine, that was how you two met."

"It sounds more exciting than it really is," Abbie said, laughing. "Some days I think I'm a glorified secretary or receptionist or professional baby-sitter for whatever model or celebrity is in town. Occasionally, I can do my job and edit stories and work with contributors. It's long hours, but I like it." She paused then surprised herself by admitting, "My real dream is to open my own publishing company." She didn't tell many people her aspiration. She had the strange belief that if she told too many people, her dream would never come true.

"Excellent." His one simple exclamation gave her the courage to continue.

"I want to give unknown authors a chance," she continued, in spite of herself.

Abbie hadn't realized they had stopped walking until she found herself staring directly into his eyes. She forgot what she wanted to say next, as she stared at his full lips. Everything about him was perfect, from his lips, to his nose, to his eyes. She wondered if he was just a dream. She wondered if she would wake up on her living room couch, slouched over work, having dreamed this entire night.

"Whatever you want to do, I know you'll do well," he whispered, leaning closer to her.

Abbie tore herself from the depths of his brown eyes as she saw a black van wildly careen around the corner at the end of the street. Davis turned at the sound of the screeching tires then grabbed her arm as the van jumped the sidewalk and squealed to a stop in front of them. The door slid open and three men dressed in all black, with ski masks over their faces, jumped from the back carrying large machine guns.

Abbie felt fear squeeze her heart and she instinctively moved closer to Davis. Davis pushed her away from him.

"Run!" he screamed at the top of his lungs and lunged at the closest man. Abbie was unable to move. She was frozen with fear and disbelief. Davis kicked another man in the stomach and glanced at her. She could see the panic and fear in his eyes. "Abbie, run!" he commanded.

Abbie gasped as the third man rammed the butt of his gun into Davis's midsection. Davis bent over in pain and the second man kicked him in the face, causing him to fall to the ground. Abbie felt the pain, almost as if she had been kicked herself. She didn't think, but reacted, and she jumped on the back of the man who pointed a gun at Davis. She dug her nails into his eyes through the mask and heard him yell.

From the corner of her eyes, Abbie saw a large dark-skinned man sprint toward the group from across the street with a gun in his hands. He shot the gun and one man fell off Davis. Another gun appeared through the driver's window and shot at the other man. He stumbled and fell to the street, completely still.

Abbie screamed as the man she clung to rammed his back, and consequently her, against the solid wall of the van. She abruptly released him as the breath momentarily left her body. She slid to the ground and saw Davis collapse to the ground unconscious, before she closed her eyes and surrendered to the darkness.

THREE

Even before Davis opened his eyes, he could feel a dull pain radiating from the right side of his face. He tentatively felt the area and winced in pain from the touch of his own fingers on the sensitive spot. He checked his body for any further injuries and was grateful that his hands and feet responded. Davis finally forced his eyes open and squinted from the bright sunlight that filled the empty, carpeted room. He rubbed his eyes to clear the double vision, then he noticed the swaying motion of the room.

Davis stood from his position on the floor and stumbled to the small, round window. For miles and miles, all he saw was crystal-blue water and the white foam that flew from underneath the speeding boat he was now a passenger on. Davis groaned and hit the plastic window in frustration. He struggled to open the window but there was no latch, no opening. He suddenly heard a groan behind him and whirled around, prepared for an assault.

Davis's heart sank. Abbie lay on the floor in the far corner of the room. He quickly ran to her side as she struggled to sit upright. She focused on him, confusion and the first sign of fear apparent in her eyes. Davis called himself every dirty name he knew, in both English and French, for allowing her to be caught. He didn't know where they were, where they were headed, or who had captured them. And because of him, Abbie was involved too.

Davis gently smoothed hair from her face until she moved from his hands. She shook her head, obviously trying to clear away the cobwebs.

"What happened?" she murmured, rubbing the back of her neck.

"You didn't run." Davis knew his voice sounded more harsh than he intended but he was too angry with himself to care about her narrowed eyes. "I'd say we've been kidnapped."

"Kidnapped," Abbie repeated, standing. She limped across the room to the cabin door and pulled helplessly on the knob. She grimaced and weakly pounded on the door. "I feel so groggy."

"I think they pumped us full of drugs before they transferred us to this boat." Davis stood and walked to the window, motioning to the ocean.

Abbie joined him at the window. "Where are they taking us? Do you think we're still in America? Do you think the drugs will have any side effects? I think I'm allergic to penicillin. Is that a drug kidnappers would normally use?"

Davis hit the wall in frustration and paced the length of the room. "I don't know. I don't know. Stop asking me questions I can't answer."

"Who am I supposed to ask, Davis?"

Davis heard the anger in her voice and he glanced at her. She never looked more beautiful. Even with the groggy look in her eyes, her mussed hair, and torn shirt, Davis became aroused just by looking at her. Then he noticed her grimace and place a hand on her lower back as she tried to stretch, and he remembered she was in pain because of him. He should have listened to Lowell and left her in the restaurant. Then she would be safe at home, instead of trapped on a boat with him.

"Are you okay?" He hid the worry from his voice, but he watched her.

"My back hurts."

"We have to get out of here." He stated the obvious. Davis pulled on the door knob, his anger increasing as the door refused to budge. He released a string of curses, surprising himself by his lack of composure. He was supposed to be prepared for this situation. He was supposed to be calm and rational, not insane with worry. He turned to Abbie to apologize for his language, but she didn't appear to be listening to him.

Abbie finally looked at him and admitted with a sigh, "I'm sorry, Davis, but you're here because of me."

Davis would have laughed, if she didn't look so serious. "Why would you think that?" he finally asked, when he noticed her expression didn't change.

"One of my brothers is an undercover DEA agent. Obviously, someone's trying to get to him through me. Because you were with me, you were taken too."

"That's an interesting theory," Davis muttered, not hiding his smile.

"Why are you laughing?" she asked angrily, crossing her arms over her chest. "You don't believe my brother works for the Drug Enforcement Agency? He does, and with his attitude, I'm certain he's angered a lot of people."

Davis didn't answer as he heard a key jiggle in the knob. He quickly stood in front of Abbie, who angrily pushed him aside. Davis temporarily forgot whoever was on the verge of entering the room and glared at her.

"What the hell are you doing?" Abbie demanded.

"I'm trying to protect you."

"Protect me?" One of her eyebrows raised in disbelief. "How are you going to protect me?"

Davis felt his anger increase another notch. "I wouldn't have to worry about it, if you had run when I told you to run."

She didn't respond as a painfully thin man, with a reddish tint to his brown skin, entered the room. He carried a tray of food, which made Davis realize how hungry he was. Another larger man, holding a semi-automatic weapon, stood in the doorway and glared at Davis and Abbie. Davis didn't recognize either man as someone from Juhatu or one of the people he had met or talked to in America. Davis cursed himself even more for his impulsiveness and impracticality. He had made himself a sitting duck for any lunatic, who wanted to use him as a pawn against his kingdom.

The small man bowed as he set the tray on the floor in a corner of the room. "Your Highness, I apologize for the sparse accommodations," he whispered in Davis's native French.

"What did he say," Abbie whispered to Davis, glancing at the small man.

"I am Pasel," the man continued. "I am the cook on this boat."

"Where are we going?"

"I'm afraid I can't answer that question, Your Highness." The man wouldn't look Davis in the eyes. Pasel's distinctive Juhatuan French accent and his recognition of Davis's title made Davis realize these men were from his country. The thought that his own people would betray him sickened him.

"What do you people want of me?" Davis demanded.

"Your Highness, please don't ask me such questions."

Davis balled his fists in frustration then noticed the guard in the doorway, staring at Abbie's breasts. Davis glared at the guard, until the man cleared his throat and looked at the ground. Davis knew the only protection he could give Abbie was the awe and respect his position inspired in people. He hoped these men wouldn't realize that he was flesh and blood, just like them, until Abbie was safely off the boat. Davis looked back at the cowering chef.

"I demand to see the leader of this doomed operation."

"That's not possible, Your Highness, I'm sorry," Pasel replied, still avoiding Davis's eyes.

"I refuse to accept your apology. Tell Kevin that I wish to see him." Davis had only taken a guess but judging from the chef's suddenly wide eyes, Davis was right. Davis knew Kevin Munji would not allow his father's death to pass without some retaliation on his part. He could only guess what thoughts were brewing in Kevin's arguably insane mind.

"Your Highness?" the chef croaked.

"He'll see me."

The chef quickly bowed at Davis then ran from the room. The guard took one last lascivious stare at Abbie then closed the door.

"Did that man just bow to you?" Abbie questioned amazed.

Davis tucked his shirt into his pants and straightened his tie, trying to ignore the confusion on her face. He wanted nothing more than to take Abbie into his arms and pretend they were anywhere but on a boat with a deranged lunatic, but he couldn't. He had to deal with Kevin, save his kingdom and Abbie, all while trying not to be killed himself.

Davis reached into his pants, ignoring Abbie's shocked expression. To his relief, none of the guards had bothered to search him. The long knife he always kept attached to his right thigh still rested in the sheath. Davis pulled the knife out and Abbie gasped, staring at him with wonder. Davis tried not to notice the unease on her face, or the panic in his stomach at the thought of her having to wield a knife because of him. He pressed the knife into her cold hands.

"When I leave, knock on the door and ask the guard to take you to the rest room. When he leads you to the bathroom, make certain you stand behind him. Press the knife here." He placed his hand against the jugular vein on her soft neck. A soft sigh escaped her lips and Davis couldn't help but caress her neck, reveling in the soft feel of her skin. He had felt women before, but for some reason, he couldn't remember any woman feeling as soft as her, any woman whose lips alone drove him insane with want. He noticed the dark passion fill her eyes and mingle with the fear. That fear made Davis clear his throat and continue. "You have to be quick, Abbie. That guard wasn't a professional. I could tell by how he held his gun, but you have to be quick because he's bigger and stronger. Take his gun—"

"I can't—"

Davis placed his fingers on her lips to stop her protests. "You have to. Take his gun and lock him in the bathroom. Be very quick, before he has time to think about it. There has to be a small dinghy somewhere in the back of the boat. Get on the dinghy and get as far away from here as possible. Understand?"

"I can't do that," she whispered.

Davis grabbed her shoulders and slightly shook her. He welcomed the anger in her eyes. If she was angry, maybe she would leave without another thought about him. "There's no other option, Abbie."

"I'm can't run and leave you here—"

"You have to. We may not have another chance like this and without you here, I can concentrate on escaping myself."

"How can you escape if I take the only extra boat?"

Davis gently squeezed her shoulders as the volume of her voice increased. "Lower your voice," he whispered through clenched teeth, glancing at the closed door. "You don't want everyone on the boat to know our plan."

"I can't leave without you."

"You have no obligation to me," Davis spat out. He saw a strange expression cross her face and she moved from his grip. Davis physically felt the loss, but forced his clenched fists into his pockets. "Besides, I'll move faster on my own."

"So I'll just slow you down, is that right?" she asked softly. Davis could hear the steel underneath her voice.

"No, Abbie—" The door swung open and the same guard as before motioned for Davis. Davis looked back at Abbie, willing her to understand. She met his eyes and simply nodded then walked to the window. Davis hesitated then walked out of the room. He glanced back at her one last time as the guard closed the door and locked it.

The guard roughly grabbed Davis's arms and led him up a narrow hallway. Davis took in as many details of the boat as he could. The brightness of the sun, compared to the shadows of his room, caused Davis to squint when he finally reached the deck and the fresh sea air. Davis glanced around the large luxury boat. The vast blueness of ocean as far as the eye could see dashed any hopes of jumping overboard and swimming to shore. There were also two men, with pistols tucked in their pants' waistbands, playing cards near the bow of the boat. Their complete attention on their card game boded well for Abbie.

The guard pushed Davis from his still position and toward the door that led to the observation room. The two entered a narrow hallway and Davis could hear voices from an open door a few feet ahead of them. The obvious wealth of the boat confirmed for Davis that Kevin Munji was definitely involved.

"That woman is yours?" the guard asked in French. Davis refused to answer him. "She must keep you warm at night. We've been at sea for a while. Me and some of the others are missing our women."

Davis did look at him and saw the lust in his eyes. "You touch her and I'll kill you."

The man pressed the nozzle of the gun into Davis's neck, pressing Davis against the wall in the narrow hallway. The man coldly smiled as he leaned closer to Davis. "I have the gun here."

After hours of training with Hiram, Davis was prepared for this exact scenario. He drove his elbow into the guard's stomach, causing the man to grunt in pain. Before he could recover, Davis grabbed the man around the neck and turned, slamming him into the wall. The guard struggled, trying to scream, but Davis's hand around his neck cut off any air to his throat. Davis was just reaching for the gun the guard had dropped when he felt the cold steel of a gun nozzle on the back of his neck.

"I wouldn't if I were you, Your Highness," came a quiet voice at his ear.

Davis muttered a curse then reluctantly moved away from the guard, who fell to the ground, gasping for air. Davis turned to face the second man, who was much more careful about keeping distance between them.

"Bravo, Davis," came a cheerful voice from inside the room. Davis walked into the room, ignoring both guards, as he recognized the cultured voice of Kevin Munji, who lounged on a plush couch in the middle of the opulent room as if he were a king. Many women thought Kevin was handsome with vanilla-colored skin, black curls, green eyes and wide, full lips but sooner or later Kevin's mask of good graces would slip and the women would see the true madman that lived underneath the facade. "I knew Adrian was too inexperienced to guard you. You didn't disappoint me."

Davis would have charged at Kevin at that exact moment if it weren't for one man who sat in the corner of the room, with a gun resting in his lap. Davis knew they wouldn't kill him yet but they could definitely make life uncomfortable for him. For that reason, he stood his ground and waited.

With a friendly smile, Kevin stood from the couch and

held his arms out to Davis. Davis gritted his teeth in disbelief as Kevin embraced him.

"You look well, Davis," Kevin said, grinning. He motioned to the couch then sat down himself. Davis remained standing. "You certainly have gained that royal stare. That look that tells an average man, you're better than him, because you were next in line in heaven when the Beriyia House needed a baby boy."

Davis heard the familiar jealousy in Kevin s voice. Ever since they were children, Kevin had never been able to successfully hide his envy of Davis. Even though Kevin did the same things as Davis, went to the same schools, traveled to the same places, tried to be with the same women, things had always been harder for him. People naturally didn't trust Kevin, didn't like him, while most people felt like they had to, at least, accept a crowned prince. And while Davis tried to avoid the fame that went with his title, Kevin sought a portion of it every day of his life.

"Whatever you hope to accomplish by taking me, Kevin, it won't work. My father will know you're responsible if anything happens to me," Davis finally spoke. Kevin glanced up at Davis then abruptly stood and moved to the bar, obviously uncomfortable with Davis looming over him.

"The beauty of my plan is I want your father to know exactly who is responsible for his son's disappearance and, if need be, death."

"Why?"

"I want your father to admit his responsibility in my parents' deaths and recognize the Munjis as the true line to the throne."

Davis shook his head, amazed by the man's warped mind. "Your mother died in a car accident, Kevin. No one in the palace had anything to do with it. And I am sorry for your father's death, but there were confirmed reports that he was negotiating for chemical weapons—"

"Telling lies will only make me angry," Kevin warned in a tight voice.

"Your father spent half his life trying to turn Juhatu into a representative democracy like America. He would roll in his grave if he knew a Munji sat at the head of the institution he wanted to abolish."

"You know, as well as anyone, my father wanted the throne for himself. I know you better than you know yourself, Davis. Don't play coy with me."

"I won't allow you to use me as a bargaining chip to terrorize my family."

"You're confident for a man in the middle of the ocean with several guns pointed at his head."

"Since you know me so well, you must know I'll do what is necessary to protect my family's honor and the throne of Juhatu." The two men stared at each other for an interminably long period of time. Davis saw the recognition and belief in Kevin's eyes.

Kevin finally smiled, breaking the tense moment, and indicated the array of bottles of alcohol on the bar. "Would you care for something to drink?"

Davis continued, ignoring Kevin's offer. "My suggestion is for you to jump off this boat into the ocean and pray a shark eats you before anyone in Juhatu finds out what you've done."

Kevin laughed then looked at the two guards, who obligingly laughed with him. "I thought they taught you negotiating skills in those how-to-be-a-prince classes you took as a child."

"I had very knowledgeable tutors. The first lesson I learned was never negotiate with a crazy man."

A glint entered Kevin's green eyes and Davis prepared himself for a blow. There was a tense silence in the room as the guards seemed to cringe, waiting for Kevin to explode. Kevin abruptly smiled and patted Davis's shoulder. "I forgot what a formidable debating partner you are."

"At the very least, before someone truly is hurt, release the American woman to safety."

Kevin took a sip of the dark liquid in the glass and made a show of thoroughly enjoying it before he finally looked at Davis. "The American woman . . . I'd almost forgotten about her. She's really beautiful but then you always did surround yourself with magnificent women. Nothing but the best for His Royal Highness. Isn't that right, Davis?"

"There's no need to drag her into this. She means nothing to me."

"Oh, really?" Kevin said doubtfully. "In that case, you wouldn't mind if I had dinner with her tonight."

"She's a friend I met in Los Angeles. She has nothing to do with Juhatu or our political problems."

"For someone who you don't care about, you are rather persistent about her freedom."

"I can accept your illogical explanations about my capture but not hers," Davis lied. He quickly glanced out the galley windows, half expecting to see Abbie run past. He hoped she wouldn't stubbornly refuse to leave. Then he remembered her angry expression as she watched him leave the cabin. She probably flew onto the dinghy without a second thought of him. He tried to ignore the loneliness and rejection that followed that image.

"When I'm eating lobster tonight with the woman, I'll see what her story is," Kevin said then smiled again. "Who knows? After an evening with me, she may not want to leave."

Davis tried not to laugh as he imagined Abbie sitting across the dinner table from her captor. Davis almost felt an obligation to warn Kevin. Instead, he murmured, "We all can dream, Kevin."

"Do you think only you can charm a woman like her? Do you think she wouldn't have time for an ordinary man like me?"

"There's nothing ordinary about you, Kevin," Davis replied, which Kevin took as a compliment and smiled accordingly.

"Thank you, Davis. You're full of compliments today. Maybe I should've allowed you to teach Adrian the lesson he deserves." Kevin turned back to the bar.

Davis looked behind him for the towering guard and a ball of fear lodged in his stomach. The guard, Adrian, no longer stood behind him. Davis looked out the windows and only saw the two men still playing their card game. Adrian was nowhere in sight. Davis remembered the look in Adrian's eyes when he looked at Abbie.

"Where is the coward?" Davis asked carefully.

"Probably licking his wounds," Kevin dismissed. "By the way, I've seen your betrothed, the lovely Lady Sophia. Does our lovely American bundle know about her?"

Davis's heart froze but he kept his voice carefully neutral. "Of course."

Kevin turned to Davis with an attempt at a smile. "You always did have luck with the women." Davis hoped Kevin never figured out how unlucky he had been with Abbie.

Abbie stood in the middle of the room for a few seconds after Davis left, still trying to comprehend what exactly had happened since she woke up with a head that felt the size of a melon. The tiny man that had brought them food had acted as if Davis were royalty. He had bowed in his presence. Abbie remembered Davis's own reaction. He hadn't been surprised or embarrassed, almost as if he were accustomed to such treatment.

Abbie shook her head and sank to the floor. Her entire body still screamed in pain. She was tired, hurt and, now, she was confused. She didn't know what to think. She was in the middle of the ocean, locked in a room with a man who she had thought was a simple handyman but who wasn't surprised when peopled bowed to him. The only explanation she could come up with was there must have been some sort of mistake. These men weren't her brother's enemies but obviously thought Davis was someone important. Abbie knew once Davis explained the truth, they'd be released.

Abbie laughed to herself at the impossibility of the idea. These men didn't look like they'd laugh and stop at the closest harbor and wave goodbye to Abbie and Davis. Either way she and Davis would be hurt unless they escaped. Hurt or dead. Tears filled her eyes and she cursed herself. She never cried. She refused to start now. She suddenly remembered the knife that she unconsciously clutched in her hands.

Abbie stood as she remembered Davis's plan. He wanted her to escape and she would. She'd go straight to the police and lead them back to Davis. Abbie ran to the door but stopped herself. She couldn't leave Davis. She remembered the image in Los Angeles of the man running across the street to help them and the way his body jerked when he was shot. Abbie would not leave Davis with these murderers. She would still try to escape but now she would take a detour to find Davis.

Abbie raised her hand to knock on the door when it suddenly swung open. She stumbled from the entrance, hiding the knife behind her back, as the man who made her skin crawl stood in the doorway.

"I was just about to knock on the door," Abbie said in an overly cheerful voice. "I need to use the bathroom."

The man stared at her, uncomprehending. He moved into the room and closed the door behind him. Abbie felt a ball of fear lodge in her throat but she tried not to show it. She gripped the handle of the knife tighter. "Um . . . You speak French, right?" She tried to remember her high school French classes from more than ten years ago and said, "Est-ce que je pourrais aller aux toilettes?"

"No," the man said with a sneer that made Abbie take

a few steps away from him. He said in broken English, "You are very pretty, no? I am Adrian and I want you."

Abbie could hear her heart thud in her chest. She took another step away from him and bumped into the wall. "Please, no."

With a quickness that made her scream, Adrian moved across the room and held his gun underneath her chin as he ripped open her cardigan. Abbie gasped as buttons from her cardigan flew onto the floor and the cool air of the room hit her bare chest, now only covered by her bra.

"Beautiful woman," the man said, licking his lips.

He reached for her and Abbie drove her knee into his groin, as hard as she could. He groaned in pain and bent over. Abbie pushed him and he fell to the ground. She ran to the door and tugged on the knob, which wouldn't turn. Abbie hadn't realized she was crying until she felt the salty tears on her lips. She screamed as the man, still on the ground, grabbed her ankle.

Abbie grunted in pain as he pulled her to the ground and she landed on the floor with a violent thud. She lost her grip on the knife, which flew to the ground and landed unnoticed by Adrian, next to his feet. She pounded her fists on his chest as he dragged her under him. She could feel his heavy weight practically squeeze the breath from her body as his hot breath thundered on her face. Abbie tried to push him from her but she might as well have been battling a brick wall. The man no longer smiled but looked ready to strangle her.

"You shouldn't have done that, *belle*," he muttered.

In one motion, Abbie grabbed the knife from the floor and swung it at Adrian's face. Adrian screamed as a thin line of blood crossed his face where the knife had dug in. He ripped the knife from her hands and threw it against the wall, then turned to her with rage brewing across his face.

Abbie screamed just as the door flew open, bouncing

against the wall. Abbie didn't have time to think as Adrian was pulled off her and thrown against a nearby wall. There was a sickening crack as his head hit the wall. He crumpled to the floor unconscious. Abbie stared at Davis in relief as he stood over her, the anger still apparent in his eyes and his heaving chest. Davis grabbed her arms, and pulled her from the floor to her feet. She had never been so happy to see someone in her entire life.

Abbie moved to throw her arms around Davis until she noticed a handsome man, wearing a tailored suit, standing behind him. The man stared at her as if she was a curious lab experiment. She quickly pulled the halves of her torn sweater together and wrapped her arms around herself.

"What the hell is going on?" Davis demanded. He stormed across the room and picked up the unconscious man. "Is this who you hired, Kevin? Is this who mans your great liberation force?"

The man named Kevin pulled off his suit jacket and offered it to Abbie. She hesitantly took it from him then glanced at Davis who watched her with an unrecognizable expression in his eyes.

"I apologize for my comrade," Kevin said softly. "I assure you he will be punished."

"This is why you must let her go, Kevin," Davis said, standing beside her. "Detaining her on a boat full of men only invites disaster."

"I, personally, guarantee no man shall harm her while she sails with me." Kevin motioned to two men standing in the hallway and the men walked into the room and pulled Adrian out. Abbie watched Davis stand in the corner of the room, as far away from her as possible. She tried not to feel hurt. She cursed herself for needing Davis to comfort her.

"I can arrange for you to have other clothes. If you'll follow me," Kevin spoke to Abbie as if they stood in the middle of a country club.

Abbie remained in her spot, holding the coat tightly. "Wait . . . I think there's been some mistake about our identities. I think you're under the mistaken assumption that Davis is royalty or something. He's not. He's a handyman at my apartment building and I'm an assistant editor for a magazine. If you'll just drop us on the nearest populated island, we can all forget this little incident occurred."

Kevin laughed, thoroughly amused. Abbie looked at Davis confused. He simply stared at Kevin. "She doesn't know, Davis? You were playing the role of a handyman? You were playing the pauper? What would your subjects in Juhatu think?"

"What are you talking about?" Abbie demanded then glared at Davis. "Davis, tell him the truth. Tell him who you really are."

Davis looked her directly in the eyes and said softly, "I am the crown prince of the House of Beriyia, of Juhatu."

Abbie forgot about the attack, the fact that she was in the most dangerous situation in her life, the fact that no one knew where she was. She only felt the betrayal in her heart as she realized Davis had lied to her. "What?" she whispered more to herself as tears filled her eyes.

She felt a hand on her shoulder and looked at Kevin. She stepped away from him, barely registering the anger that flashed through his eyes. "You're upset at the prince's dishonesty and I don't blame you. Please have dinner with me tonight and in the morning we'll drop you off at the nearest harbor." Kevin walked out of the door and waited patiently for her on the other side of the threshold.

"Don't trust him, Abbie," Davis said.

"I haven't lied to her, Davis," Kevin said smoothly. "It seems that of the two of us, it's you she can't trust."

Abbie looked at Davis, expecting him to protest or defend himself. He only stared back at her, not apologizing or explaining. Abbie shook her head, then walked out of the room. Another man with a gun closed the door then stood in front of it.

"Follow me, Abbie," Kevin said with a friendly smile. Abbie glanced at the door once more then followed Kevin down a narrow hallway. He unlocked a door with a key and opened it. With a tired sigh, Abbie noticed the plush bed that dominated the small room. She hadn't realized how tired she was until she saw the bed. Abbie tried to hide her fatigue as she turned to Kevin. He smiled gently, almost as if he knew what she thought.

"There's a bathroom through that door. You may take a shower and utilize all the amenities and you'll find clothes in the closest. They're my clothes and probably will hang off you but it'll be an improvement over a torn sweater. Dinner will be served in two hours."

Abbie barely heard a word Kevin said as she thought of Davis as a prince. "Is he really the prince of Juhatu?"

"I'm afraid so."

"And that's why you kidnapped him?"

"Among other reasons."

"What do you expect to achieve by holding him? Most nations refuse to deal with terrorists and I doubt Juhatu is any different." Once more Abbie saw his features tighten before he smiled.

"I'm not a terrorist, Abbie, I'm a freedom fighter. Besides, Davis is the only child of the king and queen, the heir to the throne. They will do whatever is necessary to guarantee his safe return." Kevin moved to the window to pull back the curtains and smiled at the ocean view. "Gorgeous, isn't it? The open ocean on an early evening. There's not a better sight in the world."

"What exactly are your demands?"

Kevin sighed, obviously bored with the subject. "I want the people to know who their monarch really is—a murderer. The King of Juhatu killed my mother and when my father came close to finding the evidence to indict him, he was killed."

"Why would the king kill your mother?"

"The Munjis are the true rulers of Juhatu. The king was warning us. He knows if we told the people of Juhatu about our legitimate claim to the throne, the people would overthrow him in seconds."

"By kidnapping Davis, you think his father will hand over the throne?"

"I know King Henry, Abbie. I've studied him for years. It will tear him apart to think that any harm would come to his son. He'll do whatever I want him to do, as long as I have Davis."

Abbie shuddered and wrapped her arms around herself. She didn't know what the truth was, if Kevin had a legitimate argument with the royal family or if he was maniacal. Abbie only knew that any man who raised Davis couldn't be capable of murder. It wasn't much to base her convictions on but it was all she had. "You aren't going to hurt Davis, are you?"

"He's no good to me injured or killed. I definitely don't want to make him a martyr." Abbie released the breath of air she didn't know she held. "Enough of this depressing talk. Dinner will be served at 7:30, until then, please relax." Kevin hesitated then walked from the room, closing the door.

Abbie ran to the door and pounded the solid wood in frustration as she heard the lock engage from the outside. She began to do the one thing she vowed she wouldn't do—cry.

FOUR

"You still look tired," Kevin remarked as Abbie walked into the dining room. Abbie smiled uneasily at him as the large man at her side shifted his gun out of the way in order to pull out a chair at the polished wood dining table. Abbie sat in the seat and met Kevin's smug expression. If the two had been sitting in a restaurant in Los Angeles, Abbie would have thrown a glass of champagne in his overconfident face and stormed from the restaurant.

But, they weren't in Los Angeles and Abbie couldn't storm anywhere. She also hadn't been able to sleep since all she could think about was Davis alone in the room. She didn't know why she cared. He obviously thought she was another stupid American who he could have a good time with then tell his friends back home about how she fell in love with him. Abbie tried to hate him but the one person she wanted to see at that exact moment was Davis.

"This is a beautiful boat," Abbie said as Pasel set plates of salad in front of them. "Is it yours?"

Kevin smiled and winked at her. "You know I can't answer that question, Abbie. When we release you, I can't have you leading the authorities directly to me."

"Where exactly will you be releasing me?"

Kevin laughed and poured bubbling, clear liquid from a champagne bottle into the long-stemmed glass in front of her. "You are clever, Abbie. No wonder Davis deemed you worthy of his company. How exactly do you two know each other? You mentioned he was a handyman. What is that?"

"I don't want to talk about Davis."

"He really affected you, didn't he? Were you in love with him?"

Abbie glared at him and set her fork down on the plate. "Even if I was that's none of your business."

"Are you so in love with him that you couldn't give another man a chance?"

"I never said I was in love with him."

"You have to know His Royal Highness would never be serious about someone like you. You're a nobody in the grand scheme of things. You hold no rank, no title, you don't even have money. To someone like Davis and his parents, you may as well not exist."

Abbie refused to allow Kevin to know how much the truth hurt her. She glared at him. "Thank you for your concern, Kevin."

"I would like to do an experiment," Kevin continued, as if she had never spoken. "I consider myself something of a scientist, a subject that Davis has absolutely no knowledge of. I bet I could take your mind off Davis."

"I don't want any part of your experiment. In fact, I've lost my appetite. I'd like to go back to the room." Abbie tried to stand but the guard immediately came to her side and placed a restraining hand on her shoulder.

"You seem to be under the mistaken presumption that you have a choice in the matter."

"You promised no harm would come to me on this boat."

"And I'm a man of my word. What harm would come from a simple dinner with Davis and me?"

"I don't want to have dinner with you, Davis, or anyone else," Abbie said as calmly as possible.

Kevin shook his head, obviously amused by her. "Byron, please bring Davis for dinner." The guard immediately disappeared and Kevin clapped his hands. The cook ran from the kitchen, trembling in his shoes. "Pasel, prepare another place setting for our royal guest." The chef quickly pulled another set of utensils from a nearby drawer.

"What are you hoping to accomplish with this?" Abbie demanded. She couldn't understand the panic that seized her heart at the prospect of seeing Davis. She'd rather listen to Kevin's rants than stare at the man who had betrayed her trust.

"Davis and I have a little . . . friendly competition. He gets a girlfriend and I take her away."

"I'm not his girlfriend. I'm not his anything."

"But, you want to be," Kevin whispered with a conspiratorial wink then grinned. "Trust me, Abbie, by the end of the evening, you won't care about Davis. You'll see him for the fake coward that he really is."

"You are an ass, Kevin." Abbie regretted the words the instant they left her mouth. Pasel froze in the act of setting silverware on the table and stared expectantly at Kevin.

Surprisingly, Kevin only laughed. "You do have great spirit, Abbie," he said.

Davis walked into the room and the guard, Byron, automatically held out the third chair at the table. Davis didn't look at Abbie as he sat down. He kept his eyes on Kevin.

"I don't believe I asked to be brought here," Davis said.

"You're welcome, Davis, for being able to join us," Kevin said, smiling. He motioned to Abbie at the other end of the table. "Doesn't Abbie look breath-taking tonight? There's something about a beautiful woman wearing a man's undershirt in candle light that makes a man proud to be alive."

"Kevin, I'm only going to say this once more. Stop this charade before it goes too far."

"It's already gone too far, Davis. Did I neglect to mention that your friend and stooge, Hiram, is dead?"

Abbie saw the anger pass over Davis's face before he quickly composed himself. Underneath the table, Abbie took his hand. She was surprised when he didn't pull away.

"You killed Hiram?"

"I'm an excellent shot and Hiram made an excellent target."

"You are dead, Kevin," Davis said through clenched teeth.

"You continue to amaze me with your self-delusion. I'm the one who has the power to have you killed and you're at my mercy—you and Abbie—yet you continue to threaten me."

Davis yanked his hand from her grip under the table. "You're releasing Abbie tomorrow, remember?"

Kevin grinned. "I remember. I still doubt she'll want to leave. Abbie, herself, commented on what a beautiful boat this is."

"Not beautiful enough to stay a prisoner," Abbie said.

"You wouldn't be a prisoner by then, my love."

Abbie shivered with disgust as the endearment slid off Kevin's tongue. "I'm not your love, Kevin. Please lock me up in the room."

"I've hardly had time to compete for your affections. That's not exactly fair to me."

"Compete against me, Kevin?" Davis asked, comprehension dawning in his eyes. He laughed bitterly. "I told you, she means nothing to me. She's not my girlfriend or a friend. She's someone I met a few weeks ago, someone to pass the time with. Once more you're inventing a competition where none exists."

Abbie bit her bottom lip as the anger and hurt stabbed

her heart with each word. She knew Davis went overboard in his denial of her to protect her from Kevin but it surprised her how the harsh words affected her.

Kevin's lower lip snarled. "You've been trying to show me up since the day you were born."

"Which hasn't been a difficult task."

A vein throbbed in Kevin's right temple and for the first time Abbie was truly frightened of him. "Watch yourself, Davis. You don't have the palace guard to protect you here."

"I don't need the palace guard to handle you."

"You and your father handle threats to your power exactly the same way: murder."

"My father did not murder your mother, Kevin. He had no reason to," Davis said frustrated.

"I've heard that lie enough to repeat it myself," Kevin snapped then smiled at Abbie. "But, we're not here to discuss the murder of my mother or my father. We're here to give Abbie a choice."

Davis quickly glanced at her then back at Kevin. "A choice about what?"

"Who she wants to spend the night with," Kevin answered simply. Abbie gasped in horror before she could stop herself.

Davis stood and the guard immediately ran to his side. "I will not be a part of this. Abbie, are you coming with me?"

Abbie looked at Davis then back at Kevin. She didn't like the challenging expression on either man's face. There was no doubt in her mind that she would rather spend a night arguing with Davis than drinking wine and eating food with Kevin, but her feminine pride would not allow Davis to use her as a trophy against Kevin, no matter how much she disliked Kevin.

"Abbie?" Davis repeated, tearing his gaze away from Kevin to glare at her.

Kevin suddenly laughed. "As usual, Davis, a woman has come to her senses and seen through you."

Davis didn't look at Abbie as he turned and stalked from the room. The guard quickly ran after him.

Kevin smiled at Abbie, which made her shudder in disgust, then he raised his wineglass. "Here's to good choices and the destruction of the reliable arrogance of royalty."

She straightened her shoulders and met his eyes. "I never told you my choice, Kevin. I choose Davis."

Kevin threw his napkin down and jumped to his feet. Abbie watched in horror as the mask of civility and good graces slowly slipped from Kevin's face, revealing the madman underneath. He threw plates off the table on the floor, glasses, champagne bottle. For five minutes, he flew into a rage, knocking over everything in his sight. Abbie tried to stay as still as possible and hoped he wouldn't notice her.

Finally, Kevin seemed to snap from a trance and looked at Abbie. His face was flushed red as sweat covered his brow, making his hair damp. He smiled as if nothing had happened and slowly straightened his tie and tugged on his jacket.

Abbie looked at the broken glass on the floor and the general upheaval of the room, as tears filled her eyes.

"Lucky for him," he said calmly, then walked from the room.

Abbie waited several seconds then ran to the door. She pulled on the knob but the door refused to budge. She rolled her eyes in frustration then turned as the chef, Pasel, walked into the dining room. From his frightened expression, Abbie could tell he had heard Kevin's tantrum and had waited until the coast was clear.

"Are you all right?" he asked.

"You speak English," she said gratefully.

Pasel shook his head and placed a finger against his

lips to convey silence. "My grandmother lived in America for forty years. She taught us English when she would visit for the summer. Did Munji hurt you?"

"No, although I'm afraid you'll never be able to use these dishes again." Pasel smiled and bent to collect the shards of broken glass and china. Abbie bent next to him and helped.

"Please, you'll cut your hand."

"I'm a grown woman, Pasel." She continued to place the broken pieces in a plastic bag. "How old are you?"

"Seventeen."

"You're young."

"My mother warned me not to come with Munji but I . . ." Pasel's voice trailed off as he glanced around the room. "You really shouldn't be doing this."

"Where are we, Pasel? Where is Kevin going to drop me off?"

Pasel looked pained as he shrugged. "You know I can't answer that."

"I'm worried about Davis. I won't . . . I just want to make sure he'll be safe."

Pasel blurted out, "You aren't being let off. Kevin's going to lock you in the state room. He'll tell His Royal Highness that he let you off. Then when we dock in Natillas tomorrow, he plans to sell you to El Jaffe."

Tears blurred her vision and she quickly wiped them away. "Who's El Jaffe?"

"You don't want to know, and you don't want to be anywhere with him." Pasel suddenly jumped to his feet and ran into the kitchen.

Byron walked into the room. Abbie smoothly slid a shard of glass into her pants pocket and stood. "Kevin wants you back below." Abbie ignored him and walked from the room.

* * *

Davis scrambled to his feet as the door flew open. He could only see the outline of two people in the darkness of the room. Then he smelled the scent of roses and knew Abbie had walked into the room. The door closed behind her and relief flooded through Davis's body. He had been in hell for the past few hours, wondering if she were hurt or if she were safe. Davis trusted Kevin about as much as he trusted a fox. Davis couldn't completely relax, given the circumstances, without feeling Abbie next to him. When he had seen her at the dinner table, he had almost dropped to his knees in relief.

"Abbie?" he said, reaching for her. The only light in the room came from the moonlight that shone through the round porthole.

"It's me," came her voice from the other corner of the room. "I guess I've been sent back to detention."

Davis laughed to himself. It was a good sign that she still maintained her sense of humor. He admired Abbie's courage. She had adapted remarkably well to the circumstances. She didn't cry or complain. She sat in the dining room like a gracious princess, never betraying the tremors Davis felt racing through her skin when she took his hand.

"Did Kevin hurt you in any way?"

"No."

"Your voice sounds strange," Davis noted, making his way to the dark corner. He reached for her face, darkened by the room's shadows, and he immediately felt the dampness on her incredibly soft skin. Davis's heart tore as he realized she was crying. He wrapped his arms around her, more to comfort himself than her. He cursed himself and his birth right for dragging her into this. "I'm sorry, Abbie. If there was anything I could do to make you safe, I would do it." It took Davis several seconds to realize she was struggling against him. He abruptly released her and she stormed across the room away from him.

"Why didn't you tell me who you were?" she demanded angrily. Davis could practically feel the daggers her eyes directed at him. "I looked like a giant fool, telling that maniac you were a simple handyman. I've looked like a fool ever since I met you. Why me? Why did you have to bother me? Did you think I'd give you the least resistance because of your dashing good looks? You wanted to have a quick roll in the hay so you could go home and tell everyone how easy American women are."

"Don't you think we have more important things to discuss right now?" Davis said annoyed.

"Is that a royal dictate that must be obeyed upon fear of death?"

"Abbie—"

"Are there still beheadings in your country? One wave of the royal hand and off with my head?"

"We can discuss this later."

"I want to discuss this now," she shot back. "What exactly were you doing in America, Your Highness? Why were you playing the role of a handyman? Who exactly is Lowell? A royal page or advisor or seer?"

Davis clenched his jaw as she made him feel more and more guilty with each word. His guilt left his mouth sounding like anger. "Are you finished?"

"No, I'm not," Abbie responded bitterly. "You're a liar and a fake. You're everything Kevin said and more. And the only reason I'm in here with you, instead of with him, is because he's a lunatic."

"Are you finished?" Davis repeated in a louder voice.

There was silence in the room and Davis heard each heavy breath she took. He knew he should have apologized or offered an explanation but he just shoved his hands into his pockets before he grabbed her and kissed her senseless.

"I guess I am," she finally said then added in a whisper, "You could have at least told me the truth when we woke up on this boat."

Davis tried to act like the future king of his country and said, "I am sorry you're involved in this." He couldn't resist adding, "But, if you had run—"

"If you say that one more time, I swear I'll scream," she interrupted him.

Davis barely withheld his own laughter, with the help of years of Lowell's strict training. "Kevin said he's allowing you off the boat tomorrow. Maybe—"

"Davis, with everything I know, do you really think Kevin is going to allow me to leave this boat?"

Davis felt his heart stop as he understood the truth of her question. In a burst of violence unknown to him, he kicked a nearby wall and cursed. "I knew I shouldn't have trusted that bastard. I just thought he'd have the common decency to . . . to. . . . We have to escape tomorrow morning."

"What can we do against men with machine guns?"

"Whatever we have to. I will not allow that maniac to use me against my father and my country or to hurt you. I would never be able to live with myself."

"He told me the Juhatu throne really belongs to his family and that your father had his mother murdered. Is it true?"

"Only in the demented mind of the Munjis. Kevin's father, Albert, was always a harsh critic of the royal throne. Eight months ago when his wife died in a car accident, he became deadly. He believed my father had his wife killed as a warning to stop his protests against the royal family. My father dismissed him, at first, because the whole country knew of his devotion to his wife. But, his threats became more violent and serious. Secret intelligence confirmed Albert was making plans to acquire chemical weapons. While Albert had always been deadly,

Kevin is ambitious. Kevin believes the throne belongs to his family, not mine."

"He's not going to let you go, Davis, no matter what your father does."

"I know."

"Pasel told me that we're heading for Natillas."

"Natillas is in the Bahamas, near St. Moritz. Many royal people from Juhatu frequent St. Moritz . . ." Davis couldn't remember his train of thought as he suddenly smelled the soft scent of her hair and felt the warmth of her body. He never thought he'd be frightened in this situation. His training at the palace had prepared him for the possibility of kidnapping since he was a child but Davis never thought he'd have a woman like Abbie with him. A woman who he cared for more than he dared to admit. Davis took several steps away from her seductive pull. "I smuggled a butter knife from the dining table. I'm going to work on the lock. You try to sleep."

"I'm not a child, Davis. I can do something."

"Like what?"

"I don't know, but anything except lying here as if I'm on a luxury cruise. Do you actually think I'll be able to sleep?"

Davis groaned to himself and wondered why he ever thought Abbie Barnes was sweet and quiet. "You think of something to do while I work on the lock," he muttered then walked to the door. He felt in the darkness for the knob and cursed when he felt the smoothness. "There's no lock on this side."

"I have an idea, although in all of your royal grandeur, you would not stoop as low as to hear an idea from a commoner like me."

Davis stifled his laughter once more and wondered why her sarcasm always made him want to laugh instead of rail in anger. He had a feeling if any other person said these words to him, he would be angry. "Considering the circumstances, I suppose I'll allow it," he said with as much disdain as he could muster.

"I have this, Your Highness." He felt the cool brush of her hand then the sharp edge of glass. Davis wasn't so much shocked by her creativity as by the sparks that flew through his hand at her touch.

"What is this? A piece of glass?"

"How astute," she replied sweetly.

"Well done, Abbie, even for a commoner such as yourself." He saw the white of her teeth in the darkness as she smiled. "We should rest for a couple of hours and then at dawn we'll get out of here. If Kevin plans to dock in Natillas tomorrow, then we must be close."

Davis took her hand and led her to a corner of the room. He sat down on the hard floor then pulled her into his lap. She struggled but Davis wrapped his arms around her, restraining her movements.

"For the warmth, Abbie," he said softly, lying through his teeth. He loved the feel of her in his arms. The smell, the soft brush of her hair against his face. Davis hoped she would stop moving in his lap soon or his body's involuntary reaction would embarrass them both.

She abruptly stopped struggling but stiffly sat in his lap. Davis sighed and leaned against the wall. "Relax, Abbie. I think I'll manage to keep my hands to myself for the remainder of the night," he muttered, although he wasn't certain himself.

"I don't appreciate being manhandled," she said coldly then added softly, "Especially after the . . . the events of today and that man . . ."

Davis cursed himself for his insensitivity and abruptly released her. "I'm sorry, Abbie, I shouldn't have been so presumptuous. You have to know that I would never hurt you."

"I don't know if I can trust you, but I know you would never purposely hurt me."

Davis tried to ignore the guilt that stabbed his heart from the knowledge that she didn't trust him. He cleared his throat and asked hesitantly, "Did that idiot hurt you?"

"No." She hesitated then whispered, "I never thanked you for coming to the rescue, almost like a real live Prince Charming."

"You don't have to thank me, Abbie." Davis suddenly felt her relax against him as she rested on his chest. Davis grunted from the short stab of pleasurable pain in his stomach at the feel of her hands on his chest. He wanted to make love at that exact moment, regardless of where they were. He knew he had completely lost his mind.

"My family is probably going insane with worry," Abbie whispered.

"Would they already know you're gone?"

"I told Chris that I would call her after dinner. She probably has called my brothers by now or they have called her to see if I'm with her."

"I have two brothers and I talk to one or the other every night. Then my parents call my brothers or call me and we report on the others. We're all embarrassingly close."

"That doesn't sound embarrassing," Davis responded as he thought of having brothers to talk to or parents who cared about his daily events. Abbie didn't respond as she unconsciously squeezed his arms. Davis shifted, trying to find a more comfortable position that wouldn't have her driving him insane, but he knew that wouldn't happen as long as she was in the same room with him.

"I probably should have gone home with Chris," Abbie suddenly said, breaking the silence.

Davis allowed the laughter to bubble through his chest and out his mouth. He heard Abbie's own restrained laughter. He never knew laughing could feel so good—or so right.

FIVE

Abbie felt the thunder against her ear and almost jumped to defend herself against whatever danger approached. Then she felt the hard muscle underneath her hands and realized she heard Davis's heart beating against his chest. Abbie allowed herself to enjoy his strength, his need to protect her. Even in sleep, he kept his arms around her, holding her.

No one had ever wanted to protect Abbie before except her father or brothers. Sometimes Abbie felt her father's one goal in life was to make sure she never needed a man for anything. Abbie always felt gratitude for her father's life lessons—from changing the oil in a car to taking out the trash to self-defense lessons. Now, Abbie wondered if her father didn't take the job a little too seriously. She spent her whole life knowing she didn't need a man, that she forgot that she might want a man.

In the pre-dawn light shining through the porthole, Abbie memorized Davis's face. The long eyelashes, the strong chin and the straight nose. Abbie imagined his brown eyes—the warmth and the strength. Even the humor. She traced his full lips and wondered how they would feel on hers. How it would feel if he wrapped his arms around her, for more than warmth, and kissed her like a man kissed a woman.

Abbie couldn't resist and lightly ran her hands over his

chest. Even through the heavy cotton material of the shirt, Abbie could feel the definition and strength of Davis's chest. She ran her hands over the strength of his arms and gloried in the pleasure that raced through her body at the feel of his warm skin. Abbie forgot all restraint and placed a kiss on the small expanse of bare skin visible above the top button of his shirt.

The taste of his skin on her lips almost drove her insane. Abbie felt a heat sweep through her entire body as she licked her lips and tasted his skin all over again. Davis suddenly groaned and Abbie immediately jumped from his arms, as if scalded. She could not believe what she had just done. She had just kissed a man, without his permission, without him even conscious.

Abbie scrambled to her feet as Davis slowly opened his eyes. He looked around the room confused until he saw her. He stretched his arms over his head and yawned. "How long have you been awake?" he murmured.

"Only a few minutes," Abbie mumbled then moved to the window. "We should hurry if we want to catch them by surprise."

Davis stood and walked to the door. He lifted a hand to knock on the door then glanced at her. "If something happens to me, I want you to keep running. Understand?"

Abbie nodded, unable to meet his eyes. She knew she should be afraid. They could be killed, but with Davis staring at her, she felt invincible. Davis knocked on the door and Abbie quickly ran behind him. Davis pounded louder on the door, after several seconds of silence. Finally, they heard a key turn in the lock. Davis quickly squeezed her hand then pulled the piece of glass from his pocket.

The guard named Byron opened the door and stepped inside. He had not fully entered the room when Davis dragged him inside and stuck the jagged edge of the glass against his throat. Byron struggled and reached for the pistol in his waistband, but Abbie quickly grabbed the gun and pointed it at him.

"We don't want to kill you, we just want to get off this boat," Davis said in French.

"Kevin will kill me if you don't," Byron replied in a trembling voice.

"That is not our concern," Davis said, calmly. Abbie watched the gun waver in her hand as her arm strained from its unfamiliar weight. She could not fathom the idea that she was holding a gun, or that she pointed it at another human being.

"How far are we from the coast of Natillas?" Davis demanded.

"About an hour at our current speed," he answered, sweat pouring from his forehead.

"Abbie, grab the door keys," Davis ordered.

Abbie stiffened from the commanding tone in his voice, but obeyed. She ignored the pleading look in Byron's eyes and quickly grabbed the keys hanging from the belt loop on his pants. She glanced out the doorway at the empty hallway. She only heard the hum of the boat motor, no men's voices.

Davis abruptly brought the gun on the back of the man's head and Byron collapsed unconscious to the floor. Abbie stared at the prone man, praying he was not dead. Davis pushed her out of the room and closed the door behind them. Davis took the keys from her hand and locked the door. Abbie shoved the gun into Davis's hand and Davis glanced at her.

"What's wrong?" Davis asked, surprised.

"I don't like guns."

"If something happens to me, this may be the only thing between you and life in some Middle Eastern country as part of a harem," Davis whispered fiercely.

"Well, then, you better stick around to prevent that."

She saw his half-smile before he grabbed her hand and cautiously led her up the stairs.

Abbie flinched as they heard a pair of boots on the deck at the entrance of the hallway. They pressed against the wall and Abbie saw Davis grip the gun. The sound faded and Davis took a step onto the deck. Abbie followed him and released the breath she did not know she held as the fresh dawn air mixed with the salty smell of the sea flirted across her body.

In the early-morning light, she could see the faint outline of land a few miles away. Abbie could even smell the scent of the thick foliage at the shoreline. Even in the cool morning air, thick humidity hung around and sweat instantly pooled in the small of her back.

Davis motioned for Abbie to follow him. The two cautiously walked around the starboard side of the deck, not seeing another person. Then a man suddenly opened a door and stepped in front of them. His eyes grew wide as he came face-to-face with Davis.

"Abbie, run to the boat," Davis shouted as the man yelled to his associates in French. He swung at Davis and Davis ducked then kicked him in the face. The man stumbled several steps back then reached for the pistol in the holster underneath his left arm, just as three men ran around the corner behind him.

Abbie grabbed Davis's arm and pulled him to the rail. Davis looked at her surprised as she climbed onto the rail then he quickly followed her. Abbie stared at the fifteen foot fall to the wavy, crystal clear blue water below. The height of the jump quickly ran through her mind. She hesitated for a brief second then felt more than heard the air from a bullet speed pass her face. Without a second thought, she jumped.

Abbie didn't yell, but she heard Davis's shout as he fell through the air beside her. The two splashed into the water at the same time. Abbie wasn't prepared for the shock of the water, as the warm wetness enveloped her. Through the diamond blue depths, Abbie saw Davis next to her. Bullets continued to pierce the water above them and Abbie swam.

Abbie sputtered as she dragged herself from the pull of the ocean's waves onto the sandy beach. She thought she would never rid all the water from her lungs. Davis crawled onto the sand next to her. The two had been swimming for more than an hour. They had swum mostly under water until they circled to the other side of the island. Then they stroked the last mile to the deserted sandy beach.

Abbie groaned from pain and collapsed in the sand, still trying to expel the water from her body. Her arms ached, her legs hurt, and she was tired enough to fall asleep at that moment. She screamed as Davis grabbed her arm and dragged her to her feet.

"We have to move," he said through his heavy gasps of air. "We can't stay here. It's too exposed." As if to prove his point, they heard the low rumble of a boat motor from the water on the other side of the trees.

Abbie forced her legs to move as Davis ran for the thick forest, only a few feet from the water's edge. Abbie followed him through the leaves and trees, feeling the sting as branches slapped her in the face. Davis kept moving and Abbie watched as the leaves began to swallow him completely from her sight. She tried to move faster but she couldn't.

Abbie finally stopped and leaned against a tree. She closed her eyes and tried to rest for only a few seconds. She felt a hand clamp down on her arm and Abbie screamed until she saw Davis's face.

"Abbie, come on, just a little farther."

"I can't. I'm too tired."

"Yes, you can."

"Just a few seconds, Davis. You go on and I'll catch up." Abbie studied the wet shirt stuck to the muscles of his chest and the pants clinging to his legs. She shook her head at his beauty. Then she noticed he was staring at her breasts. In the midst of running for their lives, Abbie felt a small tingle run through her body. She glanced down and noticed her own shirt clung to her breasts, outlining her bra and her stiff nipples.

Abbie looked back at him and softly gasped as she met his eyes. She saw the passion and desire, the longing. Suddenly, a long spear landed in the tree next to Abbie's face. She screamed in terror as ten men seemed to materialize from the leaves. Davis whirled around and stood in front of her, shielding her.

The men all had the same dark skin, dark eyes, and black hair, and wore loose thin pants and oversized shirts. Abbie would have thought they were out for a stroll in the jungle except for the paint on their chiseled faces and the large guns in their hands. Abbie suddenly wished for the relative civilization of Kevin's prison. She screamed as the men surrounded them, gesturing and speaking in a foreign language to one another. As if in concert, the men suddenly grabbed Davis, who struggled, trying to move from their grip, but was quickly overpowered by the strong arms holding him.

"Abbie!" Abbie heard the terror in Davis's voice as a man reached for her. At the sound of her name, the man hesitated and studied her expression. Everyone in the clearing seemed to stop moving as the stranger hesitantly raised a hand to her face. Abbie flinched as his hard hand touched her face. There was gentleness in his touch, even with the calluses and broken fingernails.

Abbie stopped trying to escape his touch and met his eyes, which seemed to grow wide with comprehension and he suddenly dropped to his knees. The others abruptly did the same, releasing Davis, and falling to their knees in front of Abbie. Abbie dug her fingernails into the tree bark behind her and met Davis's confused expression.

"What the hell is going on?" Davis asked, glancing at the various prostrate men.

"I don't know. Should we run?"

The leader suddenly jumped to his feet and took Abbie's hand. Abbie tried to pull from his grip but he held her hand like a firm vise.

"Ab-bee," the man strained.

Abbie forced a smile and nodded encouragingly. "Yes?"

The man turned to the other men and grinned, showing several missing teeth. "Ab-bee," he screamed, motioning to Abbie. "Ab-bee." The men slowly stood and began murmuring her name with a reverence Abbie never heard men use to speak her name.

She half-laughed and half-screamed when the group suddenly picked her up and set her on their shoulders. She helplessly looked back at Davis as the men began to carry her through the bushes. Davis stood alone in the clearing, staring after her. She tried not to show her fear but finally couldn't resist and motioned for Davis to follow her. Davis nodded and chased after them.

Abbie sighed with relief as the men finally set her on her feet. She quickly moved from their circle and stood next to Davis, who barely looked at her as he glanced around where the men had brought her. Abbie had ridden on the men's shoulders through foliage, trees, and up a mountain. She'd been too frightened to try to force them to set her down.

She finally noticed her surroundings. She couldn't believe the almost primitive state of the small village that the men had brought her to. There were small huts spaced evenly in a neat row on either side of the small road. Abbie could see the small garden plots in front of the huts and the woven chairs. Dirt crunched underneath her wet shoes as she walked farther into the village. She noticed the tall totem poles with intricate designs at the end of the village, surrounded by hundreds of candles.

Before Abbie took another step, Davis grabbed her arm and pulled her back to his side. Abbie glared at him until she saw the group of people slowly making their way toward her. The people all wore the same thin clothes as their captors, although many of the men were shirtless due to the extreme heat at the top of the mountain. They all had the same look of awe as they stared at her, mesmerized.

"Should we start calling for Kevin now or wait until they tie us to a stake?" Abbie whispered, clutching Davis's sweat-slickened arm.

"I don't think they want to hurt us."

"How can you tell that?"

"The way they look at you. They act as if they know you."

"Believe me, I don't know anyone here," Abbie said, shaking her head. "And I'm about to scream and run off the side of this mountain."

"We have two choices, Abbie. Either stay here and see what this is all about or turn around and probably run straight into Kevin and his men. Personally, I prefer option one."

Abbie didn't have time to answer since a hush descended over the chattering of the village as a man walked through the villagers toward Abbie and Davis. Abbie almost laughed at the incongruity of his outfit. He wore Levi's with a white T-shirt and an ornately decorated, jeweled belt around his waist. The man came to stand directly in front of her then abruptly dropped to his knees. Abbie gasped as everyone else in the village followed suit.

Abbie sighed in frustration and grabbed the man's arm.

He looked at her, amazement filling his dark brown eyes, as he stood.

"Ab-bee," he said.

"That's me," Abbie confirmed then pointed at him. "Who are you?" The man continued to stare at her, uncomprehending.

Davis asked in fluent Spanish, "Who are you?"

The man answered, "Tazeh."

"Ask him, why have they brought me here?" Abbie told Davis.

"You speak English," Tazeh said in an heavy accent, looking at Abbie. "You come to us finally."

"Who's us?" Abbie asked confused.

"Your people," he answered, making a broad sweeping gesture toward the other villagers, anxiously awaiting her reaction. "We wait for you for hundred years. We wait for you to lead us."

Abbie glanced at Davis then looked at Tazeh. "I think there's been a mistake," she said.

"Mistake?"

"I'm not who you think I am."

"You not Ab-bee?"

"I'm Abbie, but not your Abbie."

"Follow me." Tazeh turned and the crowd parted as he took long, powerful steps toward the forest. Abbie looked at Davis, who shrugged, and they followed Tazeh. He disappeared into the wall of trees and the two followed him, almost losing him in the thickness of the forest numerous times. Finally, Tazeh stopped at a large, thirty-foot-high rock wall and pointed to the dry painting on the smooth texture.

Tazeh dramatically gestured to the rock and proclaimed, "This Ab-bee."

"It looks just like you, Abbie," Davis whispered amazed.

Abbie looked at the eight-foot-tall image on the rock face. The female face did look like her. The resemblance was uncanny. Actually, Abbie felt the painting looked like her if she were a gorgeous, powerful warrior princess. She could feel the strength and power exuding from the woman's confident smile.

Abbie touched the painting, surprised by the coolness of the rock. She looked at Tazeh. "Who is this?"

Tazeh spoke in Spanish and Davis haltingly translated, "He says, more than two hundred years ago, one of their people painted this of their high priestess, Ab-bee. She led the people to many victories over their enemies. She was their queen and died young from a fever that consumed the village. Before she died, she vowed to come back to them and lead them to another great victory. They've been waiting for her." Tazeh stopped speaking with a satisfied expression on his face and Davis looked at her, "They think you're her."

"Really? They think I'm a queen?"

Davis rolled his eyes. "Don't get too excited, Abbie. We don't know exactly what it would mean for you to be their queen. We also don't know how they'll react when they find out the truth."

"Maybe I am a queen," she replied stubbornly.

"Don't be stupid, Abbie."

Abbie crossed her arms over her chest and glared at him, momentarily forgetting Tazeh. "The only stupid thing I've done in the last forty-eight hours is walk down that street with you after dinner."

Davis narrowed his eyes. "Every time there's a problem, you're going to throw that in my face."

"Maybe I am. I think I have that right," she snapped.

In a quick flash, Tazeh flipped Davis onto the ground and held his spear to Davis's throat. Davis froze and Abbie screamed and pushed Tazeh away from Davis. Tazeh immediately moved aside for her and she dropped to her knees next to Davis. "Are you okay?" she asked concerned.

Davis nodded, then they both looked at Tazeh's angry expression as he glared at Davis. "Do you see what I mean, Abbie? This isn't a joke to him or to any of those people in that village."

"Do you have to be right about everything?" Abbie demanded annoyed, jumping to her feet. She turned to Tazeh and smiled as she asked Davis in a cold voice, "What do they want me to do?"

Davis slowly stood and spoke in Spanish to Tazeh who answered stiffly. Davis avoided Abbie's eyes as he translated. "There's a ceremony tonight."

Tazeh whistled and a group of women suddenly appeared. Abbie didn't feel fear from these people anymore. She smiled at the women who refused to look at her. They shyly took her hand and began to lead her farther into the forest. Abbie didn't want to look back at Davis and give him the satisfaction but she did. He stared after her, his arms crossed over his chest, looking annoyed and frustrated. She wondered if she would ever be able to look at him without feeling a skip in her pulse. She quickly turned around and followed the women.

Davis watched the villagers prepare food in the open air underneath the torches on the totem poles. Night had fallen but the village was as bright as day with the many torches lit throughout the village. Davis didn't like how the night was turning out. He didn't like the alcohol with the bitter taste the men kept passing around to one another. He also didn't like the way the men and women drank from separate bowls. Most of all, he didn't like the fact that Abbie was nowhere to be seen.

Davis told himself he only cared about Abbie's safety but he knew it was more. She made him feel alive. She made him feel like he could take on several men with guns and win. Davis didn't like to think about that. He instead concentrated on the wonderful feeling of being clean. The villagers had ignored him all day, almost as if he didn't exist, and he had stumbled upon a warm spring where he took a relaxing bath and tried not to imagine Abbie next to him.

Davis smelled the scent of unfamiliar food, and he was surprised his stomach rumbled in anticipation. He realized he hadn't eaten in at least forty-eight hours. Davis moved closer to the celebration, surprised by how hurt he felt as more people turned their back to him. As the prince of Juhatu, he was never ignored. Davis had never known what the opposite felt like and he didn't like it. Then Davis forgot all his feelings, the hunger, the surprise, the loneliness, with one look at Abbie.

She walked into the clearing from a large hut, surrounded by four other young women. They all wore ankle-length white shifts but Abbie's gown seemed to flow with each breath she took. Her hair flowed around her bare shoulders, like a soft wave and her smooth arms were graced by immaculate gold jewelry and bands of various jewels. Davis thought he stopped breathing as he watched the slow rise and fall of her breasts underneath the almost transparent white gown. He could almost see the darkness of her nipples against the thin material. Unconsciously, Davis took a small step toward her before he stopped himself.

Silence fell over the clearing as even the men stopped banging the drums for the first time in two hours. Abbie scanned the faces in the clearing like a true queen. Davis dared to dream that she was looking for him, but her eyes rested on Tazeh and she smiled, holding out her hand. Tazeh crossed the clearing in four steps and took her hand. The resulting cheer made Davis's ears hurt. Not only his ears, he realized, as he noticed the naked lust and possession in Tazeh's eyes.

Davis wanted to stalk away and leave Abbie with "her

people." He wanted to, but instead he moved closer toward her. Tazeh led Abbie to a small, round table and she sat. Everyone else in the village sat around the various fires, grabbing from the pots of food. Davis watched Abbie with Tazeh. He watched her laugh and smile. Davis knew that she couldn't understand a word Tazeh said, and Tazeh could barely understand her, but Tazeh was captivated. Davis didn't blame him. Then Abbie met his eyes over the fire.

Davis held his breath, waiting for her to turn from him. She didn't. She smiled and beckoned to him with one finger, like a mythical seductress. Davis could only walk toward her.

"Davis," she greeted warmly, pulling him down to the table. Davis couldn't help but return her smile. He glanced at Tazeh who glared at him. "Isn't all this beautiful?"

Davis didn't bother to look at the jewelry she motioned to, but stared at her face. "Yes."

Abbie met his eyes then blushed when comprehension dawned and she realized he wasn't talking about the jewels. She quickly looked at her food.

"Eat, Davis. The food is actually good."

Davis nodded and obeyed, unable to resist anything she wanted. He noticed the longing in her eyes and dreamed it was for him. His eyes traveled down the shift, taking in how it dangerously hung just above the swell of her breasts. His pants grew uncomfortably tight as she looked at him and ran her tongue over her lips. Davis forced himself to look away from her and eat his food, before he pulled her into his lap.

Abbie touched his thigh and Davis nearly jumped from his position on the ground. He looked at her shocked and she leaned toward him, her lips inches from his. "I don't think Tazeh likes you here," she whispered, her warm breath touching his lips. Davis could barely think, let alone worry about Tazeh. "In fact, if I didn't know better, I would think he's jealous."

She touched his bottom lip and Davis flinched, gripping the blanket underneath him. She suddenly smiled as she placed a piece of fruit between his lips. Davis automatically chewed and swallowed, for a moment tasting her finger, which still rested between his lips.

She smiled that seductive smile that made Davis want to beg for her kiss and said, "Do you think Tazeh has any reason to be jealous?"

Davis saw her wide pupils and his ardor noticeably cooled as he noticed the half-empty cup by her plate. He glanced at Tazeh and asked in Spanish, "How much did she drink?"

Tazeh glared at him then snarled, "Enough for our purposes."

"What purposes?"

"None of your business, and you won't interfere if you want to live," Tazeh warned.

Abbie suddenly grabbed Davis's arm and practically slid in his lap, her breasts brushing against his upper arm. Davis felt the shivers of lust and desire race through his body. The only thing that kept him from grabbing her was the knowledge that she would not act like this if she were sober. Abbie Barnes was drunk, and Davis could not help but enjoy her actions for a little while. He was only human.

"You know it's rude to speak another language at the dinner table, especially one I don't understand," Abbie whispered as her lips barely brushed against his ear. "Have I told you how gorgeous you are? You look like the prince every girl dreams of. I should've known who you were, the first second I saw you."

Davis felt his manhood rise another painful notch from the seductive tone in her voice. "Abbie, you're making Tazeh angry."

"I don't care." She placed a soft kiss on Davis's lips and Davis couldn't protest any more and placed his arms around her waist to steady her. His fingers unconsciously dug into the soft flesh of her hips. "Do you really hate being a prince? Was it really that horrible that you had to run away?"

"It's not horrible, just constricting."

"Why?"

"My family and too many others still believe in arranged marriages. My life is not my own. My country comes before anything, which is exactly why I can't sit here in this village while you pretend to be queen. I have to be home and warn my country about Kevin."

He expected anger but instead Abbie grinned and moved closer to him, her right leg resting on his left thigh. "You're always so serious now. Before in LA, you laughed and teased me. Is this what you're like at home? All serious and princelike."

"I'm expected to be this way. People would not want a clown running their country."

"Maybe not, but a smile every now and then wouldn't hurt anyone either."

"They call me the Stone Prince," Davis admitted shyly.

"You are beautiful enough to be chiseled in stone," she murmured then ran her tongue along the shell of his ear. "Back in LA. you wanted me, didn't you?"

Davis nervously cleared his throat as Tazeh stormed away. Abbie obviously didn't notice as she trailed a hand down the side of his face. "Abbie, you're drunk—"

"I took the most wonderful bath in a pond with these wonderful smelling leaves that lathered into soap. And the women gave me this purple liquid to drink and it made me feel warm inside," she whispered into his ear. "It made me think of you. It made me think about what I would do to you if you let me or what you would do to me if I let you."

Davis glanced over his shoulder and noticed most of the men had their hands full with women hanging all over them, kissing them. Davis glanced at Abbie's empty cup and realized why there were two different liquids served. The women were all drugged. Davis knew Abbie would be livid when she regained her senses.

"Abbie, maybe you should—"

"Will you stop telling me what to do?" She pouted and grabbed the lapels of his shirt. "If I haven't made it clear enough, Your Royal Pain-in-the-Butt, I want you."

Davis's tongue stuck in his throat as she pulled him to her and pressed her lips against his. Davis clutched her shoulders as the force of the kiss nearly blinded him. He tried not to respond and take advantage of her state, but she deepened the kiss and Davis found his hands running over her back, practically caressing her through the thin material of the shift.

Just when Davis couldn't contain himself, he felt Abbie's lips grow slack and her hands fall from his shirt. Davis pulled from her and she fell against his chest, unconscious. Davis tried to see her passing out as a blessing, but instead he cursed to himself. He looked at the other tables and noticed numerous women leading men to the various huts in the village.

Davis stood and picked up Abbie. He carried her to the hut that he saw her emerge from before dinner. He wanted to hold her all night, a rare feeling for Davis. He loved women, he loved their smell and the way they could make him feel, but usually Davis liked to spend an evening with them then return to his own life, never to see them again. With Abbie, Davis never wanted to release her. He didn't want to run away the next morning.

Davis entered the hut and in the soft candlelight saw a pallet on the other side of the hut, on the dirt packed ground. He reluctantly and carefully placed her on the pallet. Abbie moaned softly in her sleep and turned on her back, the shift barely staying above her breasts. Davis took one last look at her long legs, the full breasts, and slack mouth, and he turned and left before he did something he regretted.

Davis walked out of the hut, straight into Tazeh's massive chest. Davis immediately knew there was a problem when he saw the anger brewing on Tazeh's face. Three men stood behind him with equal expressions of hostility and contempt.

"Is there a problem?" Davis asked, with more courage than he felt.

Tazeh threw his spear at Davis's feet then spat on the ground, in front of Davis's feet. The men nodded, satisfied, then turned and left one by one. Tazeh sent Davis a smug grin as he said carefully in English, "You, me, tomorrow. You die." Tazeh turned on his heel and walked into the next hut.

Davis rubbed a hand over his tired eyes and tried to figure out what the hell had just happened.

SIX

Abbie was having the most wonderful dream. And she knew it was a dream because there was no possibility in real life that Davis would kiss her and hold her with such passion and longing. Abbie grinned, practically feeling his hands on her skin. Then she did feel his hands on her shoulders, shaking her. She also didn't feel any love in this gesture. She slowly opened her eyes, annoyed with the intrusion to her dream and stared straight into Davis's angry eyes.

She quickly moved from his grip, holding the sheet of the pallet underneath her armpits. She raked a hand through the tangled waves of her hair, annoyed with herself for trying to look better for him. Embarrassment flooded through her body as she remembered her behavior last night and her dream.

"What are you doing in here?" she demanded, noticing the sunlight breaking through the straw in the hut.

"Considering I have to fight for my life within the next fifteen minutes, I thought you should be awake for it."

"What are you talking about?"

"Do you remember anything from your performance last night?" he snapped.

Abbie gripped the sheet tighter and glared at him. "I don't think I like your tone of voice." For the first time,

Abbie noticed him sharpening the edge of a spear in his hands. "What exactly are you doing?"

"Your friend, Tazeh, didn't tell us everything about the Ab-bee legend last night. Apparently, Ab-bee doesn't directly lead her people to victory. She gives birth to the son who will."

"What?"

"And guess who the father of the future king is?" Davis muttered with a smirk. "Your good friend, Tazeh."

"I'll admit there's a small problem, but why do you have that spear?"

"Because I've insulted Tazeh's honor since you wouldn't keep your hands off me last night and now I've been challenged to a duel to the death," Davis snapped then got to his feet. He unbuttoned his shirt and ripped it from his back. Abbie was too confused by his statement to pay close attention to his bare, muscular chest.

"Are you serious?" She got to her feet, holding the sheet between her breasts.

Davis refused to look at her as he took off his shoes. "Do I look like I'm serious?"

Abbie met his grave expression and she shook her head confused. "I thought I was supposed to be a warrior queen or—I'm just a womb?"

"I told you, Abbie."

Abbie rolled her eyes then frantically searched through the contents of the hut for her clothes. "This is just a mistake. I'll explain to Tazeh that I'm not Ab-bee and, therefore, you didn't insult his honor. Then we'll be on our merry way and they can continue to wait for her to descend from the sky or emerge from the seas or whatever she's supposed to do."

"It won't matter, Abbie," Davis said with a tired sigh. "You fulfilled the ritual last night by drinking that alcohol. The only reason you passed out is because your tolerance was weak compared to the other women. For some reason, I think Tazeh allowed you to drink that much because he knew you only wanted me."

"Want you?" Abbie repeated with an incredulous, nervous laugh. "What exactly did you drink last night?"

"You and Tazeh were supposed to begin the first step toward the promised child, and I was in the way. I have to die."

"Don't I have any say in this?"

Davis shook his head in annoyance and walked from the hut. Abbie followed him, still clutching the sheet around her. She stopped abruptly in her tracks when she saw the entire village standing outside the hut. Tazeh stood in front of the villagers, wearing only a loincloth. Abbie studied his intimidating physique and noticed how thin Davis looked next to him. Normally a man of Davis's physique and stature would not be considered thin or small but compared to the mountain man, he might have been a stick.

Abbie grabbed Davis's arm as he stared at Tazeh. She could see the fear in Davis's eyes, which he tried to hide from her.

"Davis, I have a plan," she said desperately. "I'll pretend I don't want you, that I really want Tazeh, and then he'll have to let you walk away. Then tonight I'll sneak out of the village and find you. Beautiful plan, if I do say so myself."

Davis placed a hand on her face and tears filled her eyes as she felt the warmth of his skin radiate through her. "He won't let me go, Abbie. It's not about you anymore or me, it's about Tazeh's honor."

"Then I should fight him; I'm the one who insulted his honor," Abbie protested.

"Don't worry, Abbie, I'll find a way to get out of this mess."

"What if you don't?" Tazeh suddenly yelled in harsh Spanish at Davis. Abbie did not understand Tazeh's words but she knew he wanted to start the fight. Abbie glared at Tazeh then clutched Davis's arm. "Don't do this, Davis. You're no match for him."

Davis slightly smiled as he said dryly, "Thanks a lot."

"Davis, I'm not joking. He's going to kill you. This is his weapon, his village, his method of fighting. You don't stand a chance."

"I could actually win, Abbie."

"And what if you lose?"

Davis hesitated then said with a gentle smile, "Then you'll be drinking my blood tonight."

"Don't even joke about that," Abbie snapped angrily.

Davis placed a soft kiss on her forehead, which made more tears fall down her cheeks. "Everyone will be distracted by the fight. You could run."

"I'm not leaving you."

"When . . . or if I start to lose, run for the forest. If I can, I'll catch up with you later."

"Davis—"

"Think good thoughts about me every once in a while, Abbie."

Tazeh yelled again and two large men grabbed Abbie's arms, dragging her away from Davis. Abbie screamed, trying to pull away from their strong arms, but they held her tightly. She looked back at Davis who stood, staring at her, as if memorizing her every feature. She felt all the fight drain from her body as Davis suddenly turned to face Tazeh.

The villagers slowly murmured and watched as Davis and Tazeh began to circle each other. The men suddenly swung the wooden part of their spears at each other and the resulting loud clash made Abbie struggle again to free herself. She winced in pain as the hands only dug deeper into her arms. The villagers screamed with excitement, enjoying the spectacle before them.

Davis ducked as Tazeh swung the spear at his head. He

jumped to his feet and managed a well-placed foot in Tazeh's stomach. Tazeh barely flinched. Abbie admitted that Davis was not as overmatched as she originally thought. He had obviously had some training with hand-held weapons. He managed to hold his own against the larger, stronger man. Every time Tazeh moved with the staff, Davis managed to block any hits on his body.

Abbie started to almost feel hopeful for Davis until Tazeh's foot connected with Davis's head, in a lightning move that had all the villagers cheering. Davis fell to the ground, blood trickling from the corner of his mouth, his spear flying in the opposite direction. Abbie screamed at the unfairness as a woman grabbed the spear and threw it behind everyone. As Davis tried to stand, Tazeh kicked him in the stomach, causing Davis to fall back on the ground. Abbie could feel the pain in her stomach herself and tears blurred her vision. Tazeh stabbed the spear at Davis's head but Davis managed to roll away at the last second.

Except he rolled toward a group of men who stabbed their spears on the ground at him. Davis rolled in the opposite direction and got to his feet. He looked shocked at his bare hands, while Tazeh stood opposite him with a smug smile and a spear. The men holding Abbie had relaxed their grips as they became absorbed in the last few minutes of the fight. With a burst of strength she didn't know she possessed, Abbie ripped the spear from one of the men. Before he could grab her, Abbie sprinted into the clearing to stand in front of Davis, just as Tazeh advanced toward him. Tazeh stopped short as everyone in the village became silent. Abbie ignored everyone, even the protesting expression on Davis's bloody face, and she pointed the spear at Tazeh. Anger raced through her body as she saw the blood on Davis's face.

"Stop," she ordered. Tazeh froze, shock on his face, as the villagers all yelled in disappointment.

Davis struggled to his feet and Abbie glanced at him. She didn't know how or why but seeing the bruises on his face made her own body ache and made her angry. She glared back at Tazeh.

"If you touch him again, I'll kill you," she whispered, knowing she spoke the truth. Tazeh must have believed her because he took a hesitant step away from her.

"Abbie, move," Davis muttered through his bruised bottom lip, struggling to stand beside her. "Don't become involved."

"Shut up," she snapped then looked back at Tazeh. "This is over. It's finished."

"You can't do this, Abbie," Davis tried again. "We're outmatched—"

"If he wants you, he has to fight us both," Abbie said quietly, her eyes never leaving Tazeh.

Tazeh studied her for a second and Abbie prayed no one would call her bluff. She quickly realized what a foolish idea this had been, but she would do it again. She never thought she could purposely harm another human being, but if the only alternative was to allow Tazeh and the villagers to continue to beat on Davis then Abbie would kill each and every one of them. She decided to avoid thinking about this new side of her personality until she and Davis were somewhere safe.

Tazeh abruptly threw his spear on the ground and held out his arms. He spoke in a loud, resounding voice and the villagers abruptly quieted and reverently bent their heads.

"What did he say?" Abbie quickly asked Davis.

Davis looked amazed as he slowly said, "He says I won or . . . you won. Everything he has is now mine."

"What—"

Davis took the spear from her suddenly unsteady hand.

"Keep looking fierce, Abbie," Davis muttered and Abbie heard the laughter in his voice. She tried not to laugh herself as Tazeh continued to speak to the crowd of people. "Tazeh just said I own all of his twenty donkeys."

"Donkeys?"

"We can get the hell out of here tonight," Davis said nodding then suddenly winced. "Right now, I think I need to vomit out a lung."

The villagers gradually dispersed, disappearing into their huts and continuing their various chores, their disappointment evident. Tazeh bent on one knee in front of Davis and ripped an ornate ruby broach from his belt and handed it to Davis. Tazeh briefly glanced at Abbie then quickly turned and walked into the forest.

Davis waited until Tazeh blended into the leaves then fell to one knee. Abbie kneeled next to him on the ground and wrapped his arm around her shoulders. Abbie tried not to laugh at his pain, but she was so glad there was not a spear through his head that she would have laughed at anything.

"This isn't funny," Davis muttered, glaring at her.

Abbie helped him stand and began to lead him toward the small, warm stream the women had taken her to the other day. "I'm not laughing."

"If I were a different man, say a prince, I would feel very emasculated right now. Not only did you save my life but you're practically carrying me."

"Good thing you're not a prince," Abbie said, grinning. The two crashed through the trees. Even though she could tell he tried not to rest his entire weight on her, he was still heavy. She didn't care. She would have carried him on her back if she had to.

"Where are we going?" he muttered, wincing.

"You need to wash the blood off."

"He was really going to kill me, wasn't he?" Abbie realized he stared at her and she met his eyes. She quickly looked at the ground as she felt another unfamiliar rush of longing settle in her lower stomach. "You saved my life, Abbie. For that, I will always owe you."

"I was just repaying my debt to you. You saved me twice on the boat. I figured it was time I even the score."

Davis did not reply to Abbie as they brushed past the leaves to the small, rippling pond. Davis stared at the welcoming warmth of the water and he practically sighed in relief. Every inch of his body screamed with pain. He had not been close to yielding but Davis knew if Abbie had not stopped the fight when she did, he would be dead.

Davis stared at the top of her head as she fumbled with his pants button. He wanted to touch the soft strands of her hair and kiss the strong arms that supported him. He had never met a woman like her. A woman who made him want to protect her, kiss her, love her, and make her laugh. A woman who knew when he needed her help and did not hesitate to risk herself to give it to him.

Davis swallowed the sudden lump in his throat as Abbie pulled his pants down to his ankles. She looked at him as her fingers rested on the waistband of his underwear. He could see the indecision and hesitation in her eyes. He also wondered if maybe he saw a little desire that matched his own. If Davis's entire body wasn't on fire from pain, he would've done whatever was in his power to find out.

"I can manage the rest on my own," he said while fingering the soft strands of her hair that fell over her eyes. She still wore the thin shift wrapped around her body like a towel. All he had to do was pull the knot and she would be completely nude. The thought made Davis suddenly wonder if maybe he could tolerate loving her, regardless of the pain. He ran a finger down the soft column of her neck, feeling the sudden heaviness of her breathing on his bare chest. "You're pretty dirty yourself. Maybe you should join me."

"I . . ." Her voice trailed off as Davis placed a hand on the knot that held the shift together. He pulled and Abbie caught the material at the last second before Davis could see her. He couldn't hide his disappointment when he met her eyes. "You get in the water first," she said with a shy smile.

Davis didn't think he'd ever see Abbie act remotely shy around him. "You're not going to run off with my clothes, are you?" he asked suspiciously.

Abbie laughed and shook her head. "I've invested all this energy in you, I don't want you walking around in the nude."

Davis grinned and turned his back to her. He yanked off his underwear and quickly walked into the water. He was surprised by its warmth. The feel of the fresh water on his bruises and cuts made him gasp in pain but the water quickly soothed it. He sank under the water, reveling in the feel and the cleanliness that washed over him.

"You can look," came her voice behind him.

Davis quickly turned around and she sank in the water to her chin. Her hair was completely wet and slicked back from her face. Davis thought she was never more beautiful than at that moment. He wondered how she would react if he touched her. He just wanted to make certain she was real.

"I know I look pretty disgusting." Abbie mistook his awe for disgust with her appearance. "But, I have a good excuse. I've been kidnapped, attacked, I've swum a marathon, and I've been proclaimed a queen."

Davis touched her because he couldn't restrain himself. He heard her sigh as his hands touched the softness of her cheek. She turned into it, seeming to revel in the feel of it on her face. Davis stepped closer to her and the water rippled around him, cocooning them in warm liquid.

"You are beautiful," he said softly. He touched his tongue to her forehead, tasting the salt on her skin, the taste that was distinctly Abbie Barnes. "More beautiful than Juhatu on a summer evening."

She hesitantly touched the small cut at the corner of his eye and Davis instantly felt the area respond, down to his groin. Davis stepped closer to her, wrapping his arms around her waist. She didn't resist and moved closer to him, her cool skin rubbing against his.

"I was so scared when I saw Tazeh and . . ." Her voice trailed off as tears filled her eyes. Davis kissed the corner of each of her eyes.

"It's over. You saved the day," he replied gently.

She glared at him and he saw a fire gleam in her eyes. "I wanted to kill him, Davis, for hurting you. And I have never said that in my entire life, but I wanted to kill another human being." She placed a soft kiss on his partially swollen lower lip. Davis held her tighter as her tongue ran over his lips, soothing the area. Her bare breasts pressed against his chest, making his stomach tighten. He knew she could feel his hard length pressed against her and she didn't move from his arms in horror, like he thought she would.

"It's understandable, Abbie. Through all this, we've only had each other. Of course you care what happens to me."

She suddenly stiffened in his arms then moved from his grip. Davis stared at her confused. "What's that supposed to mean?" she asked in a low, dangerous voice.

"What?" he asked blankly.

"You think I only care if you live or die because I don't know anyone else? That as soon as we reach some type of civilization, I won't care about you? Is that how you feel about me?"

"We barely know each other, Abbie. You wouldn't even give me the time of day in California."

Her eyes narrowed, and Davis didn't know how, but he had ruined whatever had been growing between them. "Why did I even bother?" she said through clenched teeth then made her way to the edge of the water. Unfortunately, she had placed the shift at the edge and drew it around herself before she emerged from the water.

"Bother with what?" Davis asked, distracted by the shift that clung to the various curves and valleys of her wet body.

"Saving your worthless life," Abbie snapped. Davis lost all amorous thoughts and glared at her. "As soon as you're ready, Your Highness, I'd like to get away from this Godforsaken place and go home." She turned on her heel and stormed toward the village.

Davis watched her leave then slammed his fist on the water. Water splashed onto his face, serving to only make him more upset. He didn't know what just happened except he still hadn't tasted Abbie's lips.

Abbie tried not to relax against Davis as the donkey swayed beneath them. Various leaves slapped her in the face as the donkey moved through the forest on a partially overgrown trail toward the one village Tazeh reluctantly directed them to. Abbie sat in front of Davis, his strong arms wrapped around her, holding the reins of the donkey. It would have been so easy for her to lean against his chest and relax, to fall asleep and ignore the two long hours they already spent on the back of the donkey. But, Abbie had too much pride. Her father always told her that was her worst quality.

Neither one of them had spoken since they mounted

the donkey. By the time Davis returned to the village, looking too devastatingly beautiful for Abbie to turn away from, she had gotten the donkey from Tazeh and refused anything else except an ankle-length cotton dress for herself. Davis just stared at her, annoyed for some reason, then climbed onto the donkey and expectantly waited for her.

Abbie could still remember the faces of the various villagers as they waved good-bye to their supposed queen. Even Tazeh had offered her a small basket of fruit and an apologetic smile. Abbie had waved and smiled until the last branch covered them from her view, then she began the long silence.

As if reading her thoughts, Davis suddenly said, "We should only have a few more miles to go until we reach the small port Tazeh described."

"And then what?" Her voice sounded hoarse to her own ears from hours of silence.

"And then we'll pay someone to sail us to St. Moritz, where hopefully people from Juhatu will be vacationing."

"With what money?"

"You love to prove how independent you are, why don't you come up with an answer for that?"

Abbie gritted her teeth at his bitter tone. She could never understand how he could be so sweet one moment then so nasty the next. "I liked it better when we didn't speak."

She heard him sigh and felt the warm air brush the nape of her neck. "We need to be careful when we reach this place. Kevin or some of his friends could still be around. I think it's best if you wait in the forest while I try to book us passage on one boat or another."

Abbie bit her lower lip to refrain from arguing with him. She didn't know why she had such a natural inclination to argue with everything he said, even if what he said made the most sense.

Davis suddenly laughed and Abbie turned to glance at him. She almost fell off the donkey from the shock of seeing his smile so close to her. She quickly turned back around, not wanting to make a fool of herself by drooling over his handsome face. If ever there was a Prince Charming, Davis Beriyia fit the bill.

"What's so funny?" she asked, trying to sound more angry than she was.

"I don't know if you missed it but I said something a few minutes ago and you didn't contradict me or yell at me."

Abbie smiled to herself but straightened her shoulders. "I don't argue with everything you say, just when you're wrong, which is the majority of the time."

Davis laughed and Abbie felt the warmth from his laughter spread through her body from her toes to the tips of her fingers. "What were you like as a child? I bet you beat up all the little boys when they tried to kiss you or look up your skirt."

"Both were serious crimes in my father's books and worthy of punishment," Abbie replied. "My two brothers played football in high school and taught me a few defensive moves for out-of-control dates."

"What about your mother?"

"My mother was so horrified that she basically had three sons instead of two sons and a daughter. I could never stay clean, my hair was always out of place, and I beat up all the little boys on the block. While the other girls had training bras and went on their first dates to the mall, I was playing basketball with my brothers and their friends. I think she spent half my childhood apologizing for everything I did to her friends, and the other half praying to God I would miraculously transform into some girl who wore ribbons and lace. Around my sixteenth birthday, she gave up, and we've been best friends ever since."

Davis laughed again and his hands brushed the underside of her breasts as he pulled the reins. Abbie momentarily forgot the warm family memories as a spark of passion raced through her body and settled in her center. She wondered if her body would always react to his touch with such abandon. She had almost begged him to make love to her in the pond, even when she had been angered by his callousness.

"You sound like you had a wonderful family. I always wished I had a brother, preferably older."

"Why older?" She suddenly laughed as she understood. "So he could be the heir to the throne."

"Even when I was a little boy, I knew I didn't want to be king. My grandfather died when I was eight. Before he died, my father was my hero. He was my best friend. Then he became king and I lost him to the throne."

"It's your life. You should be able to live it however you want."

"I tried and look where I am now," Davis muttered. "In the middle of the jungle on a donkey."

Abbie patted the donkey's thick, searing-hot neck. "I like our friend, the donkey." She laughed as she imagined her mother's expression if she saw her riding a donkey, wrapped in the equivalent of a sheet. "My mother would have a fit if she saw me now."

"How would your mother feel about the way you've been treating me?"

Abbie laughed again. "She would kill me."

"It doesn't bother you that she disapproves of who you are."

"She doesn't disapprove of me, she loves me. She just wishes I was more like her."

"It must be nice to be so certain of your mother's love."

A hitch in his voice made her turn to glance at him. There was a faraway look in his eyes that Abbie couldn't understand. "Your parents love you, too, Davis. They wouldn't have searched all over the world looking for you if they didn't care."

"They had to find me," Davis snapped. "I'm the heir to the throne. They couldn't just allow me to wander around America. It wouldn't look good to the others, to the people."

"Davis—"

Davis suddenly smiled and tightened the reins, his arms once more brushing her sensitive breasts. "I'm just feeling sorry for myself, Abbie. I think I see a rooftop through that tree."

Abbie allowed him to change the subject even though she wanted him to talk about his family more. "Are you going to tell me how you plan on paying for anything? With your good looks?"

"You think I'm handsome?"

She could hear the smile in his voice and laughed as Davis reined the donkey in near a tree. "Answer the question, Your Highness."

Davis dismounted and stretched his arms over his head. Abbie tried not to enjoy the view but she couldn't help but watch the muscles glide underneath his skin. He finally pulled a ruby brooch from his pants pocket. Abbie remembered the jewel that Tazeh had given him.

"That is worth a lot more than a boat ride."

"You're right. It's worth my kingdom." Davis stuffed the jewel back in his pocket. "I have to get home soon. No one knows where I am and there's no telling what Kevin has told my father. I don't want my father doing anything foolish in my name."

Abbie winced as the muscles in her legs protested as she dismounted the donkey. "Be careful."

"I will. Stay here and I'll be back in an hour." He stared at her for a speechless moment then quickly turned and walked toward the town.

SEVEN

Davis had been gone for only half an hour before Abbie became nervous. She paced back and forth in front of the bored, watchful eye of the donkey. She cursed at the heat, the humidity, Kevin Munji, and most of all Davis for leaving her alone in the middle of the jungle. Abbie hated herself, too, for caring about an arrogant prince who only wanted to return home and probably never see her again.

Abbie hated how she had agreed to stay in the jungle. She hated the bugs that constantly flew around her ears, landing on her neck and arms. She wanted to scream from the inaction. Abbie was a doer. When something needed to be done, she did it. She didn't wait for a man or anyone else to rescue her. Her brothers would've laughed at her if they knew she stood with a donkey in the middle of the forest while a man tried to find them a way home.

Abbie laughed at herself, then thought about her brothers again. They were probably worried. Abbie talked to her parents or her brothers every day. Three days had gone by and she hadn't talked to any of them. Her oldest brother, Joe, would probably have driven by her apartment and gone inside with his key. He would see her unmade bed and her work spread on the table and be worried, then worry everyone else in the family. Then there were her numerous responsibilities at work.

On top of everything else, Abbie knew she was mostly worried because Davis could be in danger and she couldn't help him by standing in the shade of trees. The idea of him walking through the village, straight into Kevin's trap, made her feel more pain than anything had ever caused in her life. She hated feeling so worried about him, so concerned. She didn't want to care.

By the time Davis walked through the trees to reach her, Abbie had worked herself into a frenzy. As soon as she heard him step behind her, she turned around and swung at him. Davis barely managed to duck her blow and stumbled to the ground. He scrambled to his feet as Abbie swung at him again.

She screamed as he wrapped both arms around her and restrained her flailing arms. Abbie wriggled in his arms, kicking his shins. She heard a satisfying grunt of pain in her ears and tried to move from his grip but Davis only tightened his hold. He finally fell to the ground, his arms still tightly wrapped around her, bringing her with him. Davis grunted as he straddled her, his body weight holding her legs down, and his arms holding her hands.

Abbie quickly tired herself out as she tried to scratch his eyes. She wanted to make him pay for making her fall in love with him. Abbie stilled as she realized why she was so angry. Not because her family was worried or the work that mounted at the office each day she didn't arrive but because for the first time in her life, Abbie loved a man. And she didn't like how vulnerable that made her feel.

"What the hell is your problem?" Davis demanded angrily. "You made me drop our dinner, acting like a crazy woman. I can't tell . . ." He mumbled curses to himself as he stood over her and inspected the tortillas and baked chicken that now lay on the ground.

Abbie slowly got to her feet and tried to quiet the emotions that raced through her body. "I'm sorry."

Davis glared at her, throwing the dirty chicken against a tree. "You're insane, Abbie."

"I said I was sorry," she snapped then took a deep breath to calm her temper. "I was worried about you. I'm not accustomed to sitting on my heels while someone else does all the work, I wasn't raised that way. It made me a little crazy and I probably handled it the wrong way. I am sorry."

Davis rolled his eyes and threw his hands in the air in frustration. "A little crazy? I think you're more than a little crazy, Abbie."

Abbie sighed then raked a hand through her hair. "Did you find us a way off this island?"

Davis glared at her and Abbie could see him debate whether to speak to her. He finally relented and murmured, "I found a man willing to take us to St. Moritz. He can take us at dawn."

"Did you see Kevin?"

"No but I saw two of his guards trying to blend in, that's why we're leaving so early."

Abbie glanced at the food on the ground, now being nibbled by the donkey. "I'm sorry I ruined dinner."

"What happened, Abbie?"

"I already told you. The inactivity made me go haywire."

"And that is all?"

"And, naturally, I was worried about you. I-I only know you're one hundred percent safe when I'm with you."

Davis smiled and Abbie couldn't help but return his sweet smile. "You're my bodyguard now?" he asked with a slight laugh.

"I think I've done a pretty good job so far," she said through her grin.

"How do men in California handle you?"

"They don't." The two stood like fools grinning at each other for several seconds before Davis turned to the donkey. He busied himself by creating a pallet on the ground, from the blankets on the donkey. Abbie watched him until he glanced at her, then she quickly moved to the other side of the donkey to unfasten blankets attached to the other side of the animal.

"Do you think we'll be safe sleeping out here?"

"Yes."

Abbie waited for him to say more and when he didn't she looked over the donkey at him. She stared straight into Davis's surprised eyes. He smiled and Abbie smiled back. "We should go to bed . . . I mean sleep. We both need sleep."

Davis grinned and nodded. "Of course. We're going to have to share the blankets. Is that all right?"

"Yeah."

Davis laid on the blankets then held out his arm. Abbie tried not to want to take what he offered but she practically ran into his arms and laid on his chest. She couldn't prevent the sigh of contentment that escaped her lips as his arms wrapped around her. One of his hands slowly caressed a full circle on her arm, making her breathe faster and the twirls of passion whirlwind inside her.

"It's a beautiful night, isn't it?" Davis asked in a soft voice that made Abbie want to turn and kiss him.

Abbie stared at the full moon and the bright stars twinkling in the dark night sky. She heard the various sounds of the chirping animals going to sleep for the night. She smiled against his chest and wished it were bare like at the pond. "You definitely can't get this view in Los Angeles."

"You wouldn't give up the rat race in LA for a small

cottage in the middle of nowhere, would you?" Davis questioned, surprised.

"It would depend on what I would be sacrificing it for."

"I don't think you could ever leave your country. I'd see you leave for work each day with a smile on your face. You enjoy your job, you enjoy wearing your high heels, and being able to make people jump at the sound of your voice."

Abbie wanted to argue with him but she realized it was true. She absently trailed her finger in circles on his chest, feeling comfort from the feel of him. "How did you come to know me so well?"

"I watched you for two months, walking in and out of the apartment building. I can still remember the first time I saw you. You wore this gray suit that matched the sky that day. And your hair was in this ridiculous ball. And you looked at me like I was an intrusion in your otherwise perfect world."

"No, I didn't," Abbie protested, laughing. She had thought he was an intrusion in her morning the first time she saw him, because he was so beautiful that she knew she would think about him the entire day.

"Yes, you did," Davis said with a smile in his voice. He began to stroke her hair, gently pulling individual strands. "You didn't like me. I never could figure out why. At first, I thought it was because I was only a handyman. Then I saw how you treated the men in three-piece suits in the building and I knew it wasn't that."

"And what explanation did you finally decide on?" she asked, barely able to speak because of his roaming hands.

"I'm still deciding," Davis whispered.

Abbie stared at his lips then felt his strong hands on her shoulders, drawing her to him. She didn't resist. She couldn't have resisted even if she wanted to. Their lips touched and Abbie felt the sparks almost before she felt the full contact of his lips on hers. She didn't breathe

when his tongue briefly touched her bottom lip, tracing
the full line.

Abbie moaned and couldn't wait any longer for him
to take her mouth. She turned fully into him and pressed
her lips against his. She traced the line between his lips
with her tongue, silently demanding entrance. Davis
opened his mouth and Abbie stuck her tongue inside,
tasting the richness and fullness that was Davis. Not the
prince or the handyman but the man who had taken care
of her and cared for her for the past three days.

She ran her hands underneath his shirt, loving the feel
of his bare skin, the feel of him. His tongue battled back
with hers as his hands moved over her body. His hands
seemed to be everywhere at once, on her breasts, her
back, her shoulders, her neck. Abbie almost couldn't handle all of the pleasure at once. She wanted to scream,
she wanted to whirl into a million pieces, but she knew
if she did she couldn't hold Davis or feel his tongue in
her mouth. He loved her with his mouth. He loved her
with his hands. Abbie didn't know how much he felt for
her but she loved him.

Davis tried to be gentle, he tried not to rush her, but
with her fingernails digging into his chest and her tongue
ravishing his mouth, he couldn't do anything but follow
his impulses. Davis tried to match the hungry swipes of
her tongue in his mouth but she moved too fast. He
groaned her name in pleasure and raked his hands
through her hair, burying his hands in her soft mane.
No matter what happened he would never forget the feel
of her hair or the taste of her mouth. When she returned
to America where she belonged, Davis would spend every
night for the rest of his life trying to recapture the feeling
of having her in his arms.

His hands moved to the knot of the cotton dress she
wore. He wanted to see her body, to taste her breasts,
and to make her scream when he touched her center.

Abbie suddenly placed her hands on his and pulled away from his lips. Davis groaned in protest and reclaimed her lips in a hungry kiss. He was hungry, for her, for always.

Abbie shook her head and pushed against him. It took Davis several seconds to realize she was trying to stop and still he took her mouth. She moaned and Davis knew he had to stop or lose every ounce of respect he had for himself. Davis finally forced himself to pull away from her lips, the loss almost painful. He kept his hands on her hips as the two tried to draw the thick night air into their lungs.

"I can't, Davis, I'm sorry," Abbie whispered.

"You don't have to be sorry," he said sincerely. He carefully placed her on the ground then stood. He needed to leave her presence before he disgusted himself and tried every trick he knew to persuade her to make love. She sat up and stared at him. Her hair was still mussed from his hands, her lips slightly swollen. Davis actually felt an ache in his groin from how much he wanted her.

"I shouldn't have . . . I just don't think we should become involved when we're both going our separate ways as soon as we reach Juhatu."

Davis felt his heart stop and he stared at her uncomprehending. "What?"

"I have to go home as soon as we reach your country. My family's probably worried and my job . . . I have too many responsibilities and you have your own responsibilities. Besides, it's not like you and I could ever have a serious relationship."

Davis knew she spoke the truth but it still made him angry that she could bluntly say it without even batting an eyelash. "You overrate yourself, Abbie."

He saw the hurt cross her face then the anger. She stood to her feet, placing her hands on her hips. "What did you say?"

"I never said I wanted a serious relationship with you.

Even if I did, it would be impossible. I have to marry someone who will improve my kingdom—either politically or economically—and I'm afraid you don't fit either description. While I wouldn't mind fraternizing with you should the opportunity ever occur again, don't think it would be anything more than that."

Davis saw her hand fly in the air and he didn't bother to duck. He felt the sting of her hand on his face, more painful than he had imagined, because of the untruthful words he spat at her. Davis placed a hand to his face and squarely met her eyes.

"You're an arrogant pig," she said through clenched teeth. "If you ever touch me again, I'll cut off your hand." She marched to the other side of the donkey and threw a blanket on the ground.

Davis watched her for a second longer as she lay on the ground and turned her back to him. He cursed himself then laid back on the pallet, trying not to smell the scent of her that lingered in the blanket. Then Davis realized, it wasn't on the blanket, it was on his hands, his skin.

Abbie opened her eyes for some unknown reason. She had been sound asleep, dreaming of cheerfully strangling Davis, when she suddenly found herself wide awake. Abbie stared at the midnight-black sky and the stars. She heard Davis's even breathing and the sound of the donkey moving in the night. Abbie never thought she would find the sounds of a donkey moving around and a man she hated softly snoring, comforting. But, she did.

Abbie glanced at her watch in the dark, barely able to read the face. She realized they only had half-an-hour to reach the harbor and she quickly moved across the clearing. Abbie stared at Davis's vulnerable, sleeping form. Even though he had said such a horrible thing to her, she wanted to kiss him, to caress the frown lines from his forehead. Abbie hoped he would marry a woman who knew how to take his frown lines away with the wave of her pampered royal hand. Abbie couldn't believe she actually hated a woman who didn't even exist at that moment—the woman who would marry Davis.

Abbie didn't want to risk touching him with her hand and embarrassing them both, so she did the next logical thing. With one foot, she nudged Davis's back. Davis groaned in his sleep, then turned toward her. He slowly opened his eyes and glared at her. "What?"

"I don't know about you but I want to get off this island."

Davis rolled his eyes then reluctantly stood. "My watch was set to go off in five minutes. Would it have killed you to let me sleep five more minutes?"

Abbie ignored him. She whirled on her heel and started through the leaves toward the village. She didn't care if Davis walked behind her or not. She didn't care if she ever saw him again. Abbie continued storming through the forest, brushing leaves from her face, feeling the humidity stick to her body, to her bare skin.

Abbie stopped at the edge of the forest, staring at the small village. This was larger than Tazeh's village at the top of the mountain. There were modern buildings and several decrepit boats were moored to the docks. In the early-morning light, Abbie saw an older man slowly set up a food stand and her stomach rumbled from hunger.

Since Davis had all the money, and she needed money to buy food, she'd have to go back for him—or that's what she told herself. Abbie knew she really went back because she didn't want to go forward without Davis, even into the small town. The thought sickened her but she would deal with it later.

Abbie stumbled to a stop as she reached the clearing where they spent the night. The donkey still stood tied to a tree branch and Davis's blankets still lay rumpled on the ground. Abbie felt horror fill her throat as she realized Davis wasn't there. She ran through the leaves, heading back toward the village, hoping she and Davis had just missed each other in the thickness of the jungle. Abbie broke through the trees and stared at the dark village. The old man was still the only one visible in the street. All the other buildings looked closed. Abbie saw a short, squat man exit one building and head toward a boat, preparing to leave. Abbie knew it was their ride to St. Moritz.

Abbie stayed on the edge of the forest and ran to the other side of the village, when her heart stopped in her throat. Davis was being led into a house by two large men. She breathed a sigh of relief that he was still alive. Then Abbie realized it didn't matter because there was nothing she could do to save him. Abbie glanced back at the man waiting near the boat. She could get on the boat and ride to St. Moritz and send help. Abbie shook her head, disgusted with herself for even thinking of abandoning Davis. He wouldn't abandon her.

Abbie crept toward a window of the house, hoping the darkness covered her. She knew everyone in the house could hear her beating heart as she stopped outside the window. She leaned against the wall and rolled her eyes in disbelief. Since when did Abbie Barnes race to save the day? Since she had stared down a high priest with a spear, held a gun, and conversed with a madman.

Abbie prayed for courage and peeked inside the window of the house. The two men were tying Davis to a chair with coarse thick ropes. Davis looked angry and upset. No doubt because he felt he was too princely to be tied up by anyone. Abbie laughed at the arrogant disdain on his face then sank back to her knees, checking the road behind her. She looked back into the window then felt a heavy hand on her shoulder. She tried to scream but another hand covered her mouth. She struggled free and whirled around to look straight at Tazeh.

He smiled then placed a finger to his lips to convey silence. Abbie grinned and wanted to kiss him, but also didn't want to give him any ideas again.

"Davis," Tazeh whispered, pointing to the house.

Abbie nodded. "Help me, Tazeh, please."

Tazeh nodded then patted her cheek. He motioned for her to knock on the front door. Abbie nodded her understanding then grabbed his arm. "I won't owe you a baby after this, will I?" she asked suspiciously. Tazeh stared at her, confused. Abbie racked her brain for the few Spanish words she had picked up around Los Angeles. She rocked her arms as if she cradled a baby then whispered, "No *bambino*, no?"

Tazeh abruptly grinned and shook his head. Abbie sighed in relief then ran to the front door. Her heart thudded against her chest and the sweat beaded on her forehead. She wondered if she could knock, if she could find something to say to help Davis. She didn't know if she could, but she would, because her Davis was inside. She finally accepted that for him she would do anything.

Abbie took a deep breath then knocked on the wooden door. She heard chairs scrape on the floor then the door opened. She slightly recognized the man as one of the guards from the boat. He instantly recognized her and dragged her into the room. Davis glared at her and shook his head. She knew if there hadn't been a bandanna stuffed in his mouth, he would have yelled at her for coming to the house. She could see the anger in his eyes from across the room.

"You are stupid lady," the guard declared, shaking her. "We let you go and you come to us."

"I want to make you an offer," Abbie blurted out, praying she hadn't misunderstood Tazeh's motions.

The other guard stood and walked over to her while

Davis's eyes bulged. "What type of offer?" the other guard asked, his English considerably better.

"Anything you want, for as long as you can handle it." She tried to look sexy, tossing her hair over her shoulder, like she had seen Chris do numerous times. Lust immediately appeared in the two guards' eyes while Davis began to thrash around in his chair. Abbie couldn't understand why men would become so excited over a simple movement. She continued speaking in the same, throaty voice she had heard Chris use. "In return, you have to let the prince go."

"We could just take what we want right now," the guard replied, making certain to direct his gun at her.

Abbie's legs shook but she kept a confident smile on her face. She placed her hand on the gun nozzle and pushed it away from her face. "But, it wouldn't be half as fun."

Tazeh jumped through the window with a loud, warrior yell. He rolled to his feet in one motion, throwing a knife at the first guard's chest. The guard fell over dead. The second guard shot at Tazeh but Abbie pushed him just enough for the shot to harmlessly end in the ceiling. He reached for her but Tazeh ran over and hit him on the back of the head. He fell over unconscious.

Abbie ran to Davis and quickly untied his ropes as Tazeh ripped the bandanna from his mouth. Davis jumped to his feet, ignoring the fallen bodies and pinning Abbie with a hard glare. "You are insane, woman! What are you doing here?"

"Saving you," Abbie replied simply, then smiled at Tazeh and said, *"Gracias."*

"I don't need you to save me," Davis yelled. "I don't need you to care about me. The only reason I allowed those men to take me is because I knew you'd be on that boat and be safe."

"I don't like your attitude," Abbie said annoyed. "I just

wasted a lot of energy trying to save you and that man is dead . . ." Her voice trailed off as she glanced at the man with the knife in his chest. She had never seen a dead man in such close proximity. She was mesmerized by the vivid color of the red blood and the man's blank stare. Tears filled her eyes and she wondered if she would faint for the first time in her life.

Davis quickly moved to her and took her suddenly cold hands. He forced her to look at him, which broke her almost hypnotic trance with the dead man as she stared into the warmth of his brown eyes. He caressed her face then whispered softly, "We need to leave. They called Kevin and he's on his way."

Abbie nodded and quickly walked from the room before she was tempted to look at the dead man again. Davis and Tazeh followed. She watched the two men softly converse in Spanish then briefly embrace each other.

Davis grabbed her hand and led her through the village to the boat. The boat owner yelled in Spanish, gesturing toward the slowly rising sun. Davis handed him several more bills and the man quieted and started the boat motor. Abbie sat in the corner of the boat and Davis quickly sat beside her, pulling a dirty blanket over her.

"You've never seen a dead man before?" Davis asked as the boat slowly pulled through the harbor.

"Not that close. On TV and . . . not that close."

"I remember the first time I saw a dead man. I used to hunt with my friends and the older people. One day, a man accidentally killed his brother. Shot him straight through the forehead because he had heard a sound. I stopped hunting that day. I stopped using guns that day."

Abbie nodded and wiped the tears from her face. Davis pulled her to his chest and gently stroked her hair. "Do you know what Tazeh said before we left?"

"What?" she asked, not caring but knowing he wanted to take her mind off the dead man.

"He said, you're a beautiful woman with the spirit of a warrior and that's what makes good sons." Abbie laughed in spite of her shock and sadness and she felt Davis's grin against her forehead. "I thought you'd appreciate that."

Abbie smiled and relaxed against his chest. For the first time in three nights, Abbie fell asleep feeling safe and right where she belonged.

EIGHT

Davis helped Abbie off the small boat in the busy harbor of St. Moritz. A crowd of people wandered through the harbor, buying from the vendors and heading for various pleasure boats. This was a definite change from the smallness and slow pace of Natillas Island. Davis almost missed the quiet stillness of the small island, the huts and wooden houses, and the chance to be alone with Abbie.

St. Moritz was a tourist stop for many cruise ships and was a fairly large island. Davis had visited the tropical island many times with his parents and later his friends. He'd grown sick of the overpriced hotel rooms and crowded beaches a few years ago and had found another haunt for the wealthy and bored. Davis never realized how shallow his life was until that moment.

"I feel so dirty," Abbie whispered as a woman in a gold bikini top and shorts walked past them.

"We slept in a jungle for the past two nights," Davis said then groaned as he recognized the one hundred and thirty five foot luxury yacht moored in the harbor.

"What is it?" Abbie asked, a frightened tremor in her voice.

Davis smiled to ease her nerves and rubbed her neck. He felt the tense muscles underneath the skin and had the sudden urge to massage her entire body until every worry and tension she felt floated away. He didn't care if it took all night or several nights, as long as he could touch her skin. "I see something more scary than Kevin, Tazeh, or anything you could imagine. The yacht of Countess Jana Van de Owtis."

Abbie laughed and looked at the white luxury boat he pointed to. "Who is she?"

"A woman you could only find in royal circles. She's Russian nobility, although Russia hasn't recognized her or her family for about eighty years, but they still retain their title. She travels from one royal circle to the next, all over the world, searching for a husband who'll allow her to park her yacht outside his palace. She's been married three times and each time her husband gets older and older, although she's been known to keep several younger lovers on the side."

"How old is she?"

"I'm not certain with all the plastic surgery. I can tell you she was a . . . a mature woman when I was a boy."

"Who cares about her morals? We need help." Abbie headed for the yacht but Davis grabbed her arm. She laughed at him. "I promise I'll protect you from the evil claws of Countess Jana Van de Owtis."

Davis laughed and brushed her hair from her eyes. The only woman he needed protection from stood right in front of him. "I'm not worried about her, I'm worried about my mother. When she hears I went to the countess for help, she'll have a panic attack."

"Considering the circumstances, I think your mother won't mind too much."

"Prepare yourself," Davis said, taking her hand. "You're about to get your first introduction to Juhatu court life."

Davis climbed onto the yacht and Abbie followed him. An attendant, dressed in white shorts and a tight white T-shirt that strained against his massive chest, immediately appeared at the entrance of the boat. Davis took one look at the outfit and knew it was probably the Countess's mandatory uniform for her men servants. "May I help you . . ." The man's voice trailed off as his eyes grew wide. The young man obviously recognized Davis and bowed respectfully. "Your Highness, forgive me. I didn't know it was you."

"Is the countess here?"

"She went shopping, Your Highness, but . . . but Sir Francois is here. Should I wake him, Your Highness?"

"Francois Kent?" Davis tried to stifle his laughter and squeezed Abbie's hand. She looked at him curiously while the attendant withheld his own laughter. "Please bring him here. We'll wait in the sitting room." The attendant quickly ran into the boat and Davis led Abbie into a plush room.

Abbie sank into the velvet couch with a grateful sigh that made Davis's blood sing. He wanted to make her sigh like that. He clenched his fists and stuffed them in his pants pockets.

"Please tell me this is the end of a long road."

"It's the end of a long road. Just don't stare at Sir Francois too much."

Abbie opened her eyes and glanced at him. "Why?"

"He's married and . . . not to the owner of this boat. This is our secret."

Abbie frowned and shook her head. "Do many men in your country vacation with women other than their wives?"

"I guess it depends on the wife," Davis mumbled as the door opened and Sir Francois Kent walked into the room. He stood tall and proud, betraying his military career. He had black hair and crystal-blue eyes, and many women in Juhatu blushed whenever Sir Francois happened to glance in their direction. Sir Francois had long been a good friend of Davis's family. His family had fought with the Beriyias hundreds of years ago to drive the French from their land.

"Davis," Francois greeted embracing him. He placed a kiss first on one cheek, then the other. Francois held him at arm's length and looked over his clothes with distaste. He asked in French, "What happened to you? You look like a beggar on the streets."

"You haven't been home lately?" Davis asked.

"No, not for two months."

"What of Angelique?"

Francois frowned at the mention of his wife's name. "She takes her own vacation with Baron Putrow this time of year."

Davis saw the pain in Francois's eyes and once more Davis vowed never to marry for love. He'd rather marry for business and economics than be a slave to his heart. "I am in a bit of trouble, Francois."

Francois glanced at Abbie. Davis didn't miss the appreciative gleam in his eyes as the older man visibly examined every inch of her body. Davis also saw Abbie stiffen and glare at Francois. "Does your trouble involve this beautiful woman?"

"We were kidnapped from America by Kevin Munji and his men four days ago," Davis continued. "I think they drugged us and we flew to Florida or somewhere on the Atlantic coast. Then we sailed to about five miles off the coast of Natillas where Abbie and I were able to escape."

Francois shook his head confused. "You go too fast. What were you doing in America?"

"That's not important," Davis said, dismissing him. "I must contact my father immediately and tell him I am safe. I was supposed to return to Juhatu with Lowell four nights ago and no one has heard from me since. Kevin Munji wanted to use me as leverage in demands with my father. I want to stop anything that may transpire in my name before it is too late."

"I understand the urgency. We can use the radio in the next room."

"Thank you, Francois. My family will not forget you."

"This time the Munjis have gone too far," Francois said, slamming his fist on a table. "They must be stopped, eliminated."

"Kevin is a sick man, as was his father. We can't blame them for their actions."

"Maybe you can't, but I will. Jana and I will return home with you at once."

"I must wait until my father can send the palace guard and our plane. Kevin Munji and his men are still in the area. I refuse to place you or the countess in any danger."

"I dare that coward to set foot on this boat. I will rip his head off and eat it with my morning cup of coffee," Francois proclaimed then suddenly grinned and glanced at Abbie once more. "You and this woman escaped from Kevin Munji. Who is she?"

Davis glanced at Abbie's angry expression. He knew she did not speak French but, from the hard glint in her eyes, she knew they talked about her. "A friend I would be dead without. Someone once told me she has the heart of a warrior."

Francois grinned as he stared at Abbie. He shook his head. "She definitely doesn't have the body of one." He gallantly bowed at Abbie who rolled her eyes. Francois laughed then patted Davis's arm. "Follow me."

Davis turned to Abbie who glared at him. "What were you two talking about?" she demanded angrily. "That man kept looking at me like I was dinner."

"Francois has always appreciated a beautiful woman," Davis murmured more to himself than to her. He cleared his throat then said, "Francois and I are going to contact my father by radio, then I'll arrange a hotel room for us, and we'll finally have a decent meal."

"And when will I be in America?"

Davis felt a stab in his heart at the thought of her leaving him. He tried not to care but he did. "Within the next seventy-two hours."

Abbie sighed in relief and grinned. "I have to call my family as soon as possible. I know they must be worried sick."

"As soon as we reach the hotel." Davis forced himself to smile then walked from the room. He closed the door with a slam then ran a hand through his hair. He didn't need Abbie. He didn't want Abbie. Davis pushed any contrary thoughts out of his mind.

Davis sighed with something akin to relief at the first sip of the dark brandy as the two men sat in Davis's hotel suite. From across the room, Sir Francois grinned and raised his glass in salute, enjoying the view of the ocean from the windows.

Davis had gotten Abbie far away from Kevin with all of her appendages intact, his father had yelled at him for only two minutes, which almost made Davis think his father cared about him, and now he sat in his favorite hotel suite in St. Moritz with a view of the ocean sparkling in the moonlight, and a glass of the best brandy he could ever remember tasting in his hands. He even had on a clean suit, and a shirt that did not stand stiff from its own filth. His only problem was that the wrong person sat next to him. Davis liked Sir Francois. He respected him. But, the person he wanted beside him was on the other side of the door that connected their rooms—only twenty feet away. Davis knew this because he had envisioned himself crossing the distance about two hundred times in the last three hours since they had arrived at the hotel.

"It is a beautiful night, Your Highness, is it not?" Sir Francois commented, glancing out the balcony doors at the diamond-accented night sky.

"Wonderful," Davis murmured, thinking of the night he and Abbie had spent in the jungle. He abruptly cleared his throat. "My father told me to express his gratitude for your assistance in my situation."

"I would do anything for your father, king or not," Francois replied.

"Why?" Davis looked at his hands as Francois shot him a look of censure. Davis finally met the older man's eyes again. "I know you respect my father, Francois, a lot of men do. But, I wonder how many men like him. I wonder how many men . . . or women, for that matter . . . will like me."

"Like Sophia?"

Davis set his glass on the table, completely disgusted with himself for mentioning personal subjects around Francois. Francois was an old, dear friend of the family, but he was not a Beriyia. "Forget I mentioned anything, Francois—"

"Have you told your father how you feel?"

"About what?"

"About that young woman in the next room," Francois said, bluntly.

Davis laughed awkwardly then picked up the glass again. "I have no feelings for that woman besides gratitude and respect."

"She's quite beautiful."

"So is Sophia."

"Sophia is also a brainless twit," Francois said.

Davis tried to be offended on behalf of his future fiancée. "Watch how you speak of my intended, Francois."

Francois was not impressed or intimidated by Davis's cold tone. "She's a twit, Davis. I know it, you know it, and believe it or not, your father knows it."

"I cannot believe that my father would want me to marry someone he does not like."

"Maybe he's waiting for you to say something," Francois pleaded, almost desperately. "Whether you believe it or not, your father loves you."

"He must," Davis said bitterly. "I am the heir to his throne."

"If your father were a high school teacher and your mother were a housewife, they would still love you, Davis. They may not show it all the time. In fact, I'm not entirely certain either of them would know how, but they do, Davis. I had never seen your father cry in my entire life until the day you were born. Your mother had a lot of complications. . . . The doctors weren't entirely certain that either of you would make it."

"I'm certain the idea of losing both the queen and his heir upset him," Davis muttered.

Francois glared at him. "Watch how you speak of my friend, Your Highness," he said through clenched teeth. "At that moment, when your father almost lost both you and your mother, he was no longer the King of Juhatu. He was no longer a Beriyia. He was a man whose entire world was on the verge of collapsing. He and your mother want the best for you, Davis. Don't ever forget that. Don't ever allow anyone to make you forget that either."

Davis's sarcastic retort fell from his mouth when Countess Jana breezed into the hotel room. Davis refrained the urge to groan as she immediately headed toward him and enveloped him in a mass of frosted-blond hair, full lips, and a twice reconstructed bosom.

"Your Highness," Jana exclaimed, as she placed wet kisses on both his cheeks and then an uncomfortably long one on his lips. "It is such an honor to have you and your lady friend join us."

Davis politely but firmly placed distance between them. He noticed Francois's attempt to cover his laughter by lighting a cigarette. "Thank you for being a gracious host, Countess Jana."

"Anything I can do for Your Royal Highness," she replied, then added in a seductive whisper, "Anything."

Davis smiled at the older woman because they both knew she only spoke the innuendo because it was expected of her. "I'll remember that," Davis replied smoothly.

"You'll make me jealous, Jana," Francois remarked lightly.

Jana sauntered across the room to him and placed a kiss on his cheek. Davis had to admit that the countess made a nice picture—tall and curvaceous with the right amount of hips and even with all the blond hair, she always looked sophisticated and classy.

"You know you're first in my heart this month," Countess Jana said to Francois.

Francois shrugged at Davis. "She says this month, Your Highness. And they call us men callous."

"Now, Your Highness, where is this lovely creature I've been hearing about?" Jana demanded, with a pleasant smile. "Francois has told me she's quite delectable."

"She's not food. She's American," Davis replied lamely.

Jana broadly grinned then glanced at Francois. "It also seems as if this American has a way with Juhatuan men. She already has both His Highness and Francois wrapped around her finger."

"She's preparing for dinner," Davis said quickly, as Francois roared with laughter at Jana's teasing.

Jana glanced at both men's dark suits then at her own evening dress. The smile faded as she glared first at Davis then at Francois. "Does the American have anything to wear to dinner?"

"I told her to charge whatever she wanted from the boutique of the hotel—"

"Did you also tell her that we would be dining in the five-star hotel restaurant?" Jana demanded.

"Why is that important?" Davis asked blankly. "I'm certain she bought a dinner dress."

"Men," Jana mumbled to herself then began to speak in Russian as she stormed toward the door. She finally turned to them with an insulted heave of her shoulders. "Do either of you have any sense?"

"Jana," Francois protested.

"Sometimes I wonder if any of you are worth more than the arm to escort women into a room." With that final snort, she stormed from the room.

Davis and Francois stared at each other, then shook their heads. Francois settled on the black leather couch and asked companionably, "Did you catch much of the American football while you were in California?"

Abbie thought the bubble bath was positively sinful as she sank in the silky bubbles in the hotel room. She closed her eyes as she inhaled the flower scent of the soap. Not only was the bath large enough for several people but her hotel room was larger than her apartment at home.

She grinned as she remembered the telephone conversation with her family. Her two brothers and her parents had all been at her apartment, tearing the place apart, looking for any clues as to where she was. For the first fifteen minutes, Abbie sat silently on the phone while they each took turns yelling at her about her disappearing act. Abbie didn't tell them the truth because she didn't want them to worry further. She also knew if her father thought she was in any danger, he would send her brothers to bring her back home. Since there wasn't any more danger, Abbie refused to waste her brothers' time or unnecessarily worry her family. Abbie told her family that she had needed time off and had flown to St. Moritz for a vacation. Her younger brother, Adam, obviously hadn't believed her, but thankfully he didn't grill her like he usually did.

Plus, Abbie reasoned, she wasn't entirely lying. Apart from the kidnapping and the Natillas incident, this hotel room definitely qualified as a vacation. Abbie couldn't believe Davis lived like this, with friends as handsome and rakish as Sir Francois, hotel rooms large enough to get lost in, and the bowing and scraping of various servants. Abbie shuddered in disgust at the memory of the awe in men's eyes when they looked at Davis, of the whispers that followed them when they walked into the hotel. Davis was recognized on this small island wherever he went. People stared at him as if he were an animal in a zoo.

If Sir Francois had not requested the island police to escort them to the hotel, Abbie had no doubt the people would have crowded around Davis to get a closer look. Not to speak to him or be friendly, but to stare at him like a lab rat. Abbie hated the invading looks from everyone. She suddenly felt a new respect for Davis and how hard it must be for him to live in a world where he was treated like a statue by virtually everyone. People wanted to look at him, but not care for him. Not that she felt too sorry for him. She couldn't feel sorry for anyone who could afford an opulent hotel room like this.

Abbie reluctantly stepped from the bath and wrapped the hotel's plush terry-cloth robe around her. She felt as if finally all of the grime and dirt from the past few days was washed off her. Because she felt clean and comfortable, she wondered what Davis was doing. Their two rooms were connected by a single door that Abbie half-hoped and half-feared Davis would knock on. After spending almost seventy-two straight hours with him, Abbie felt lost without him. She knew he was safe and probably sleeping next door but she wanted to hear his voice and see the exasperation that crossed his face when she ignored whatever he wanted her to do.

There was a knock on the hotel door and Abbie moved to answer it. She told herself she was safe, that Kevin Munji couldn't possibly know where she was, but her hands still trembled as she opened the door.

A tall, blond woman breezed into the room in a wave of floral-scented perfume and large breasts. Abbie smiled because she knew without a doubt that this woman was the infamous Countess Jana Van de Owtis. The woman grinned and set a package on the bed. She made a loud hiss of glee as she twirled Abbie around. She excitedly clapped her hands together, a bundle of energy that made Abbie tired again.

"You must be Countess Van de Owtis."

"Everyone calls me Countess Jana," the woman responded in heavily Russian-accented English. "You must be Abigail, a beautiful French name. Francois was right, you are ravishing."

Abbie could feel the flush cover her face and she clutched the lapels of the robe closer together. "It's nice to meet you, Countess Jana."

"I didn't want to interrupt your preparations for dinner, but I had to meet the woman who has placed such a gleam in the Stone Prince's eyes."

"Stone Prince?"

"That's a pet name some of us have for Davis. He can be quite a cold young man when he wants. I saw him smile twice when your name was mentioned."

Abbie laughed at the image of Davis smiling at her name. "He was probably laughing because he wants to kill me."

Countess Jana gently patted Abbie's right cheek and smiled. "He wants to do something to you and it doesn't involve killing you." She grinned as Abbie's mouth dropped open when she understood the meaning. The Countess laughed then practically whirled around the room to the closet. "Now, show Countess Jana what you will wear to dinner tonight."

"Dinner? What dinner?"

Countess Jana sighed in exasperation and rattled on for a few seconds in Russian. She rolled her eyes then said in English, "Men. I arranged for Francois and Davis to come up with the idea to take us to dinner. Of course, neither man thought of what you would wear. But, once more, Countess Jana to the rescue. I brought my dresses that I have outgrown . . . or shall we say, matured out of. I can't bear to part with most of them because they have such good memories, such romance, such passion. But, I guess it is time for Countess Jana to move on to a new chapter in her life. Francois told me your measurements and I knew these would fit. Pick one."

Abbie didn't know which she was more depressed by: that Francois knew her measurements or that she would have to spend another evening pretending not to be affected by Davis.

An hour later, Abbie stared at herself in the room's full-length mirror, and she was absolutely speechless. Abbie had never thought of herself as particularly beautiful or worthy of a second look, especially compared to Chris or some of her other friends. But, tonight, Abbie thought she was gorgeous. The long, almost sparkling, white gown Countess Jana had chosen for her, emphasized the positive attributes of her body and hid the flaws. For once her height seemed like an asset, her legs were emphasized and visible through the high slits on either side of the dress, her body encased by the tight dress. The dress even made her neck appear long and graceful, instead of just long, like she usually thought.

Abbie studied her face in the mirror. She never wore makeup, except the occasional mascara and lipstick, but Countess Jana had artfully applied the full package. Even though it looked like Abbie wore no makeup, Abbie could see the change in her face. She looked beautiful. She looked like the type of woman that would interest a prince, the type of woman who could handle a prince with one arched eyebrow. Abbie couldn't wait to see Davis's reaction when he saw her.

Countess Jana stood next to her with a proud smile, as if Abbie was her own creation. "You look like a princess."

Abbie grinned at the older woman. "I feel like a princess." She gently touched her hair, which fell in soft, gleaming waves to her shoulders. "What did you do to me?"

"What do you mean?"

"I-I've never looked like this before."

Countess Jana shot her a strange look at the comment then smiled. "I'm not a fairy godmother, Abigail. I'm about as far from a virginal, magical fairy as one could possibly be. You're a beautiful young woman, Abigail. Not only that but you're smart and independent. You remind me of myself when I was younger. Maybe that's why I like you so much."

Abbie abruptly threw her arms around the woman as tears sprung to her eyes. Countess Jana laughed then delicately wiped Abbie's tears away. "No crying is allowed. We women cannot cry and mess up our makeup."

"I'm sorry," Abbie said, smiling through her tears. "It's just that for the first time in my life when I look in the mirror I like what I see."

Countess Jana sobered. "You're serious, aren't you? This isn't some false show of humility." Abbie nodded unable to meet the other woman's eyes. She had always successfully hid her insecurities, and now she poured out her true feelings to a Russian countess. "Abigail, you are beautiful. The first moment I saw you, I said to myself, *Jana, there's a woman who could have given you a run for your money if you were twenty years younger.* Believe me, I don't say that about every woman I meet."

Abbie ungracefully sniffled and smiled. "You're too kind."

"That's the first time I've been accused of that. If you don't believe me, watch the prince's eyes when he sees you for the first time. A man's eyes give away all his secrets when it comes to a woman. He can bluff his way through a game of cards, but he can never fool the woman he loves."

Abbie laughed in disbelief and pretended to straighten the bedcovers. She didn't want the countess to see her own true feelings for Davis. "Davis doesn't love me."

"If you believe that, then you're not as intelligent as I thought."

"We have feelings for each other, and we probably always will because of the experience we shared. We were almost killed."

"And your love for him is because of this shared experience?"

Abbie quickly glanced at her as a knock sounded on the hotel door. She grabbed the woman's arms causing Countess Jana to gasp. "Please, Countess, don't say anything to Davis."

"You do love the prince?" Countess Jana whispered with an amazed smile.

"Countess, this is between us. Davis must never know."

"Why, darling?"

The pounding on the door grew more insistent and Davis's voice floated through the door. "Abbie, are you okay in there?"

"Just a second, Davis," Abbie called toward the door then looked at the countess. "Please."

"You must tell him. He loves you, too, Abbie. I know it."

"I can't. Please promise me you won't say anything." Abbie pleaded silently with Countess Jana until she reluctantly nodded. Abbie released her arm then crossed the room to open the hotel door.

She smiled when she saw Davis and Francois standing in the hotel hallway, both wearing black tuxedos. She barely noticed Francois. She only saw Davis and how incredible, how beautiful he looked in the tailored suit. She knew whatever happened, she would remember this night for the rest of her life, especially his eyes as he looked from her right leg visible in the slit of the dress to her full breasts molded against the material.

Abbie hid her smile when he finally met her eyes, a shocked expression on his face. "Good evening, gentlemen," Abbie said innocently. She finally understood why Chris walked around with such a confident attitude. It was very empowering to leave a man speechless.

"Belle," Francois complimented, taking her right hand and placing a kiss on the palm. "You look absolutely breathtaking." Davis continued to stand in the doorway with a confused expression on his face.

Countess Jana floated through the door, expectantly holding out her hand to Francois who obligingly kissed it. "How do I look, Francois?"

"Dazzling as always, darling," Francois said smiling then winking at Abbie.

"Has the palace guard arrived yet?" Abbie asked, looking at Davis. He shook his head, still staring at her like he had never seen her before.

"They shall arrive within the hour," Francois answered for Davis. "They recommended we stay in public until they are present. It is harder for Kevin Munji and his men to try anything with people around. The St. Moritz police will escort us until the palace guard arrive."

"Great. I'm famished," Abbie said, closing the hotel door.

"We have reservations at the restaurant downstairs. Magnifique," Francois said then offered his bent arm to

Countess Jana. She winked at Abbie then linked arms with Francois and the two walked toward the hotel stairs.

Abbie started after them but Davis grabbed her arm. She gasped from the shock of his touch then met his eyes. She wanted to run away when she saw the blatant desire in his face. She wanted to run because she knew it would never work, but running was the farthest thing from his mind.

"I wish . . . I can't describe how beautiful you are," Davis said in a low voice she had never heard from him. "I thought in the jungle with your hair wild, and your face flushed from the air that you were the most beautiful vision I'd ever seen in my life. But now . . . now, I . . . you're like the stars, Abbie. Simply heavenly and not of this world."

Tears filled her eyes at his beautiful words and she took his hand in hers. "You clean up pretty nice yourself, Your Highness."

Davis laughed then kissed her hand that rested in his. "Shall we pretend to enjoy dinner now?"

Abbie nodded silently because she understood and wanted the unspoken "after" that they both knew would come that night. Davis brushed an errant curl from her face then led her down the hotel stairs.

NINE

Davis could barely eat like a mature adult while sitting across the dinner table from Abbie. He always knew she was beautiful, but tonight in the long dress and with the soft sheen on her hair, Davis couldn't remember the names or faces of any other woman in his life. He knew he was acting foolish and Francois would probably tell everyone in Juhatu about his behavior but even Davis couldn't understand why he acted like a child.

He could only mechanically stuff whatever food he had ordered in his mouth and pretend to follow the conversation. Every time Abbie looked at him or smiled at him, he would lose all trace of the composure he had gained since the last time she had looked at him. Davis finally stopped berating himself and started enjoying the evening. The four sat at a round, discreet table in a dark corner of the restaurant. Candles glowed throughout the room, the open patio doors allowed the salty ocean breeze into the room, and Davis was with the woman he loved. He could admit he loved her. He had probably loved her since the first moment he saw her. Only with Abbie did he let his wall down, lose his cool, act like Davis, instead of the crown prince of Juhatu.

"Your Highness," a deep voice said behind him. Davis turned in his seat and stood when he saw Edward Getrin, the captain of the palace guard. The two men shook hands and Edward smiled with obvious relief, speaking in French. "It's good to see you are well, Your Highness."

"Edward, I'm very happy to see you, as well." Davis motioned to his dinner companions, his eyes lingering too long on Abbie. "You know the countess and Sir Francois. I would like to present Abigail Barnes."

Edward smiled at Abbie and kissed her hand, lapsing into flawless English. "You must be the woman who accompanied the prince on his adventure."

"Adventure is an interesting way to describe it," Abbie said, smiling.

Davis didn't like the sight of another man touching Abbie, no matter how innocently, and quickly asked Edward in French, "Are your men in place?"

"Yes, Your Highness. We shall leave for Juhatu early tomorrow morning from a private airstrip. We will be in the capital by noon. Your father is looking forward to seeing you and discussing the events of the past few days."

"Very good." Davis could see from the uncomfortable expression on Edward's face that his father's famous temper had been unleashed on the Palace Guard. Davis began to sit then touched Edward's arm. "I am sorry about Hiram. He was a good man and was my friend."

"What happened to Hiram. . . ?" Edward's voice trailed off and he suddenly grinned. "No, Your Highness, Hiram is still alive. He was shot in the stomach but he survived. He's in a Monboit hospital, complaining about the food and itching to get back to work."

Davis grinned and looked at Abbie. "He says Hiram, my bodyguard who was shot in Los Angeles, is still alive. He's in the hospital and doing fine."

"That's wonderful, Davis," Abbie said, smiling.

"We'll escort you to your rooms when you're ready. We've also placed guards at the countess's yacht." Edward smiled at the others then crisply turned and made his way around the other tables.

Davis sat back in his seat, his eyes once more wandering to Abbie. He quickly looked away when she met his eyes. He didn't want to frighten her with his intensity and strange feelings. Davis had never been in love with anyone before. He had tried not to care about anything or anyone since he realized his life as a prince wasn't his own.

"Does everyone in your country speak English so well?" Abbie asked.

"I believe so," Davis said, smiling for no apparent reason.

Countess Jana suddenly clapped her hands as a band moved to the stage in the front of the room. Soft music floated through the room. "Oh, Your Highness, they're playing a waltz. I can still remember the Christmas Ball last year at the Palace and how positively dashing you looked on the dance floor with that ditzy young woman from England. I'm surprised your suit was not dripping from her drool."

Davis forced himself to smile. "Would you like to dance, Countess Van de Owtis?"

Countess Jana giggled. "Of course not. I know I pretend to be young but you need someone as lovely as you to dance with."

Davis stared at Abbie who laughed at the Countess. "I don't know how to dance a waltz, a samba, or anything else," Abbie said, shaking her head.

"His Highness is an excellent dancer," Francois chimed in. "He could teach you anything that you do not know."

Davis abruptly stood and held out a hand to Abbie. "I don't think we'll get any peace from these two until we dance."

Abbie laughed and placed her hand in his. "And His Highness must have peace."

Davis grinned, like he only did around Abbie, as she stood. They moved to the dance floor and Davis tried to maintain a respectable distance from her, but as soon as she smiled at him, he drew her as close as possible to him. He noticed several people point toward them but Davis didn't care about royal decorum or social dictates. Abbie Barnes, the woman who stared down a pagan chief, was in his arms and he never felt more adventurous, more happy, more right with the world.

"What are you smiling about?" Abbie asked, staring at him.

Davis grinned. "I just thought of you in Natillas, threatening to kill Tazeh."

"I don't think that was funny, at all," she responded, as laughter bubbled pass her lips. "I was so scared, Davis. I thought I was going to drop the spear."

"I was pretty scared too."

"You finally admit it."

"Did you see that man? He could've eaten me for breakfast."

"Why did he help us? Did you ask him?"

"He said he owed you. He recompensed me but since you won the fight, those are his words, you deserved some recompense yourself."

"I'm glad to see someone recognizes me as the true winner of that fight," Abbie said as her hands moved in circles on his back. Davis could feel the heat from her hands, almost as if she touched his bare skin. Davis knew this was unacceptable affection in a public place, but he couldn't force himself to say anything. Her hands moved to his face and she briefly touched the still-sensitive bruise on his chin. "You still have a bruise. I should've killed him."

Davis grinned and whispered, "I didn't think I'd ever hear a woman say that. At least, not the women I've known."

"I'm nothing like the women you've known," she responded with a secret smile.

Davis couldn't stand the anticipation anymore and

pressed his lips against hers. A shocked gasp escaped her lips and Davis took the opportunity to plunge his tongue in her mouth. She slowly responded and Davis drew away from her before he made love to her on the dance floor.

"I want you, Abbie," he blurted. "I've never wanted anyone like I want you right now and to be perfectly honest, I doubt I ever will again."

Abbie grinned and Davis held his breath as he waited for her response. He hadn't meant to put his feelings on the table, to make her uncomfortable. He also didn't know why her answer was so important to him.

"How long do we have to pretend to enjoy dinner?" she finally said, repeating his words from earlier that evening.

Davis laughed, as a wave of relief washed over him. "I'm a prince, didn't you hear? I don't have to sit at dinner if I don't want to."

"Well, I'm not a princess, which means I have to be polite, which means we're going to be here until dessert. Try to eat fast, Your Highness." She slowly moved from his grip and walked back to the table. Davis grinned as he watched her hips sway across the room. He suddenly realized he stood alone on the dance floor, grinning like a fool. He straightened his jacket and walked to the table.

Abbie felt the butterflies flutter in her stomach as the guard opened her hotel door. Davis followed her into the room and closed the door with a note of finality. Abbie knew she couldn't back out now. She knew Davis would never make her do anything she didn't want to, but she also knew once she was alone in the room with him, she would lose all self-control.

The nerves and the passion all mingled in her stomach as she moved to the hotel bar and pretended to examine the labeled liquor. "Would you like anything to drink?" Even she could hear the nerves in her voice.

Davis didn't answer and Abbie dared to look at him. She slightly choked on the lump in her throat when she saw his eyes darken. He stalked across the room like a hunter and placed his hands on her shoulders. Abbie couldn't stop herself from flinching and he smiled.

"Is my warrior princess suddenly shy?" he asked softly. His voice sent bursts of tingles through her body. His hands moved to her shoulders and he rubbed them gently. "We don't have to do anything you don't want, Abbie. Relax."

"I'm not shy," she said defiantly.

"No?" Davis touched his tongue to her ear and Abbie blushed as she jumped again. Davis grinned and gently bit her ear, making her moan in pleasure. "I was beginning to think you weren't scared of anything but you are. You're scared of me because of how I can make you feel."

"I'm not afraid of you." The tremors in her voice betrayed the truth and Davis smiled again.

"Come to the couch." He took both her hands and led her to the couch several feet from the bed. He gently pushed her to lay on her stomach on the couch and she trembled, unable to see him, as she felt the weight of the couch shift as he sat next to her hips.

She didn't know what he was doing until she heard the buzz of the zipper and felt his fingers brush her bare skin as he slid the dress down. Abbie knew she should've protested but she only shifted her body so he could slide the dress fully off. She shivered from the cool air on her bare skin and the feel of his intense eyes as she lay in only her bra and panties.

Her eyes slid closed as his hands began to massage her shoulders and back in slow, erotic circles. Every concern and worry Abbie felt about her family, her job, even Davis drifted out the window with the ocean breeze. She could feel his hands down to the balls of her feet, as her body confused itself with love and desire.

"You're too tense," Davis whispered. "It's a good thing

I've trained to be a masseuse, in case this prince thing doesn't work out."

Abbie laughed, relaxing even more. She hadn't been with a man since her last boyfriend over two years ago and the few previous times, she had never laughed before making love. The men always made her feel it was a serious, somber undertaking and she should lie in one place and allow them to work their magic.

"Well, if you ever need a recommendation, give me a call." Davis laughed as he unhooked her bra. Abbie clenched her fists on the sofa but lifted so he could remove her bra. His fingers fluttered around the waistband of her underwear for an unbearable moment then he slid them down her legs. Abbie lay on the couch, completely nude before his eyes. And she flowed with too much warmth to feel embarrassed or worry about whatever body flaws she imagined she had.

Davis placed a kiss between her shoulder blades and Abbie whispered his name. He alternated between kissing her back and shoulders and massaging the area with such tenderness that she felt like the consistency of gelatin. Abbie knew the only reason she didn't melt was the thought of never feeling his touch again.

"Will you turn over for me?" he asked her, breaking the silence in the room.

Abbie slowly turned over, still laying on the couch. Davis's eyes traveled over her body then he smiled at her. Abbie returned his grin and caressed his face, loving the feel of his skin underneath her hand. Davis deliberately took off his jacket then tie. Abbie helped him with the buttons on his shirt and within seconds, he was as deliciously naked as she was.

Without any shame, Abbie looked over every inch of his body with a smug smile. He was as beautiful as she had imagined, as she had dreamed. With a mind of their own, her hands ran over his body, over his shoulders, around his stomach, down the length of his legs. It was a cramped position on the couch but neither could stop touching the other long enough to move to the bed.

As Abbie explored the muscles and hardness of his chest, Davis took her mouth in a passionate kiss. Abbie welcomed him, wrapping her legs around his waist and trying to pull him as close to her as possible. She wanted to chain him to her forever. She wanted to always feel like she felt at that exact moment, like she would explode into a million pieces were it not for Davis's weight on top of her.

His hands moved all over her at once, from her neck to her breasts, even down to her toes. Then his lips took over. His tongue dipped into her navel and Abbie trembled from the shot of pleasure. She ran her hands over his strong shoulders as his mouth traveled down to her center. He teased her for several seconds, as he breathed onto her opening, his breath tickling her and driving her completely insane.

Abbie couldn't stand the warmth any more and pulled his face back to hers. Davis grinned as his lips rested inches above hers. Abbie tried to smile back but she could only run her tongue over his lips and kiss him.

Then she felt him enter her. Abbie gasped from the intense pleasure that washed over her. All thoughts fled from her mind as he moved in her. His eyes bore into hers and she quickly closed her eyes, not wanting to look at him. She knew her body told him about her love but she didn't want him to see it in her eyes. Abbie dug her nails into his shoulders and used him to anchor her to earth before she floated into the sky and never returned.

Then the swirls of euphoria began. It started in her toes and her fingertips then centralized in the place that called his name. The circles became more and more intensified, almost painful, until the beautiful release came.

Abbie screamed his name over and over as she felt him fall over the edge right after her.

Neither Abbie nor Davis moved for several moments, trying to recover from the feelings still racing through their bodies. Davis looked at Abbie and she met his eyes with an amazed expression. He tried to think of something, anything, to say but he could only brush a few sweat-dampened strands of hair from her eyes. Abbie grinned and Davis's body began to respond before his brain could.

"Well," Abbie said then burst out laughing. Davis laughed, too, feeling the same pleasure move through his body as when they just made love.

"That would describe it," Davis finally said then abruptly stood. He picked her up and walked across the room to the bed.

Abbie wrapped her arms around his neck and when he laid her on the bed, she pulled him on top of her. "Now that you've got me in bed, Your Highness, what do you plan to do with me?"

His mind answered in a million different ways but he could only kiss her and try to convey his thoughts through the kiss. With his tongue, he explored the depths of her warm mouth as his hands continued to run over her body, remembering every curve and valley.

One of her hands covered his manhood and Davis's mind went completely numb as her hand moved over the length. His legs trembled as her hand erotically tortured him. Davis managed to smile at her. "I guess you're not shy any more," he said.

"I wasn't shy before," she muttered, her hand momentarily squeezing his length. Davis gulped in pretend fear then laughed. Abbie grinned then pulled him to her lips. Their tongues clashed and Davis slipped into her again. Davis moaned from the pleasure and the pain and bit his lower lip before he blurted out his love for the one woman who would never have him and he could never have.

TEN

Abbie slowly opened her eyes, as her hand rubbed the empty pillow on the bed next to her. The empty white sheets and the empty room confirmed her worst fear— Davis was gone. She tried not to care. She tried to tell herself she had gone into the situation with her eyes open but she still felt the pain stab her in the heart.

Abbie dragged herself from the bed and quickly wrapped a robe around her body. She could still feel his hands on her, his lips against hers. Abbie wanted to take a shower and erase every memory of last night, although she knew one shower wouldn't do that. Abbie walked into the bathroom and turned on the hot water. Steam quickly rose from the faucet as she stared at herself in the mirror.

Abbie couldn't bear to face her reflection and quickly turned away from the mirror. She had broken her own cardinal rule by sleeping with a man without really knowing him. For that, she would never forgive herself. Then Abbie remembered their lack of protection. Not only had she been impulsive but she'd been foolish. Abbie placed a hand over her stomach at the possibility of having Davis's baby. It disgusted her that the thought made her smile. She wondered what their child would look like. Would their son or daughter have Davis's beautiful eyes and smile?

Abbie quickly shook her head to clear away those thoughts and untied the knot on the robe. There was a knock on the bathroom door and Abbie quickly retied the knot and cracked the door an inch. She almost slammed the door when she saw Davis, looking too handsome for his own good in a black suit, standing on the other side. The only reason Abbie didn't close the door was her pride. She wouldn't allow him to know how much last night affected her.

"I just wanted to make certain you were awake," he said stiffly. "We have to be at the airstrip in forty-five minutes."

"I'll be ready."

"It will be a five-hour flight to Juhatu. We have two flights a week to the United States. You'll miss the flight today but you'll be able to leave on Monday."

"Thank you."

"I took the initiative and bought several outfits for you from the hotel boutique."

"You didn't have to do that."

"Yes, I did."

"As soon as I get home, I'll send you a check to cover the full amount." Abbie felt the tears pushing against her emotional wall and she cleared her throat as he continued to stare at her. She could tell he wanted to say something and she prayed he wouldn't mention last night.

"About last night . . ." His voice trailed off and she saw the discomfort and shame on his face. Abbie knew she would lose whatever composure she had managed to retain if he told her he felt guilty or that last night was a mistake.

"We're two adults who acted on an attraction that resulted from extraordinary circumstances. I'll return to California and you'll rule your country and we'll both remember our time together with a smile. That's what happened last night." Abbie dug her fingernails into the palm of her hand to restrain her tears as she retained a friendly smile on her face. "I need to get ready to leave." She closed the door and the tears immediately rained down her face.

Abbie glanced out the airplane window as the pilot announced their descent into Monboit, the capital city of Juhatu. She gasped at the tree-covered hills and the sparkling blue ocean that surrounded the island. She could even see the tall white columns of what she knew was Davis's home, the palace of Monboit.

She wanted to ask Davis hundreds of questions about his country, about the terrain, the economy. She wanted to know about the customs and traditions but she hadn't spoken to him since leaving St. Moritz. They had shared idle conversation and one-word exchanges, but she had never stared him in the eyes and she had never seen him looking at her.

Abbie tightened her seat belt as the plane lowered to the ground. She smiled at Edward, who sat across from her. If Edward hadn't been on the flight, she probably would've jumped from the airplane to escape the tense silence.

"I think you will enjoy Juhatu," Edward said, smiling. "We have beautiful beaches, exquisite shopping, and wonderful mountains. You can take your pick of which activity to enjoy first—horseback riding, hiking, lying on the beach."

"It sounds wonderful but I have to return home. My family won't be satisfied until they see me in the flesh, and I have work."

Edward shrugged. "Maybe another time."

Abbie forced a smile then stole a quick glance at Davis, who was reading a magazine and ignored them. She sighed and stared out the window again. She imagined laying on the beach with Davis, feeling the sun on her back. She rubbed her eyes before a tear could escape because she knew it would never happen.

"We want to keep this incident with Kevin Munji out of the media," Davis suddenly said, still not looking at her. "The palace has leaked that I went to America with full knowledge and approval from my parents. You are described as a friend who wanted to visit Juhatu."

Abbie didn't respond but stared at her hands.

Out of the corner of his eye, Davis saw Abbie clutch the arm rest as the plane landed on the ground. He always found it fascinating when she showed any hint of fear or nerves. Davis thought she was invincible. She certainly had emotions of ice. Davis could barely function after their night, while Abbie joked with Edward Getrin, promised to pay him for clothes. He would've bought her the entire boutique if he thought she would've accepted it.

As the airplane rolled to a stop on the runway, Davis glanced outside the window and groaned. A group of men and women in suits stood behind the fence waiting, as well as a whole unit of armed guards and the multitude of press. He couldn't believe he could wake up after the most invigorating experience in his life and immediately head back to his cage.

Davis forced a smile as one of the guards opened the door and the warm Juhatu breeze rushed into the airplane. Davis didn't look at Abbie, for fear he would hijack the plane and demand to be taken anywhere with her, and walked down the stairs. He waved to the people with the practiced insincerity of a person who was forced to do it thousands of times. His mother, Queen Lissette, met him in the middle of the red carpet. He could tell she had worried about him by the dark circles around her hazel eyes, marring her otherwise smooth vanilla complexion. Despite her apparent concern for him, she still looked impeccable as usual, her sandy blond hair swept into the usual intricate chignon. Davis placed a kiss on her cheek and was surprised when she squeezed his arms, a divergence from their usual formal greeting.

"I'm glad you're well," she whispered in his ear.

Davis smiled at her then was enveloped by a blur of black curls and expensive perfume. He returned the embrace of Sophia Zidane for fear of any misinterpretation or embarrassment for her to the press but he made a mental note to talk to whoever had approved her presence at his welcoming. In the months before he left, Davis couldn't turn around without Lady Sophia Zidane shoving her breasts in his face.

"Next time you leave for an impromptu skiing vacation, at least have the decency to write, Your Highness," Sophia scolded as she placed a kiss on his right cheek.

"I apologize, Sophia," Davis said then walked toward the car before he ran onto the plane screaming. Nothing had changed, not that he expected anything to, but the reality only depressed him more. His mother walked beside him.

"Your father can't wait to talk to you," Lissette said in a neutral tone.

"That doesn't surprise me." Davis heard the numerous reporters call his name from behind a barricade and he dutifully waved to them. A guard opened the waiting car door and Lissette slid into the backseat. Davis looked behind him to help Abbie into the car and frowned. Edward was already opening the door of the car behind them. Davis clenched his jaw to prevent himself from commanding Abbie to ride with him. Instead, he slid into the car with his mother. He certainly didn't want to give the press anything to write about by singling out Abbie.

* * *

Abbie pushed aside all the pain from Davis ignoring her as soon as they landed and stared out the window as the car weaved through the quaint, clean streets of the capital city. Abbie instantly fell in love with the small city. The clean streets, the beautiful people; she could see the sparkling-white sand in various glimpses between the split-level buildings.

She smiled in amazement at the rainbow of colors of people who walked down the sidewalks of the cobblestone main street. She noticed the small, chic boutiques and the expensively dressed mannequins in the windows. She waved back to the people who sat at tables placed on restaurant terraces, enjoying the bright sun. Everyone on the street smiled and seemed to know everyone else. Abbie could tell it was a small community, where people actually knew their neighbor or the town mayor, not like in Los Angeles, where Abbie barely knew the people who lived next to her in her apartment building.

Abbie turned away from the scene on the street and stared out the front window of the car. She saw the tall mountains rising in the distance, framed by an ocean of trees at the base of the mountains and clouds that hovered at the peaks like an idyllic scene on a postcard. With the emerald blue-green ocean reflecting the bright rays of the sun, which were visible just beyond the businesses on the main street, Abbie wondered how anyone could ever leave this island.

"It does something to you, doesn't it?" From his seat beside her in the back of the limousine, Edward broke into her thoughts.

"This city is beautiful," Abbie admitted. "How does anyone do any work around here?"

"When you live in paradise, you become blasé about it," Edward said, with a laugh.

"It certainly is paradise." But no matter how beautiful the city was, it still could not erase the image of the young chocolate woman throwing her arms around Davis. She stared at her hands for a second then asked as casually as she could manage, "Who were those two women that greeted Davis . . . I mean, the prince."

"His mother, Queen Lissette, and Lady Sophia."

"Who is Lady Sophia?"

"There are rumors she is his betrothed. They say the two will announce their engagement within the month."

Another stab of disgust and pain left Abbie breathless. She gripped her fists and tried not to scream in anger. She felt betrayed, she felt less than human, like the prince's own toy. All he had to do was look at her and she fell into his arms, exactly like the stupid women she had always made fun of in school.

Abbie's thoughts momentarily turned away from her self-hatred when she saw the towering, massive structure in front of her. The palace. The building sprawled across an acre with massive columns and windows spaced evenly on three different levels. Various balconies dotted the front of the building. A green lawn surrounded the house as far as she could see, which abruptly dropped off into a cliff, in the distance, to the side of the house. The palace looked like the classical Renaissance structures that dotted most of Western Europe. Palaces that Abbie liked to dream about, wondering what life had been like for the occupants when they were first built.

The car rolled to a stop in front of the massive double door that easily could have fit several horses through the entrance. Without waiting for anyone to open the door, Abbie absently got out of the car. She noticed the intricate craftsmanship on the columns that towered over her head, and the panels that decorated the front of the palace. There was minute attention to every detail.

"It's beautiful," she gasped as Edward stood next to her. "It's like a fairy tale."

Edward smiled and placed a hand at her elbow. Abbie

noticed Davis and the two women walking ahead of them. She gritted her jaw, forgetting the beauty that surrounded her. She wanted to sock Davis and the beautiful woman who clung to his arm. Abbie reluctantly walked with Edward into the palace and once more her mouth dropped open.

Abbie knew from the foyer alone that the works of art and history inside the palace were priceless. Golden framed paintings, expensive tapestries, and gold candlestick holders decorated the massive entrance. The marble floor of the entrance led toward two different hallways and also housed the end of a large staircase that Abbie could only assume led to the private quarters of the family, although she could not imagine anyone living in the palace. There were too many beautiful things around for people to live near.

She made certain to keep her arms close to her body. The last thing she wanted to do was knock over an irreplaceable vase or crystal and have to pay the country of Juhatu twenty dollars a month for the rest of her life.

"Welcome home, Your Highness." Abbie heard the various greetings from the group of men and women standing inside the foyer. She watched Davis absently nod to various members of the group and shake hands.

A young woman, with large blue eyes and curly black hair, immediately approached Abbie and offered her hand. Abbie tried to pretend her heart wasn't breaking into numerous pieces as Davis kept his back to her, and she shook the young woman's hand with a forced smile. "I'm Josie," she said in heavily accented English. "I am to help you while you are in Juhatu. If you'll follow me, I'll show you to your room."

"Thank you, Josie."

"Abbie, wait," Davis said, without looking at her. She debated on continuing up the stairs then stopped because she imagined herself in some medieval stocks in front of the palace for disobeying the prince. "I'd like to introduce you to my mother."

Abbie glanced at the beautiful woman who eyed her like a wolf would eye an ant—insignificant. She was tall with smooth, creamy skin, shining hair, and intense hazel eyes. Abbie could instantly tell where Davis inherited the intense gleam in his eyes. Abbie liked to think she didn't intimidate easily, but Queen Lissette intimidated her without saying one word.

"Mother, this is Abigail Barnes. Abbie, this is my mother, Lissette Beriyia."

Abbie wasn't certain whether to curtsy, shake her hand or bow. She finally decided to straighten her shoulders and offer her hand.

"It's a pleasure to meet you, Your Majesty." She cringed as her voice shook. Lissette stared at Abbie's hand for a second then smiled and shook it.

"It's a pleasure to meet you, as well, Abigail. Before you leave, we'll have to have tea and discuss the specifics of your vacation."

"I look forward to it," Abbie lied.

"This is Lady Sophia, a friend of the family," Davis continued. The younger woman didn't attempt to disguise the contempt in her beautiful hazel eyes.

"You don't speak French, Abigail?" Sophia asked in perfect English.

"I took a few years in high school, but no, I don't."

Sophia instantly murmured something in French to Davis, who glared at her. Sophia smiled at Abbie with a triumphant gleam in her eyes.

"I'm sure it's been a long few days for you, Abigail," Lissette said graciously. "Josie will show you to your room where you may take a nap and freshen up. Dinner is served at six o'clock promptly. Until then, the day is yours."

"Thank you." Abbie refused to look at Davis and instead followed Josie up the stairs.

She lost track of all the beautiful vases and paintings on the wall as they walked down a hallway that seemed to continue forever. There were portraits of brown-skinned and olive-skinned men and women evenly spaced on the wall. Abbie noticed almost every man and woman in the pictures had the same look in their eyes. There was a combination of regret and pride. The same look she had seen in Davis's eyes whenever he talked about his responsibilities in Juhatu.

"Those are the past kings and queens," Josie said softly, noticing Abbie's interest. "I'm supposed to know the history of each one but I become too confused."

Josie opened a door and Abbie walked inside the most beautiful sitting room she had ever seen in her life. Through the open patio doors drifted the unique scent of Juhatu, half ocean saltiness and half pristine mountain freshness. Abbie ran a hand over the large, soft fabric of the overstuffed couch. Through an open door across the room, she could see the bedroom and the king-size, four-poster bed.

"This is for me?" Abbie asked amazed.

Josie smiled and opened a window next to the patio doors. "His Highness, Prince Davis, sent strict instructions that you were to have this room."

"It's beautiful." Abbie laughed as she ran her hand over the soft material of a chair.

"Yes, it is. Usually, no one ever stays in the same wing as the royal family. Guests are always placed in the west wing."

Abbie's smile fell from her face and she sat on a nearby couch. She didn't know why that information made her as upset as it did. "Really?" she murmured.

"I've upset you," Josie said, frowning. "I apologize, I didn't mean to—"

"You didn't upset me, Josie, I just think I would feel more comfortable in the west wing. Can you arrange that?"

Josie's eyes grew wide with fear and she vehemently shook her head. "I-I would have to ask Prince Davis and then . . . I don't know how he'll react. He gave explicit instructions that everything be perfect for you. If you have a problem with this room—"

Abbie placed a hand on Josie's arm to calm her down. "Josie, I love this room."

"Then you're not dissatisfied?"

"What woman in her right mind would be with a room like this?"

Josie rolled her eyes and muttered, "I imagine Lady Sophia would be. She finds fault with everything."

"I'm not Lady Sophia."

Josie grinned and patted her hand. "I know."

"I'll talk to Prince Davis about the room, and I'll make certain to tell him what a great job you've done in helping me adjust to everything."

"Thank you very much, Miss Barnes."

"Please call me Abbie." Abbie stood and unbuttoned the jacket of her suit. "Now, I'm going to take a shower then tour this beautiful palace and the grounds. Then I'll find Prince Davis and tell him exactly how I feel."

Josie grinned then stood to her feet, her tears gone. "Would you like me to help you prepare for your bath?"

"I've been managing by myself for years now," Abbie said, hiding a smile.

"If you need anything, just pick up that phone and ask for me." Josie walked to the door then turned to face Abbie. "Would you like to know what Lady Sophia said about you earlier in the foyer?"

Abbie laughed and shook her head. "I don't think I want to know."

Josie tried to hide a smile but was unsuccessful. "I don't

think you want to know either." She walked from the room, closing the door behind her.

Davis stared out the window of his father's office, not seeing the ocean or the mountains, only seeing Abbie. He couldn't erase her from his mind. Ever since he met her, he had thought of little else and frankly Davis was sick of himself. He refused to love anyone, to care for anyone, when his life wasn't his own, and all of sudden Abbie Barnes infiltrated his senses like a deadly disease.

Davis stood as the door opened, and his father and Lowell walked into the room. Lowell loudly sighed with relief when he saw Davis and patted him on the shoulder. King Henry merely stared at his son then sat behind the intimidating, massive oak desk.

King Henry had spent so many years behind that desk that it almost was another appendage of the older man. Despite his advancing years, Henry was still handsome. Davis believed his father would look younger if all of his days weren't filled with the burdens of running a kingdom. Henry was tall with piercing brown eyes, skin the color of polished oak wood, and thin, severe lips. Davis didn't think he had seen his father smile since he took the throne.

"I can't tell you how relieved I am to see you, Your Highness," Lowell said in a rare show of emotion. "If I had never left you that night, none of this would have happened."

"It still would have happened, Lowell, except you'd be dead or seriously injured. How is Hiram?"

"He's much better now that he knows you're home safe. The doctor in Los Angeles had to sedate him to restrain him from leaving the hospital bed to search for you."

"I will visit him as soon as possible."

Henry finally spoke. "Do you see what your imperti-nence has caused? One of our most valued guards has been injured, the palace was thrown in turmoil, and your mother didn't sleep the entire time you were gone, which meant I didn't sleep."

"I apologize for interfering with your sleeping habits, Father," Davis said through clenched teeth, barely restraining his temper.

Henry jumped to his feet, his trademark vein throbbing in his left temple. Davis had rarely seen his father upset or angry. He could count on one hand the times his father spoke in anything but an imperial commanding tone. "You were immature and childish, Davis. You have a responsibility to this country, to the throne, you cannot just run away when you feel like it. Lowell told me you were some sort of worker. You fixed drains and mowed lawns. . . . What exactly were you thinking, Davis, or were you thinking?"

Davis refused to give his father satisfaction and show any emotion. "Thank you for your concern, Father, but I'm fine. Being kidnapped and nearly beaten to death in the Natillas jungle was nothing more than a pleasant experience."

"What the hell are you talking about?" Henry demanded.

"Your Highness, please—"

Henry interrupted Lowell. "And who the hell is this American woman you dragged into this? It's hard enough explaining your disappearance but trying to explain her presence in this household is another matter entirely."

"If it weren't for that American woman, I'd be dead or still be held captive by Kevin Munji."

Henry calmed himself and sat back in the plush leather chair. "I trust she's leaving Monday on the flight to New York."

"Yes, sir," Davis muttered.

"Fine." Henry ran a hand over his immaculate hair then opened a folder on his desk. "We have begun a complete investigation of all palace personnel to determine how Kevin knew Lowell found you. We also have doubled the guard around the palace and your own security force."

"What about Abbie?"

"Who is Abbie?" Henry asked impatiently.

"The American woman, Your Majesty," Lowell interjected.

"What would you like me to do, Davis?" Henry asked, studying the papers on the desk.

"I want her to have her own security detail. The best we have."

"We can't spare that—"

"Father, have I asked you for anything in the last five years?" Davis demanded, his emotions escaping his iron-tight control. Henry did not move, but Davis saw a brief flicker of surprise move across his face. "I have done everything you've ever asked me, in serving this country. I am going to marry the woman you want, I am going to trot around the globe like a circus animal for this country, and the one thing I want is to keep the American woman safe. Is that too much to ask?"

There was a tense silence in the room and Lowell nervously cleared his throat. Davis noticed the change in his father's eyes and realized that he had gone too far. He straightened his jacket. "I apologize for raising my voice but I would appreciate it if Abbie had an experienced and trusted security detail. She is involved in this mess because of me and I'd like for her to return home safely."

"Of course, Davis," Henry finally responded then motioned to one of the chairs across from the desk. "Will you sit down now so we may continue filling you in on the news you've missed since you began your ordeal?"

Davis quickly glanced at Lowell, who pretended to be absorbed in his notes. Davis nodded at his father and sat in the chair.

ELEVEN

After three hours of tedious meetings, Davis finally gained his freedom. He could still see the strange expression on his father's face when he practically ran from the office. Davis never enjoyed the meetings with his father and Lowell, but this day he almost itched to get out of the room. Davis didn't understand why until he realized he was searching for Abbie.

He prowled the palace like a cat until he glanced out a window and saw a lone figure standing on the edge of the cliff. Davis would recognize Abbie anywhere. His heart pounded against his chest as her hair trailed in the wind behind her and her ankle-length flowered dress molded to the curves of her body. Davis took a deep breath for the strength not to make love to her on the spot, and he walked outside.

Abbie didn't turn to him when he stood beside her and that made him more surprised than angry. He wasn't accustomed to being ignored.

"You're welcome," Davis finally said, with more bitterness than he intended. Abbie finally glared at him.

"For what?" she demanded. Davis recognized the anger in her voice and he almost smiled. "For ignoring me for the last few hours, for decreeing I stay in the room next to yours, embarrassing me in front of the palace staff? What exactly should I be thankful for, Prince Davis?"

Davis pretended to think for a moment then he abruptly nodded. "For all those reasons, actually."

"I also forgot to mention your conveniently forgotten fiancée, the gracious and friendly Lady Sophia."

Davis stopped smiling. "Who told you Sophia was my fiancée?"

"You didn't and that's what matters." Abbie turned to walk toward the palace then glared at him. "I want a room in the west wing. I want to be as far away from you as possible. In fact, I don't want to see you as long as I'm on this stupid island." She turned to walk away but Davis grabbed her arm. Abbie glared at him then stared pointedly at his hand on her arm. "Take your hand off me right now."

"You seem to have forgotten something," Davis said calmly. "We're not in a jungle anymore, or on a boat in the middle of the ocean. You are in my country and I will not be dictated to by anyone, especially an American woman. If I want you in the room next to mine, you will be in the room next to mine. If I want you in my room, you'll be in my room. Do you understand?"

"When hell freezes over." She yanked her arm from his grip and stalked toward the palace.

Davis walked after her, anger screaming through his body. He knew he wasn't supposed to lose his composure or raise his voice above a controlled tone but where Abbie was concerned, Davis never did anything he was supposed to do.

"You are treading on thin ice, Abbie."

"What are you going to do?" She stopped in her tracks, waving her arms in the air. "Throw me in the dungeon, lock me in a cell and throw away the key?"

"I might."

"You and how many of your guards?"

Davis's mouth dropped open as he stared at the one woman who didn't tremble in his presence or acquiesce to his every whim. What was even more amazing to him was that in the midst of his rage and her anger, he still could only think about making love to her. He suddenly noticed several faces peering from the windows of the palace. He was too far away to distinguish their features but he knew whoever they were, they'd tell of his very public argument with Abbie and how he lost.

Davis took a deep breath and tried to calm himself. "I should have told you about Sophia and I apologize for that, but you cannot move from that room. The highest concentration of guards resides and works in the east wing. I only want you to be safe. When you reach California, you can do whatever you want. But, for now, I feel responsible for you. As medieval and archaic as that may sound to you, that's how I feel."

Abbie crossed her arms over her chest and refused to meet his eyes. "I accept your apology."

"You only have two days here. I hope I haven't ruined it for you."

"I hope so too."

Davis rolled his eyes and threw up his hands in frustration. "I give up, Abbie. I try to apologize and be nice and what do I get in return?"

She raked a hand through her hair then asked helplessly, "What exactly did you hope to accomplish by coming out here?"

Davis couldn't answer truthfully that he only wanted to see her face, to maybe hold her. He glanced back at the palace windows. While the faces weren't visible, he knew they were still there.

"I suppose I-I wanted to make certain you knew that you're welcome in any room in the palace. My home is your home for the length of your stay here."

"Thank you," she said, stiffly. Davis glanced at his

watch, although he had nowhere to be for a few hours. Fortunately, Abbie didn't know that.

"I have a meeting," he lied smoothly. "If there's nothing further . . ." His voice trailed off as she turned back to the ocean, effectively dismissing him.

Davis wanted to touch her. He wanted to talk like they did in the jungle or on the boat or in America, but once more his position erected a barrier between him and anyone he could care about. He stared at her hair billowing in the wind then he turned to the castle and returned to his duty. His life.

Abbie stared out the balcony doors of her room, as the early evening light cast numerous colors over the expensive furniture. She had wanted to take a nap before dinner that evening. She had wanted to rest, but all she could think about was Davis. His face filled her mind. His smell drifted through her room. Erotic images from their night together tortured her. No matter how hard she tried, she remembered each second they had spent together. She remembered all of their kisses. She remembered all of their arguments. And she knew, from the hard glint in Davis's eyes that afternoon, that he remembered none of that.

While Abbie couldn't sleep, Davis probably was entertaining his beautiful fiancée. As much as Abbie disliked Sophia, she could admit that Sophia looked every inch royalty. She belonged on the arm of a prince. Sophia would know how to handle other royalty and state dinners. She would know what Davis talked about when the glare of the spotlight became too much. Sophia could offer him everything that Abbie could not.

Abbie rose from the bed. Even though she was surrounded by more wealth and beauty than she had ever imagined, she had never felt more empty and alone in her entire life. She stared at her reflection in the mirror. She was in a castle on a tropical Mediterranean island for forty-eight hours. Abbie vowed to not spend that forty-eight hours in her room, dreaming about Davis Beriyia.

An hour later, Abbie stared at a wall-length painting that hung in a room she had labeled the study. It was the third study she had come across in her exploration of the palace. When she began exploring, she had expected to be stopped or arrested, but most of the servants and security guards barely glanced at her. After her initial fear, Abbie had begun to enjoy herself. She had also become more aware of Davis's history and the background that followed him everywhere he went. Each room seemed more beautiful and filled with more gold than the next.

The painting she stared at now was of a coronation. There were more than two hundred life-sized figures, each in amazing detail, down to the sparkling white gloves some of the women wore. The king's long royal red coronation robe trailed several feet behind him as he stood at the altar, prepared to receive his crown. Even through the painting and hundreds of years, Abbie could see the intensity in the handsome king's eyes as he stared at the crown.

For some reason, Abbie was more fascinated with the queen, who stood to his left and slightly behind him. Her black curls tumbled down her back and her distinctive features showcased her beauty across the painting. What intrigued Abbie the most was that while everyone else in the painting stared at the crown, the queen stared at her husband.

"Beautiful painting, is it not?" came a voice from the doorway. Abbie almost screamed, until she saw the friendly face of the woman standing in the doorway. Abbie recognized her as one of the people who had greeted Davis that morning at the front door.

The woman was short, she barely reached Abbie's

shoulder. She had gray hair that was pulled into a severe bun at the nape of her neck and brown eyes that twinkled in the light of the study. The woman walked across the room and extended her hand to Abbie.

"I am Estelle," the woman said, as her large hand enveloped Abbie's. "I am the head chef for the palace."

"My name is Abbie."

"I know who you are, dear, everyone knows," Estelle said. Whatever she thought of that fact was not betrayed by her still twinkling and friendly eyes. "I went to your room to introduce myself and ask if you would like a snack, and you weren't there. I asked myself where would a lovely, young American woman wander off to, alone in a gorgeous palace? I immediately came here."

Abbie smiled at the energy that radiated from the older woman. When she smiled, all of her wrinkles seemed to disappear. Abbie had a feeling that many people would pour their hearts out to Estelle.

"This place is amazing," Abbie said, staring at the sculpted ceiling.

"Do you really think so?" Estelle's right eyebrow raised in surprise at Abbie's statement.

"Of course," Abbie gasped, placing a hand over her heart. "The beautiful artwork and decorations. . . . Every room is a treasure in itself. I could spend the entire day staring at this one painting."

"I heard a baron once call this captivating," Estelle mused, with a nod in the direction of the coronation painting. "It was done by Arnoldo Raggazi. He was an Italian who adopted Juhatu as his homeland in the 1600s, and is still one of our most celebrated artists."

"I've heard of that name," Abbie murmured. "I've seen his work in the Louvre."

Estelle nodded proudly then continued. "This is a depiction of the coronation of His Majesty, Lionel the Second in 1622. He was twenty-one years old when he became king. He is still one of the most popular kings in the island's history."

"What was the queen's name?"

"Regina. She was nineteen. Together, she and Lionel brought this island into a new era of peace and prosperity. They negotiated a profitable deal with France that has kept us close allies until this day."

Abbie smiled at the almost lyrical quality in Estelle's voice. She figured Estelle probably knew the history of each item in the palace.

"She's very beautiful," Abbie murmured, looking back to the painting.

"Every woman in the Beriyia family has been breathtaking," Estelle said. "I guess, when there are amazing men, they only choose amazing women."

Abbie's smile disappeared as she thought of Sophia. Sophia would certainly blend in with all the other portraits on the wall.

"Davis chose well," Abbie whispered.

"Looks are not everything," Estelle said. Abbie stared at Estelle, while Estelle continued to stare at the painting. "The queens of Juhatu, the queens who contributed to the growth of this country, were not just beautiful women. They had dignity and style and . . . and compassion. Something our dear Sophia would not know if it . . . bit her in the ass."

Abbie couldn't control the rumble of laughter that spilled from her mouth. She placed a hand over her mouth, as her laughter echoed throughout the high-ceiling room. She continued when she noticed Estelle's shoulders trembling from laughter.

"I should not have said that," Estelle said, although Abbie could hear no remorse in Estelle's voice. "Although, I can never pass up a chance to use an Americanism."

"An Americanism?"

"My nephew lives in New York City. Whenever he visits, he brings me a new Americanism, like 'bit her in the ass.' I really like that one." Estelle smiled proudly as Abbie laughed. Estelle suddenly became serious as she studied Abbie's face. Abbie's laugh became nervous chatter as she grew uncomfortable under Estelle's intense scrutiny. Estelle finally said, "I've worked in the palace more than forty years. I started as an assistant to my father in the kitchen, then when he died, God rest his soul, I became head chef. I remember when King Henry paced the foyer, the night before his wedding to Queen Lissette."

"I've seen kings and queens, princes, barons, and dukes in these halls. And, I've learned that looks, breeding, and rank mean nothing. To be truly beautiful, there must be a light inside. And no matter how beautiful one is, if there is no light, there is no true beauty," Estelle concluded.

"Which is Sophia?" Abbie asked, even as she told herself not to.

Estelle smiled just as there was a hesitant knock on the door. Josie walked into the room, looking more nervous than the first time Abbie saw her. Blood drained from Josie's face when she saw Estelle.

"Madam," Josie greeted Estelle, with an awkward curtsy. Estelle shot Abbie a long-suffering look then clucked her tongue at Josie.

"How many times do I have to tell you to curtsy to royalty, not me," Estelle sighed.

"I apologize, madam," Josie said, with an identical curtsy. Estelle rolled her eyes then turned to Abbie and placed a soft kiss on each cheek.

"Remember, dinner at six. There will be twenty people dining with you and the royal family tonight. Considering the possible guests, consider yourself fortunate for this lively bunch." Estelle sent one last glance at Josie then walked from the room.

Josie practically ran across the room to Abbie and clutched her hands. Abbie almost screamed from the strength in Josie's grip. Only the terror in Josie's eyes made her withhold her scream, for fear she would scare Josie even more.

"I did not mean to leave you alone for so long, Abbie. Please forgive me," Josie pleaded, with wide eyes. "I saw you go for a walk . . . then you were talking to the prince, and I definitely could not interrupt and—just tell me you're not angry with me."

"Of course I'm not, Josie," Abbie assured her. Abbie knew her brothers would have laughed at the picture of Abbie as the calm one. Usually, Abbie was the one who ran around the room in frenzied circles, while everyone else attempted to calm her down.

"I promise I will no longer neglect my duties as your assistant," Josie said solemnly, then asked uncertainly, "Would you like to see the rest of Juhatu? We have world-famous museums and . . ."

Abbie watched as Josie winced, obviously at a loss for words. Abbie smiled and took Josie's hands, causing Josie's eyes to widen. Abbie was tired of following Davis's perfect plan for her. She didn't want to have dinner with his parents and Sophia, no more than she wanted to have her fingernails peeled off.

"Josie, forget the royal-dictated tour. I want to see the real Juhatu, your Juhatu."

"I don't think the prince would approve," Josie said, shaking her head. She pulled a crumpled, much-folded sheet of paper from the pocket of her silk dress. She quickly unfolded it and said, in a shaky voice, "Prince Davis specifically instructed me to take you to the art museum, the natural history museum, the boutiques on Champs Avenue, where you can buy anything you desire on the royal account . . ." Josie's voice trailed off as Abbie ripped the paper from her hand and crumpled it into

a ball. Abbie almost relented when Josie began to gasp
for air. Then Josie smiled and looked at her.

"Abbie, what are you doing? The prince himself wrote
that," Josie whispered hoarsely, as she shot quick glances
at the closed doors as if expecting the royal SWAT team
to burst in.

"It's Friday night, Josie," Abbie said excitedly, as she
thought of her chance for escape. "I know there is something more exciting to do in Juhatu on a Friday night
than tour museums."

"No . . ."

Abbie narrowed her eyes and assessed Josie, which
made Josie tremble. "How old are you, Josie?"

"Twenty-one."

"At twenty-one years old, you go to the museum on
Friday nights?" Abbie asked doubtfully. Josie's averted
eyes were the only answer Abbie needed. "I only have
two days of my vacation left. I want to have fun."

"I'll be fired."

"Davis—the prince—would not fire you for taking me
where I want to go. There must be somewhere we can
go and have fun."

"My mother is having a birthday party for one of my
brothers. Practically the whole island will be there," Josie
reluctantly confessed.

"A real party?" Abbie asked, practically jumping up
and down. She tried to imagine Davis at an island party.
Even when he had been on the mountaintop with her
and Tazeh's people, he had still been separate from everyone else. Abbie doubted Davis would ever fit in at something as frivolous as a party. She doubted he would even
want to.

"Abbie, I don't think. . . . You're supposed to attend
dinner tonight with the royal family. Everyone will expect
you there."

"Somehow, I doubt anyone will miss me." Abbie

squeezed Josie's hands and tried to hypnotize her into agreeing. Abbie wanted to leave this place. She needed to leave. She knew if she stayed and had to watch Davis and his perfect fiancée during dinner, she would embarrass herself by crying or lunging across the table for Sophia's throat. "Come on, Josie. No one will know."

Josie bit her bottom lip then reluctantly nodded. "I have to warn you, Abbie. We . . . my family can get a little out of control."

"That's exactly what I'm counting on," Abbie said, laughing. "Now, what should I wear?"

TWELVE

"She is where?" Davis screamed at Hiram, as he ripped off his tie.

The two other security guards in the room flinched at Davis's bellow, while Hiram remained in the same position and met Davis's hard glare. Davis looked away first.

"Abigail Barnes is at the Bettrand party on the north beach," Hiram repeated calmly.

Davis felt the rage build. He could practically feel the anger course through his veins and hit his body. He had been in the lounge with the other dinner guests. He had forced a smile and dealt with Sophia longer than he intended, all because he waited for Abbie. Normally, he would have waited until social convention screamed at his absence before he would deal with exchanging forced pleasantries with that night's dinner guests. But, tonight, Abbie was supposed to be there. He didn't know what made him more angry: the fact that he had to endure social interaction with Sophia and the other dinner guests or the fact that Abbie had never showed.

"Three of our best guards are at the party. There is no need to worry about Abigail's safety, Your Highness," Hiram said, calmly. "Three of the four Bettrand sons are in the royal military, and Josie, the only daughter, works here in the palace. There are far more dangerous places on the island Abigail could have wandered to."

"I'm not worried about Abigail," Davis snapped, rubbing a hand over the back of his neck.

He rolled his eyes in frustration and stared out the windows of his office. His office stared over the north beach, although separated by trees and large mountains. But, Davis could almost see Abbie. He didn't know what happened at beach parties in Juhatu, but he did know Abbie was supposed to be with him, and not at a party. His jaw clenched at the idea of one of his subjects approaching Abbie. He could almost see the man's hands traveling over Abbie's back, her behind, into her hair. The images of Abbie with another man made him slam his fist into the wall and whirl around to Hiram.

"We have no other choice. We must retrieve Abbie," he said, firmly, as he pulled on his suit jacket.

"Your Highness, dinner starts in less than twenty minutes."

"A dinner that my mother and father are expecting Abbie to attend. My parents have extended their kindness to her, and I will not allow her to embarrass me. She will be at dinner tonight in the royal palace, and she will like it."

Davis glared at Hiram and the other two guards for any hint of an argument, then he stormed from the room. He was the prince of Juhatu. When he ordered a woman to dinner, she came to dinner.

Thirty minutes later, Davis trudged through the sand toward his first beach party in Juhatu. There was a large bonfire in the sand where most of the hundred or so guests gathered, drinking and dancing to a band that played on a makeshift stage. The people who weren't dancing ran in the surf or stood in groups laughing and talking.

As Davis walked toward the center of the party, surrounded by ten security guards, with another ten circling the area in cars, the partygoers stopped talking and pointed to him. Davis ignored the stares and peered through the darkness for Abbie. He couldn't help but feel a little out of place in his suit, surrounded by other men in suits, while most of the partygoers wore little more than bathing suits. It was like all the pictures and movies he had seen of parties. People were laughing and having fun, and Davis almost wished he could join them.

"There is Josie," Hiram said, standing to Davis's right. He pointed to the young woman, who stood near the fire, laughing with three tall men.

Davis's entourage made its way toward her, plowing a path through the human trail. Davis noticed most of the talking and laughing stopped when he reached Josie. The fire's light was very bright and anyone who could see far enough could tell who he was. Davis realized that he had effectively brought the party to a dead halt. He was the prince. He shouldn't care, but he almost felt embarrassed by the disruption his presence caused.

Josie seemed to be the last one at the party to realize the crowned prince of Juhatu was in their midst. She followed everyone's gaze and stared at Davis. She immediately dropped the cup in her hands.

"Your Highness," Josie squeaked.

"Where is Abbie?" Davis demanded, ignoring their audience.

"Abbie?" Josie repeated, with an audible swallow. Davis could see her tremble even in the moonlight.

"You are aware that she is expected at dinner at the palace tonight," Davis said, with one raised eyebrow. The young girl nodded, with wide eyes, making Davis feel like an evil ogre for frightening her. He tried a gentle tone. "I know she's here, Josie."

His gentle tone brought tears to Josie's eyes. She bit her lower lip then pointed toward the ocean, where a group of people splashed in the water, obviously unaware of the latest guest.

Davis didn't bother to thank Josie and risk having her die of shock, so he turned to the crashing waves. He and his men walked toward the ocean, with most of the guests on their heels. Davis stopped in his tracks when he saw Abbie.

She wore white shorts and a white bikini top, both of which were wet. In the moonlight, her skin glistened with water as she jumped in the waves with a man. The man and Abbie laughed together, then linked hands and jumped over another small wave that harmlessly crashed to the sand. The man had to die, Davis decided as soon as the man's hands lingered longer than necessary on Abbie's bare shoulders as he helped her maintain her balance in the churning water. Davis envisioned a nice, long death in the stockades. Since Davis didn't know if there were still stockades on the island, he stepped closer to the water's edge and called Abbie's name.

She turned at his voice. And he almost smiled at the guilty expression that crossed her face.

"Davis," she muttered. She began to walk toward him, as one of his security guards directed the man in the opposite direction. The other guards formed a barrier between the partygoers and Davis, and motioned for the party to continue, while Hiram maintained a close but discreet distance from Davis. Within minutes, conversation and dancing resumed, although Davis knew people still watched.

"You found me," she said, with a tired sigh. Against his own will, Davis's eyes dropped to her breasts. He could see her pebble-sized nipples through the wet material, which made his manhood rise and his anger grow red hot.

"You're supposed to be at the palace preparing for dinner right now," he said, through clenched teeth.

"I know," she admitted, with a careless shrug. "Josie mentioned it was her brother's birthday, and I forced her to bring me. The poor girl had absolutely no choice—"

"Josie will be fired," Davis said flatly. He watched amazed as Abbie's features hardened in a split second.

"You will not fire her."

"You keep forgetting that I'm the one in charge on this island, not you."

"I will lose all respect for you if you fire that girl for following my wishes," she warned in a raspy whisper.

Davis wanted to throw her respect for him in her face, but they both seemed to know it was the one threat she held over him. For some reason, Davis craved her opinion of him. She was an American. Nothing she thought about should have mattered, but it did.

"Since I know firsthand how stubborn you are, I cannot blame Josie for disobeying my orders," Davis said quickly, before he thought about how Abbie made him withdraw one of his decisions. "However, I can and I will blame you. My mother invited you to our table for dinner, and you will be there."

"Why, Davis?" Abbie demanded. Davis quickly glanced at his guards at her loud tone. Several of them quickly looked away. No one was supposed to yell at the prince of Juhatu. "So, I can toast your engagement to Sophia?"

"Why do you care so much about whom I will marry?" he asked, with a smile he could not resist. The idea of Abbie being jealous made it almost worth the ruined shoes on his feet.

"I don't," Abbie retorted, as she crossed her arms over her chest.

"Then return with me to dinner," he shot back.

"I refuse to spend one of my two nights in Juhatu in the gilded rooms of the palace. As beautiful as the palace is, unlike you, I'm actually interested in the real lives of your people."

"Be careful," Davis warned, stepping closer to her. Abbie didn't move, but met his gaze. Davis realized his mistake. Her seductive scent, mixed with the moonlight and ocean air, wrapped around him and pulled him closer.

"Do you even care about this island and the people? Or is Juhatu just a pile of rock for you to claim as evidence of your pedigree, Your Highness?" Her eyes flashed as he took another step closer to her.

"I care about my people."

"Which is why you need half of the palace guards to walk in their midst?"

"It's not that simple. In case you forgot, we were being held hostage not more than three days ago." Even in his own ears, his excuse sounded weak. Davis tried to remember the last time he had shaken hands with anyone, other than a politician.

"Why do you think everyone—the media, the people, the palace staff—calls you the Stone Prince?"

Davis hurt more from the accusation in her eyes than from the thought that people regarded him as emotionless. He had duties. He had obligations. He wasn't supposed to be regarded like other men. Those reasons had always made him brush away his image in the media—until Abbie.

"This is not America, and I am not one of your American politicians," he sneered, not bothering to hide the contempt from his voice. "In Juhatu, we believe the political system should have integrity and honor. I know this is a hard concept for an American to understand, but it means that I am not like everyone else. I am held to a higher standard than my contemporaries, and if fulfilling—"

"Go back to your castle, Your Highness," Abbie interrupted, with a wide yawn. "You're boring me, like you bore everyone else."

Davis sputtered in outrage at her obvious sign of disrespect. He glanced around to make certain no one else had witnessed Abbie's serious breach of protocol. Only Hiram openly watched them and, as usual, his eyes were unreadable. The rest of the people had gone back to their party, resuming the drinking, laughing, and dancing in full force.

"What would you have me do, Abbie?" Davis demanded, through clenched teeth.

"Dance with me," she said simply.

"Dance with you?" He laughed in disbelief and shook his head. "Do you have any idea how absurd that is? I can't dance . . ." For the first time, he studied the people gyrating around him. They moved to the beat of the loud music, moving on top of one another, with one another. Men and women had their arms wrapped around each other, some with their legs entwined. But, all moved to the music. And, Davis noticed that they were having fun. More fun than he could ever remember from dancing.

"What would dancing with you prove to anyone?" he finally asked uncertainly, glancing back at her.

"Nothing, but it would prove to me that these people, this country means more to you than a set of rules and responsibilities."

"I don't owe you anything," he shot back. He strongly wanted to believe that, but as the moonlight highlighted her lips and wide eyes, Davis knew he would do anything to make Abbie respect him. Because after everything they had been through together, Abbie's opinion of him was more important than he cared to admit.

"Then why are you still here?" she asked softly, crossing her arms over her chest.

He held up one finger and said firmly, "One song."

Her smile was the best reward he could hope for. She grabbed his hand and pulled him into the middle of the crowd, which parted majestically when people saw the prince of Juhatu.

Abbie stopped then turned to him and began to move to the music. Davis hesitated, as he stared at the crowd of people that gathered around them. Once more, the entire party had ground to a stop as people waited for his next move. Davis saw his guards move closer toward him, as their sharp eyes surveyed each and every face. Then Davis noticed something. The people weren't waiting for an opportunity to make fun of him. They were smiling. They were waiting for him to allow them to welcome him.

Davis looked back at Abbie, who grinned at him and continued to move to the music. Josie and a tall, older man, who must be her father, emerged from the crowd and began to dance next to them. Slowly, other couples circled them and began to move to the music. Davis even noticed a few of his guards discreetly moving their broad shoulders to the music, while maintaining their sentinel poses.

Abbie wondered if she had finally pushed Davis too far. She had known that he would come after her. She had hoped that he would come after her, but she had never decided what she would do once he arrived. Then seeing him on the beach, looking uncomfortable in his suit surrounded by sand and crystal-blue waters, Abbie had wanted him to do anything but leave.

She had thought she was over him. After his dismissal of her at the airport and his imperial commands, Abbie had wanted to believe she could come to Josie's family party and when Davis arrived, she had planned to send him away with a sweet, unremorseful smile. However, when Davis had arrived, the only thing Abbie could do was attempt to find a reason for him to stay. She told herself challenging him to dance was weak, but the alternative of him sitting across from Sophia at dinner was unacceptable. The only alternative was to embarrass him.

"I can't do this, Abbie," Davis suddenly said, moving closer to her to whisper in her ear. His warm breath caressed her ear and the loud music seemed to dim in the background as she stared into his eyes. "I can't dance like this. I've never danced like this. I . . ."

His voice trailed off as Abbie placed her arms around his neck. He was like a magnet. She couldn't resist him even when she tried. He was in her world, the world of non-royalty, and instead of laughing at him, Abbie only wanted to protect him.

"We danced in St. Moritz," she reminded him.

He smiled for the first time since they reached Juhatu, and Abbie's eyes blurred with tears as she realized how much she had missed his smile. His hands drifted around her waist and he pulled her closer, until there was no space between them. Her breathing increased as she tried to draw air into her suddenly constricted lungs.

"Except, now, we aren't surrounded by your usual environment. Now, it's just you and me, the ocean, normal people, and . . . and the music." His eyes slid closed and he pressed his forehead against hers. She swallowed the lump in her throat and continued softly, "Can you hear the music, Davis?"

"Yes," he whispered, as they slowly began to move. As the wild beat raged around them and other couples danced with energy, Davis seemed to want to move slow. His fingers flexed on her waist, and he pulled her even closer. She inhaled the spicy cologne that she knew she would never smell on another man.

"Davis . . ."

He pressed his lips to hers, effectively silencing her. Abbie could feel the strong undercurrents in the kiss, the passion that raged between them, but for some reason, Davis would only allow the chaste kiss. When he removed his lips, Abbie opened her eyes and gasped at the desire she saw in his.

Davis suddenly glanced around, and Abbie followed his quick looks. No one watched them. No one seemed to care, but Davis stepped from her, removing his hands last. She bit her lower lip to withhold the scream of frustration.

"I guess I'll never learn how to dance." He glanced at his watch, a sign Abbie had learned he used for escape when a situation became uncomfortable. "If I hurry, I can still be there for dessert."

"Or you can stay here and taste the delicious food." She cringed at the desperation in her voice, but Abbie still couldn't beae the thought of him returning to the palace. "And Josie will bring out the cake for her brother in a few minutes. She says—"

"Do you really want me to stay?"

She clutched his arm at the uncertainty in his voice. "Of course."

"You actually want to be seen with the Stone Prince?" he asked, with a teasing smile. His smile suddenly disappeared as he moved several strands of hair from her eyes toward her ponytail. His fingers lingered on her face as he said, "I'll stay, Abbie."

"Your Highness," Josie squeaked, as she tapped Abbie on the shoulder.

Davis jumped from Abbie as if he had been burned, and turned to Josie. Abbie cleared her throat as the heat from his touch warmed her face. She was almost grateful for Josie's disruption, even if Josie seemed on the verge of collapsing from Davis's hard stare.

"Yes, Josie?" Davis demanded, his imperial mask once more in place.

"I'd like to introduce my father, Petra, and my brother, Maurice," she whispered.

Abbie had met the two boisterous and friendly men earlier. She laughed at their sudden transformation from loud military men to intimidated and quiet subjects. She was more surprised when Davis offered his hand, with as much of a smile as he could manage.

"Captain Bettrand, I have heard much of your proud

accomplishments in our military. You continue to represent this nation in a manner that makes us all proud," Davis told the older man. Abbie watched Petra Bettrand's hazel eyes light with pride that made his chest expand. Davis turned to the younger man, who smiled at his father then looked surprised when he found the prince staring at him. "Lieutenant Bettrand, I have heard that you are equally as skilled and honorable as your father. The nation of Juhatu is blessed for having had the Bettrand family in its service for so many generations."

Josie, Petra, and Maurice seemed frozen as they stared at Davis, as if he had sprouted another head. Davis glanced at Abbie, and Abbie cleared her throat to hide her laugh at the long-suffering look in his eyes. Davis grinned at her then turned back to the Bettrands.

"If it's not much trouble, I would like to stay and celebrate your birthday, Maurice. I would be happy to repay any food or financial losses my guards or I—"

Petra Bettrand finally seemed to reanimate and he abruptly grabbed Davis's hand and pumped furiously. "It's such a pleasure to meet you, Your Royal Highness," Petra said excitedly. "I met your father and mother once . . . I mean, I met their Royal Majesties once and—"

"Of course, you can stay, Your Highness," Josie interrupted her father, placing a comforting hand on his shoulder. "Our family would be honored to have Your Royal Highness and your guards as our guests."

Abbie grinned as Josie looked surprised at her own smooth delivery.

"Thank you, Josie," Davis said, nodding. "Excuse me for a moment." He walked over to Hiram and the two quietly conversed for a moment.

Abbie watched as Josie and her family barely maintained their control.

THIRTEEN

Abbie sat in the back seat of the limousine, as far across the seat as possible from Davis. He hadn't looked at her since they had left the party, where he had unsurprisingly been the star attraction. What had surprised Abbie was how easily he communicated with the guests, once the guests had the nerve to approach him. With a smile or a well-placed pat or wink, Davis made everyone feel like they weren't talking to a prince. Abbie had been completely wrong about him, and she had been the only one at the party who had kept her distance. Everyone else ran to him; they all found a reason to talk to the prince. Abbie couldn't blame them, but she hadn't found a moment alone with Davis, not that she wanted one.

Abbie heard every move he made in his corner of the limousine, but she couldn't bring herself to look at him. She didn't want to scare him with the need that coursed through her veins, the need that she needed to control. Instead, she focused on the beauty of the island at midnight, as the limousine sped through the streets of downtown Juhatu toward the palace. She gazed at stars she couldn't see in Los Angeles, bright, shining stars that made her sigh and think of paradise.

"I should have told you about Sophia," Davis said quietly. Abbie forced herself to look at him and found him staring at her. The shadows of the limousine partially covered his face, but Abbie could feel his eyes on her, almost as if his hands touched her.

"It doesn't matter—"

"I didn't tell you because . . . she means nothing to me, Abbie."

"She's your fiancée," Abbie snapped.

"It doesn't mean I love her."

"Can you love anyone?" Abbie demanded, then immediately regretted her question at the hard glint that entered his eyes. She forced herself to continue. "You hide behind your supposed obligations to your country, but do you think any of the people at the party tonight would care if you married Sophia or not?"

"Once more you overstep your place, Abbie," he snapped, his rage barely contained

"Did you see their faces, Davis? I was wrong. Those people don't think of you as an untouchable Stone Prince. They think of you as their son, their brother, and their best friend. They want you to be happy, Davis."

"You know nothing about my people or me."

"Stop the car," Abbie commanded.

"Excuse me," Davis said, with one raised eyebrow in disbelief. "Did you issue a direct order to me?"

"Stop the car," she repeated, more slowly. "I'll ride in the other limousine, with your guards."

"You will not further humiliate me this night."

"Go to hell," she snapped. "Tell the driver to stop the car."

"What is the problem now?" Davis demanded, the frustration evident in his voice. "You have no right to tell me how to rule my country."

"I don't have to have a degree in royalty to know how people feel about you. You've convinced yourself that you have to marry Sophia, so you can continue your self-sacrificial role as the prince of Juhatu," she shot back angrily.

"You know nothing about my duties as prince," Davis roared.

If Abbie had not just spent several days dodging bullets with Davis, or one beautiful night making love with him, she would have been frightened by his yelling. Instead, she said as clearly and firmly as possible, "You're right, Davis. Only royalty would understand people or their behavior. The rest of us are too common and simple to know anything."

"You underestimate yourself, Abbie. You're not simple."

Abbie didn't miss how he didn't attempt to refute the rest of her sarcasm. She clenched her hands into fists and demanded, "Stop the car now."

"No."

"I'll only tell you one more time, Davis. Have the driver stop the car."

"I'll only tell you one more time, Abbie. I am the only one, of the two of us, who gives orders. You are here by my graciousness. Remember that."

Abbie wanted to control her temper. She wanted to discuss their differences in an adult and mature manner, but his imperial, smug smile made hot disgust run through her body. She glared at him then lunged for the telephone that connected to the driver on the console near his legs. Davis reacted by grabbing her arms. Abbie screamed and tried to struggle from his strong grip. As a result, they both tumbled to the floor.

Abbie screamed in outrage when she found herself on the floor of the limousine, with Davis hovering above her. She scrambled and struggled, but his grip only tightened on her wrists as he raised them above her head. She tried to move under his body weight, but Davis refused to budge. Abbie stopped moving to gather her strength for one final assault, when she saw the change in his expression. There was no longer murder raging in his eyes. Instead, he stared at her breasts, only protected by the bikini top since her shirt had come unbuttoned during the struggle.

Abbie's anger melted as one of his hands trailed from her lips down her neck and in between her breasts. She wanted to scream. She wanted to be powerful enough to push him off and call him a pig, but she could only whimper in pleasure when his lips followed his hands.

She squirmed as his tongue touched her neck then left a moist trail down her chest to the indentation of the bikini. His hands moved down her legs, branding them through her white denim shorts. Abbie tried to move her arms to tell him no, but her hands only clutched his neck and pressed him closer to her. She felt the familiar heat, the familiar desire. Only Davis could make her feel this way, could make her flow with desire with one touch.

He met her eyes then moved his fingers to her lips. Abbie opened her mouth and took one of his fingers into her mouth. She reveled at the grainy feel of his finger in her mouth. His eyes widened at her actions then he replaced his finger with his tongue. There was as much rage and passion in his kiss as there had been in their conversation. He wanted to control, to dominate her. Abbie would allow him to do that for now.

Abbie clutched his shoulders as the kiss grew deeper. His hands were everywhere at once on her body. As he stole her soul with the hungry kiss, his hands drove her body insane. His lips were on hers, his tongue swiped and invaded, and his hands manipulated her body to his touch. Abbie was lost. She was found. After a full day without his touch, her body drank from him as if he was water in a desert.

Then as quickly as he started, Davis stopped. He moved from her and returned to his seat. Abbie wanted to beg him to continue then she felt the limousine stop. She quickly moved to her seat as she saw the towers of the palace through the tinted windows. She refused to look in his direction as she buttoned her blouse and ran trembling fingers through her hair.

The door to the limousine swung open. Without a backward glance, Davis stepped from the limousine and walked into the palace. Abbie pounded the seat and cursed herself for once more falling prey to his charm.

"I thought I would find you here," Lowell said, as he walked into Davis's favorite room in the palace. His heels clicked on the floor as he walked across the room to stand next to Davis at the window.

Davis always found it slightly strange that he felt more comfortable in the palace's main ballroom than he did in his own living quarters. The ballroom was probably the size of his entire apartment building in Los Angeles, and the ceiling stretched to the same height as a three-floor building. Glass chandeliers hung from every inch of the ceiling and were reflected in the gleaming, white floor. Long windows, ten on each side of the room, that offered the best views of Juhatu in the palace, led to balconies.

Whenever Davis needed to think or be alone, he would come to the ballroom. He would sit on one of the window seats or on a balcony and dream. The ballroom was the largest room in the house and the most isolated.

Immediately, after he had fled from the limousine, Davis had run to the ballroom before he pulled Abbie into his arms and begged her to make love to him. He knew he should not have stayed at the party. He knew he should not have kissed her or touched her. But, where Abbie was concerned, his body and his head took separate courses.

"Let me guess, my father wants to lock me in the dungeon and throw away the key." Davis only half-joked and Lowell didn't laugh.

"His Majesty is very upset with you," Lowell said tiredly. He sighed as he settled onto the window seat next to Davis. "The ambassador from Spain was in attendance tonight. He was quite charmed with Sophia."

"He must be the only one in the entire kingdom," Davis muttered. Lowell didn't answer, but pulled a gold cigarette holder from his coat pocket. He offered one to Davis, who shook his head. Lowell found his gold lighter in a coat pocket then lit a cigarette.

"How many times have we done this?" Lowell asked, as he leaned his head on the window and stared at the ceiling. "How many times have we sat on one of these seats at such a late hour and talked . . . or not talked?"

"Is my father very angry?" Davis tried not to sound concerned, but Lowell wasn't fooled.

"His Majesty was more angry when our source at *Juhatu Daily* called to tell us that your picture will be on the front page tomorrow morning . . . with the American."

Davis muttered a curse then buried his face in his hands. "And Mother?" he moaned behind his hands.

"The queen instructed the staff to hide tomorrow's paper from Sophia. Of course, Lady Sophia will see the news on television or hear from her friends or her family, but Queen Lissette hopes she will have softened the blow."

"What am I going to do, Lowell?" Davis looked at Lowell when, for the first time in his life, Lowell didn't have an immediate answer.

"About Lady Sophia or the American?" Lowell finally asked, glancing at him from the corner of his eyes.

"There's nothing to do about Abbie," Davis snapped.

"Are you absolutely certain about that, Your Highness?"

"Abbie is my friend, the first real friend I think I've ever had. She cares nothing about my rank or my title. You should hear the way she speaks to me, Lowell. Sometimes, I think she has no idea who I am and . . . and, for some reason, I like that. I like that I can tell her whatever I'm feeling or thinking, and she'll tell me whether I'm being dumb or an idiot." Davis smiled as he thought of her anger in the limousine. His smile quickly faded when he remembered the erotic kiss that followed. He cleared his throat when he found Lowell watching him. "Everyone needs a friend like that, even a prince."

"I certainly would want a friend like that, Your Highness," Lowell agreed then said with a slight smile, "I suppose I already have a friend like that. My wife, Liza. After a day in the palace, with all the headaches and worries and stress, especially about runaway princes, I can go home and tell Liza everything. Or tell her nothing. And either way, I feel better."

Davis didn't answer, as he stared at his hands. A hand clenched around his heart at Lowell's softly spoken words. Davis knew he would never have that type of relationship with Sophia. Davis had met Lowell's wife, Liza, many times. The two had been in love since childhood, and the love was apparent in every move the pair made. Davis had known at a young age that he, as the prince, would never have that type of relationship.

"Every man needs a woman to talk to at night," Lowell said in the deep silence. "If he wants to have a life worth living."

"Sophia and I will never have that," Davis said, softly.

"Probably not, Your Highness. Will you be able to handle a life without love?"

"Sophia loves me," Davis protested blandly then added through clenched teeth, "in her own shallow, superficial, Sophia-like way."

"I think she does, too, Your Highness," Lowell said, with a hint of a smile. "But, the true question is, do you love her?"

"Does it matter?"

Lowell hesitated then answered softly, "Not if you think it doesn't, Your Highness."

"Why were you trying to find me, Lowell?" Davis asked, clearing his throat and switching to a safe subject.

"I made a change in your calendar for tomorrow, Your Highness," Lowell said, standing. "Instead of a breakfast meeting at the palace tomorrow at ten o'clock, you have a meeting at the Beriyia Building downtown starting at seven in the morning. Now your schedule is full until eight o'clock . . . until dinner."

Davis grinned. Lowell had always protected him from the full wrath of his parents, and Davis knew Lowell would do it for his entire life. If Davis was gone before his parents woke up, and if he didn't return until dinnertime, Davis wouldn't have to deal with his parents until they'd had a chance to calm down.

"Good night, Your Highness." Lowell moved to pat Davis's shoulder then hesitated and walked from the room.

Davis sighed and stared out the window at the beautiful ocean.

FOURTEEN

Abbie almost choked on the piece of croissant in her mouth when she opened the morning newspaper that rested on the breakfast table. She had been awake since five that morning, day dreaming about Davis and their kiss in the limousine. When she could not stay in bed any longer, she had thrown on clothes, intent on running for a few miles, but the sight of the delicious pastries and fruit on the table in the dining room had stopped her in her tracks.

Then Abbie had seen the newspaper. There was a picture of her and Davis at Josie's party on the front page. The photo had been taken at the most inopportune moment when Davis had kissed Abbie, when they had shared the most innocent kiss that could have been between two friends, except somehow in black and white, the two didn't look like friends. They looked like a man and woman wrapped in each other, not caring about another soul in the world.

She gulped down her coffee and winced as she read the article. There weren't many facts, but the writer was liberal with innuendo. This Michel Wotre hinted at a possible affair, which he blamed on Abbie's relentless pursuit of the prince. Michel Wotre also mentioned Sophia, the "potential fiancée" of Prince Davis, and portrayed her as the virginal noble lady left in the palace, anxiously awaiting her fair prince. Abbie was more hurt than she thought she could have been.

"Abbie," Josie gasped as she ran into the room. Her cheeks were flushed and her hair in disarray as she ran to Abbie and grabbed the newspaper from her hands. "I am so sorry."

"I . . . I didn't see a photographer last night. I didn't even know someone took our picture," Abbie whispered, shaking her head. She glanced at the picture again and anger flared through her body. The picture took something innocent and turned it into something cheap and wrong. "What are libel and slander laws like in this country?"

"Libel . . ." Josie shook her head in confusion and grabbed Abbie's hands, with a frantic expression. "We must leave. We have a full day ahead of us."

"I can't leave these walls," Abbie protested. "I'm too embarrassed. This man portrayed me as a—I didn't lure Davis into my American trap. I'm his friend, nothing more."

"You must go to your room and prepare for our day," Josie said hurriedly. Abbie noticed Josie's frantic look at the door.

"Do you realize what happened here, Josie?" Abbie asked in disbelief. "Your entire country thinks I'm a seductive witch. They probably all hate me. While Sophia, the most obnoxious woman I've ever met in my life, is portrayed as Miss Susie Sunshine."

"Susie Sunshine?" Josie repeated uncertainly then shook her head with a dismissive wave of her hand. "We must leave the palace before Queen Lissette arrives for breakfast."

Abbie saw the frantic expression in Josie's eyes. Abbie didn't have to ask to know that meeting Queen Lissette at breakfast that morning would not be a good thing.

"I'll be ready in five minutes," Abbie muttered, then ran up the stairs.

Two hours later, Abbie wished she had braved a confrontation with Queen Lissette rather than allow herself to be dragged from one museum gallery to the next. Josie didn't know much about Juhatu royal history, but she certainly knew a lot about art. Too much about art, as far as Abbie was concerned. After the first hour of Josie explaining the difference between the cubism of two artists that Abbie had never heard of, she knew she would never escape. Abbie had laughed when she noticed three of the guards assigned to protect her cringe when Josie opened the door to a third room.

Abbie had almost cried in relief when Josie suggested lunch at an outdoor cafe on the beach. Josie ordered lunch for them in her native Juhatu and the waitress left to place the order, with a quick glance in Abbie's direction.

"Did you see the way she looked at me?" Abbie whispered to Josie.

"Who?" Josie answered innocently.

"The waitress. She read the newspaper this morning."

"Everyone reads the *Juhatu Daily*. It's the only newspaper we have on the island," Josie said simply.

Abbie groaned and rolled her eyes, "Then everyone thinks I'm a prince-stealing whore."

"No one thinks that, Abbie." Josie patted her hand on the table with a comforting smile. "Most everyone on this island knows Lady Sophia."

Abbie laughed at Josie's innocent statement. "So, I'm the lesser of two evils. An American over the hometown witch?" Josie laughed but refused to answer.

Abbie stared at the ocean, at the sunlight shimmering on the crystal-blue waves. Two little children splashed in the water as their mother watched from her seat on the sand. In the miles-long stretch of smooth sand, only these three people occupied the beach.

"This place is paradise," Abbie sighed.

"You really do like Juhatu," Josie said, surprised.

"What's not to like about paradise?"

"I love Juhatu. I could never live anywhere else. But Juhatu is an island. A very small island, especially for someone like Prince Davis."

Abbie's warm feelings floated away with the ocean breeze, as she glanced at the royal guards stationed near her table. They sat at their own table, wearing sunglasses and impressive suits. Abbie didn't doubt any of them would unhesitantly kill a man.

"I don't know how he can handle all of it," Abbie murmured. "The constant scrutiny, the press, the guards."

"He's dealt with it his whole life. Maybe he's used to it," Josie said, with a shrug.

Abbie shivered in the bright sunlight as she thought of Kevin Munji. She forced a smile for Josie and said softly, "I don't think a person can ever get used to that."

"I always thought the royal family had everything, until I began to work there. I see all the sacrifices and duties and how much they all truly love this country. It can't be an easy life for them or anyone who marries into the royal family."

The waitress abruptly slammed two bottles of water on the table. She glared at Abbie then sauntered back into the restaurant. Abbie raised an eyebrow as she glanced at Josie, who tried not to laugh, but failed miserably.

"The one person in Juhatu who doesn't know Sophia?" Josie suggested, with a giggle. Abbie laughed then opened the bottled water. "I think Prince Davis will be very unhappy with Sophia," Josie said suddenly.

Abbie hesitated then said, "I do too."

"Can't you stop the prince, Abbie?" Josie pleaded, passionately.

Abbie laughed in disbelief then said, "I have no power over the prince."

"He listens to you."

"I'm a friend, Josie. I can't tell Davis what to do."

"But, the prince listens to you," Josie protested. "I've only been at the palace a short while, but I can see the difference in the prince when he's around you. Do you think the prince would have danced or stayed at the party last night if you weren't there? He's never shown that side of himself to people. It happened because of you, Abbie."

"Josie, please—"

"Granted, the newspaper article was a little harsh on you, but the article also mentioned how the prince did something that the Beriyias haven't done in centuries— be one of us." Josie took a deep gulp from her bottled water then met Abbie's eyes. "I hope I haven't overstepped my place."

Abbie placed her hand on Josie's and forced a smile. She wished Davis were her friend. She wished she could stop Davis from marrying Sophia.

"Of course not, Josie."

"I really like you, Abbie," Josie said, grinning. "I wish you could stay longer."

"Me too." Abbie couldn't bear to tell Josie the truth, that she wanted to escape Juhatu before she gave into the charm of the island and of Davis. If she couldn't keep a small part of herself secure while she was here, she knew she wouldn't leave this island with her heart intact.

Davis loosened his tie as the limousine sped down the main street toward his third meeting that day. Whenever he thought he couldn't handle one more meeting, one more minute with stiff bureaucrats and arguing politicians, he forced himself to march into another meeting.

Davis stared out the limousine window at the ocean. The sun was shining, the sky was blue, the last thing he wanted to do was spend another three hours in a meeting. Not for the first time that day, his thoughts drifted to Abbie. He wondered what she was doing. He had purposely forced himself not to ask about her whereabouts, so that he could prove to himself he could spend a day without her. Once she left the island, he would have to spend a lifetime without her.

But, as the day progressed with each boring meeting, Davis found his thoughts wandering to their erotic moments in the limousine last night. He found himself thinking about their time on St. Moritz, making love. No matter what he did, Davis couldn't erase Abbie from his thoughts. She was like a lingering scent that he couldn't ignore. Several times during his meetings that day, he found himself having to ask people to repeat questions, which would have horrified his parents.

Davis couldn't handle his thoughts any longer and grabbed the limousine telephone. He instantly was connected to Hiram in the front seat.

"Where is Abbie?" Davis hoped he hid the desperation in his voice.

"You have an important lunch meeting with the Minister of Interior in twenty minutes, Your Highness," Hiram answered.

"I know Abbie's guards report to you, Hiram. Where is she?"

"She is eating lunch with Josie at Cafe Playa." Davis could hear the resignation in Hiram's voice as he asked, "Should I have your assistant at the palace cancel your meeting with the Minister of Interior, Your Highness?"

Davis stared out the window at the ocean. He had responsibilities. He had a duty. He couldn't cancel a meeting with an important public official to eat lunch with a woman, especially a woman whom he had been photographed with on the front page of the newspaper. The more he thought of all the reasons why he shouldn't find Abbie for lunch, the more he wanted to. She would be gone the next day, and he would have the rest of his life to fulfill royal duties.

With his mind made up, Davis said into the telephone, "Have the palace cancel the meeting and . . . and tell Paulie to head toward Cafe Playa."

"Of course, Your Highness."

Davis almost laughed at Hiram's barely concealed note of censure then hung up the telephone. He straightened his tie and smiled to himself. He couldn't wait to see Abbie's face.

Davis had prepared for the usual chaos that accompanied his unannounced arrival at a restaurant downtown, but he was not prepared for Abbie's look of surprise and annoyance when he walked through the restaurant toward her table. Davis ignored the maître d' buzzing in his ear about a more suitable table inside the restaurant. Davis also ignored Hiram whispering in his handheld radio to other guards, and he ignored the other uniformed guards who moved to positions in the front of the cafe. He could ignore everything, because he had never seen Abbie look more beautiful, more gorgeous, more breathtaking than she did at that moment.

The sun emphasized the copper highlights in her hair and the sparkle in her warm eyes. She wore a gray suit, tailored to emphasize her full breasts and long legs, which seemed to highlight the recklessness that he knew coursed through her veins. He knew no woman could look more alluring and sexy in a suit than she did at that moment.

"Your Highness," Josie greeted, jumping to her feet.

Davis was disappointed with himself for not noticing

that Josie also sat at the table with Abbie. He now accepted that Abbie was driving him insane. She had controlled him since he first saw her in her apartment building. He had wanted to tear her clothes from her body since the first moment he saw her, and he decided that he would do exactly that this day.

"Please sit, Josie," Davis said, forcing a smile.

"Your Highness," the maître d' said, while pulling a chair from another table for Davis. Davis nodded his appreciation and sat in the chair.

"What are you doing here, Davis?" Abbie said, being the only one at the table who didn't smile at his presence. Josie visibly flinched at Abbie's question, while the nosy maître d' gasped in shock.

"I was hungry," Davis responded calmly, meeting her direct gaze.

"You were hungry, and you came to the same restaurant that we did? With all the restaurants in Juhatu, I find that hard to believe," Abbie flatly responded.

"Abbie," Josie warned, through clenched teeth.

Davis tried not to laugh as the wide-eyed maître d' placed a hand over his heart. Davis had never enjoyed eating on the beach, but he had a feeling he would with Abbie.

"You've been keeping tabs on me," Abbie accused, leaning across the table to glare at him. Davis clenched the chair arms as her suit jacket moved slightly to reveal a fraction of cleavage. He couldn't believe his body reacted to this brief glimpse when he, without so much as batting an eyelash, had been seduced by the world's most beautiful women.

As her eyes flashed, Davis realized that he was only fooling himself. He wanted her. He wanted her now. He couldn't pretend to sit across the table from her and eat lunch like he wasn't on the verge of grabbing her and taking her on the table.

He ignored the stares of the maître d', Josie, and the other diners at the cafe. He leaned across the table, until his lips were mere inches from hers. He was unable to draw his attention from her full lips. With his last shred of common sense, since he couldn't kiss her in full public view, he forced himself to meet her gaze. He smiled, a slow, lazy smile, because he could see the confusion in her eyes. He liked Abbie confused because it meant she wasn't rejecting him.

Davis shot a quick glance at the maître d', which sent him scurrying back into the restaurant. He then looked at Josie and raised a questioning eyebrow. Josie's face flushed red and she mumbled something incomprehensible about making a telephone call and practically ran into the restaurant. He took it as a good sign when Abbie didn't protest.

He turned back to Abbie, who still watched him. He smiled, the smile he somehow knew that he reserved just for her, then he whispered, "Come with me, Abbie."

She licked her lips then glanced around the cafe at all the curious diners. Davis saw the embarrassment flush her face. She finally looked back at him.

"Do you think that's wise, Davis?" she finally said. "We were on the front page of the newspaper. Sophia must feel—"

"Come with me, Abbie," he repeated softly. "I want to show you my country."

"You don't have to entertain me, Davis."

"I know."

Her eyes narrowed with suspicion, and Davis found himself praying that she would agree. He couldn't explain it to himself, much less her, but he wanted to see his country through her eyes. He wanted to fall in love with the place that had seemed like a burden for so long, until he had seen the wonder on her face.

She finally nodded then asked reluctantly, "What exactly did you have in mind?"

"The most beautiful spot on this island." He held out his hand and, without hesitation, Abbie placed her hand in his.

Davis hadn't been exaggerating about the most beautiful spot on Juhatu. With an entourage of cars filled with guards following them, Davis weaved his black convertible Porsche up the mountain, through the thick trees and bushes of the forest. Abbie was awed by the scenery alongside the road until Davis parked the car at the top of the mountain.

She laughed in disbelief as she stood from the car. From the top of the mountain, she could see the entire eastern side of the island. The palace, the various houses and buildings, the crystal-blue ocean that crashed on the gleaming white sands. The wind swirled around her and she wrapped her arms around her body and looked at Davis, who stood beside her. What surprised her was the realization that she wouldn't want to share this view with anyone other than him.

"Thank you, Davis."

"It's beautiful, isn't it?"

"Living in Los Angeles, I forget there are places like this on earth." She impulsively twirled around in circles, her arms spread out, trying to embrace everything about the moment. She stopped and continued to laugh as she met Davis's smiling eyes. "Each time I think I couldn't love Juhatu more, I find somewhere else to prove me wrong. How could you ever want to leave this place?"

"Abbie, I am sorry about the newspaper, about the way they portrayed you."

Abbie was surprised by his apology and shook her head.

"I should apologize to you. If I hadn't forced you to stay at that party, there never would have been a picture—"

"I was at that party because I wanted to be," Davis interrupted her, with a strange smile. "You didn't force me to do anything."

Abbie swallowed the sudden lump in her throat and asked uncertainly, "Did you get in a lot of trouble with your parents?"

Davis snorted in disbelief and said, "Lowell arranged it so I'd have meetings all day until dinner. By dinner, with all the dignitaries at the table, my parents will have forgotten about the newspaper photo. Just like they seemed to already have forgotten that I was kidnapped by Kevin Munji. I still haven't had one private conversation with my parents since we've been back. My mother is too busy meeting with socialites around the city, and any pleasantries with my father were brushed aside after the first few minutes of our three-hour-long meeting."

She placed a hand on his arm, needing to comfort him. "I saw the concern on your mother's face at the airport. She cares about you, Davis; maybe she doesn't know how to express it."

Davis abruptly laughed, but the laugh didn't reach his eyes. He shook his head as he said, "I know how lucky I am, Abbie. I'm heir to the tenth largest fortune in the world. I have nothing to complain about, but I always seem to complain around you."

"Everyone deserves to complain once in a while," she said softly then took his hands and forced herself to smile for his sake. "Let's explore these woods."

"In this?" He stared at his suit.

"Don't tell me you're suddenly afraid to get dirty."

Davis smiled and immediately took off his jacket and tie. "We have to leave in an hour to make it to the palace for dinner, and you're definitely going to dinner tonight."

Abbie didn't care about anything as insignificant as food or dinner when she held Davis's hand and the wind blew through her hair. She pulled him through the trees, deeper into the forest, not caring that the guards yelled at them. Davis laughed and propelled her faster through the trees.

The two jumped over a fallen tree branch. Abbie heard the guards running behind them, still yelling. She laughed with Davis as they practically slid down a steep slope of the mountain. She held on to his hand tighter as her feet slipped on the unsteady ground. They could easily have fallen and broken something, but all Abbie could do was laugh and hold on to his hand. She never wanted to release him and for the next hour she vowed to pretend she didn't have to.

Davis pulled her beneath the shade of a tree and Abbie laughed as the precious glow of freedom raced through her body. Davis placed a warning finger against her lips signaling silence as they both heard the crash of leaves and the guards, who ran by, looking for them. Once the last man raced by, Abbie laughed. The laughter died from her lips when she noticed the look in Davis's eyes. She recognized the passion that made his chest heave, and by the way his finger still on her lip began to stroke her.

"Maybe we shouldn't have run away from the guards," Abbie whispered, to take her mind off the sensations that instantly raced through her body. "It's still not safe. Kevin has not been caught."

"I couldn't stop thinking about you. I probably looked like an unprepared child this morning, but all I could think about was you."

His soft words caressed her neck and she tried not to respond. "What kind of flowers are those?" she asked helplessly, pointing to bushes in the distance. She didn't care, but she needed distance between them before she forgot her vows to herself.

Davis grinned, a smile that made her knees tremble and her heart race faster. "Juhatu is known as a lover's paradise. I never realized why until this very moment."

"Davis, don't—"

He abruptly moved away from her and the passion in his eyes was quickly replaced by teasing. "Do you mind getting wet?"

Abbie regarded him suspiciously. "What do you mean?"

Davis grinned as he took her hand again. "We've jumped into the water in our clothes before. This time will be no different."

Abbie didn't question but followed him as he ran through the forest. She felt like a ten-year-old tomboy, running behind a boy, glad to be free from the constraints of society. But, she was not ten and Davis was definitely not like any boy she knew when she was younger. None of the boys she had known ever made her feel so beautiful, so alive.

Abbie screamed as Davis nearly ran off a cliff. She stumbled on the loose gravel then clung to Davis to prevent him from falling over the side of the mountain into the ocean, twenty feet below. She stared at the rolling waves of the crystal-blue waters that lazily lapped onto a sandy white beach a half mile away.

"Are you crazy?" Abbie demanded, grabbing Davis's arm.

Davis grinned. "I haven't done this since I was a kid. Come with me, Abbie."

Abbie glanced at the long jump and shook her head. "We could be killed."

"I guarantee we won't be killed. Juhatuans have been jumping off this cliff for centuries. No one's ever been hurt . . . although, there was that one American woman who drowned."

Abbie saw the teasing gleam in his eyes just before he

began to laugh. She hit him on the arm. "That's not funny. Come on, let's find your security detail before they send a warrant out for me. They probably think I've kidnapped you."

Davis stepped closer to her and Abbie wanted to take a step away from him, but somehow he had maneuvered her so she had her back to the water. She decided to figure out how he did it later, but at this moment she crossed her arms over her chest and stood her ground.

"And if you kidnapped me," Davis said in a soft voice. "What would you do?"

"I don't know the etiquette for kidnapping. Am I supposed to torture you?" She tried to keep her voice light, but failed miserably as his scent swirled in the wind around her.

"You're torturing me right now, Abbie," he whispered, his breath massaging her right ear.

"Your Highness," came the cry behind them.

Davis glanced over his shoulder then turned to Abbie, with a wild gleam in his eyes. "We have to jump now, Abbie."

Abbie saw the troop of guards race across the distance that separated them. Then she glanced at Davis's pleading expression. She realized that she wasn't frightened, especially with Davis by her side. She placed her hand in his and Davis beamed, then they both jumped off the side of the mountain.

Abbie actually thought she was flying through the air with Davis, and that thought didn't seem ridiculous or impossible. She heard Davis's own laughter match her screams as they sailed through the air. She slammed into the water with a shock that almost took her breath away. Like bullets, the two plunged deep into the water. Abbie almost lost her bearing until she felt Davis tugging on her hand, leading her toward the surface.

They broke the surface, both gasping for air in between

laughs. Davis yelled in excitement and slammed his fist into the water.

"That was better than any ride," he exclaimed.

"And only slightly more dangerous," she said, grinning. She heard several men's voices calling from above and they both looked up to see all ten of the security detail staring over the edge at them. Davis started laughing as he listened to the men yelling in French, then he shouted something in reply. The men abruptly turned and ran toward the cars.

"What happened?" Abbie asked, as they paddled toward the deserted beach through the lazy waves.

"They asked if they should jump in after me. I told them to get in their cars and find us."

"Would they really have jumped in after you?"

"It's their job. They'd follow me through a tornado." Davis shook his head and turned on his back to stroke. "I've always wondered what type of man would willingly give his life for my family or me. What if they don't like us? What if we don't deserve it?"

"Then I suppose you have to live in a way that makes you deserving of their sacrifice," she mused.

"I never thought of that," Davis said, quietly. He was silent as they swam towards the shore.

The two stumbled onto the beach and Abbie laughed in embarrassment as her suit plastered against her body. She started to make a joke, until she met Davis's eyes. He wasn't smiling or in the same teasing mood as before. In fact, she would almost be scared of him—almost—if she hadn't been feeling the same desire herself. She took a hesitant step away from him, but Davis wrapped his arms around her waist and pulled her against his body. She could feel his hard length pressing through both their clothes and practically touching her.

Abbie tried to protest but his mouth covered hers and she could only wrap her arms around his neck and hold on as the sensations rocked her body. His tongue snaked between her lips and teased her own tongue into combat. Abbie tried to pull him even closer. His hands moved in between them and reached for the buttons on the front of her suit jacket.

Abbie abruptly pulled away from him. "We can't."

"Why?" Davis murmured, placing kisses on her neck.

"Your men will be here soon."

"Not for at least forty-five minutes. We could do a lot in forty-five minutes."

"What about your fiancée?" Davis stiffened but didn't release her. Abbie had tried not to think about Sophia or allow the thought of the woman to ruin her day but it was too late.

"Arranged marriages still exist, Abbie. I don't love her and she doesn't love me. How many times do I have to tell you this?"

"That doesn't make this right."

"I'm not married to her yet." Davis framed her face with his hands. "Everything I do is scrutinized, including who I spend time with. Right now, I'm not obligated to Sophia or anyone else. If I want to be with you, then I can. People can talk, but it doesn't matter to me."

Although it physically pained her, Abbie stepped from his hands. "It matters to me, Davis. I can't do this."

"Can't do what?" he asked coldly.

"I can't be so casual about us, like you can. I'm starting to care for you, Davis, and if I want to be a whole person after I leave this island, I can't continue to act like this is some fling."

"A fling?"

"Would you stop repeating everything I say?" she screamed.

"I thought we had a perfect arrangement. No strings attached."

"I thought I could handle that, but I can't."

"Are you saying that you're in love with me?" he asked, as if the idea was impossible.

Abbie refused to meet his eyes and, instead, she walked to the water's edge. She finally answered. "I'm not saying that. I'm just saying I can't treat making love like a frivolous act. It means more to me than that. I mean more to me than how I've been treating myself."

"Are you saying that I treat you like less than a person?"

Anger flushed her face and she turned to face him. "Are you deliberately trying to misinterpret everything I say?"

Davis clenched his jaw and said, "I'm trying to understand you. One second you're all over me and the next second you're the ice princess. What am I supposed to think?"

"Are you calling me a tease?" Davis shrugged and didn't answer her. Abbie took a step closer to him, her hands clenched at her sides. "You better watch yourself, Your Highness. None of your bodyguards are around to protect you."

Davis laughed bitterly then shook his head. "I've been meaning to tell you about your unrealistic sense of security in yourself."

"Don't talk to me," Abbie grumbled then walked a few feet away from him and sat in the sand, hoping he didn't touch her, because she would lose all of her resolve.

Davis muttered a curse then walked to a tree and sat in the shade, ignoring her.

FIFTEEN

Davis could barely remain in his seat at the dinner table as the usual mindless conversation lulled around him. He sat at his father's right, trying to maintain a sense of his respectability. But, he didn't know how he could with Abbie sitting at the other end of the table, looking beautiful and completely unattainable. There were ten people between them at the long dining table and Davis could still smell her scent, taste her lips. He knew what she said at the beach made sense for both of them but he didn't want to believe it. He didn't want her to think of protecting herself from him because she was leaving Juhatu.

"Davis." Davis heard the impatient tone in his mother's voice as she sat across the table and knew she had called him several times. "Are you feeling well, dear?"

"I'm fine, Mother."

"It must have been that afternoon swim that's distracted him," Henry muttered then met Davis's eyes. Davis groaned. He should have known his father would find out what happened.

"What afternoon swim?" Sophia asked from her position next to him. He had been able to avoid Sophia all day, but judging from her possessive hand on his arm throughout dinner, Davis knew she had seen the newspaper. "You went swimming and didn't tell me, Your Highness?"

"There's been a misunderstanding, Lady Sophia," Davis muttered.

"Did you or did you not go swimming this afternoon, Davis?" Lissette asked curiously.

Davis shot his father an angry look then said to his mother, "I had an impromptu swim."

"What does that mean?" Lissette pressed.

"Impromptu swim, that's a new one," Colonel Phillipe Montage said, joining their conversation. The man's loud voice carried down the table and Davis cringed in his seat. "What exactly does that mean, Your Highness?"

Davis glanced down the table at Abbie. She stared at her plate, only half-listening to the woman at her side. Davis had made certain she sat near a baroness from Austria because she spoke excellent English. Now he wondered if he made a mistake; the baroness could talk about her prized horses for hours, without any encouragement. Davis wanted to be next to Abbie. He wanted to talk to her and make her smile again.

"Davis?" His father said as he nudged his leg underneath the table. "The colonel asked you a question."

"I felt like swimming and that's what I did," Davis said impatiently. The colonel's smile disappeared and he nodded, obviously uncomfortable. His mother shot him a look of censure. Davis stuffed a forkful of fish into his mouth and prayed for the dinner to end soon.

After dinner, Davis followed his mother into his parents' private sitting room. He should have been downstairs in the library, talking with the other men about politics and economics. He was expected to be there. Davis knew he wouldn't be able to concentrate on anything tonight and was more than grateful when his mother pulled him aside.

Lissette closed the door and motioned for Davis to sit in a plush leather chair. "Would you like anything to drink, dear?"

"I'm fine, Mother."

Lissette fixed herself a drink from the mini bar in the corner of the room. "You barely looked at Sophia all during dinner. I think you hurt her feelings."

"As if anything could dent Sophia's confidence," Davis muttered.

Lissette stared at him then sat on the couch. "I'll admit Sophia has her faults, but she'll make a good wife and an excellent queen for Juhatu. You must remember that's what's really important."

"This is about the picture in the newspaper, isn't it?" Davis asked, not bothering to hide his glance at his watch.

Lissette's smile didn't change as she said coolly, "This is about Sophia and your obligations toward her. She deserves more, Davis."

"I agreed to marry her, didn't I?"

Lissette took a sip of her drink then asked, "Did you know your father and I weren't a love match?"

"No, I didn't."

"He treated me almost the same way you treat Sophia—like an after thought. But, we grew to love each other. We had a wonderful son, hundreds of memories, and years of love. I couldn't imagine my life with any other man. It just takes time, Davis. Give Sophia a chance, you may actually like her."

Davis stood to his feet, barely restraining his anger. "I have agreed to marry Sophia. I have agreed to devote my life to this country. Don't tell me who I will love and how to love her."

Lissette's eyes grew wide and she stood, laying a hand on his arm. "Are you that unhappy with the choice of Sophia as a bride?"

Davis sighed and ran a hand over his eyes. "I'm tired, Mother. I'm going to sleep."

"Is it that American woman?" Lissette asked coldly.

"Abbie?" Davis asked uncertainly. "She has nothing to do with this."

"I see the way you look at her, Davis. It's almost embarrassing. Then with the picture in the newspaper, it almost looked like you're in love with her—"

"The only reason I'm standing across from you right now is because of that American woman. She saved my life twice. I owe her for that, you and Father owe her for that."

Lissette relented. "You're right, Davis. I plan to meet with her tomorrow and express my gratitude."

Davis forced himself to smile and kiss his mother's forehead. "That's a good idea. Good night."

"Davis, if you do not want to marry Lady Sophia, you do not have to."

Davis met his mother's eyes and saw the compassion and regret. "And what would Father say?"

"Who cares?" Lissette said dismissively, causing Davis to laugh. She smiled and took his hands. "I know you and your father don't often see eye to eye, but he only wants your happiness. We both do. I can't even begin to explain how worried and afraid we were when you left for America without telling anyone and then Hiram told us you . . ." Her voice trailed off as tears filled her eyes. She moved from his hands and delicately wiped her eyes.

Davis was too shocked to speak. He had never seen his mother cry. Lissette laughed through her tears and said, "I vowed not to discuss this subject and embarrass us both. Go to sleep, darling, and think about what I said."

Davis nodded dumbly and walked from the room. He stood on the other side of the door for a moment, listening to his mother's sobs.

"Hello?" Abbie breathed a sigh of relief upon hearing her older brother's familiar voice. After enduring the torturous dinner, Abbie excused herself from after-dinner drinks and ran to her room to call her family. She hunkered in the bed in pajamas and knew she had to talk to her brother.

"Hi, Joe."

"Abbie!" Her brother's excited voice made her smile. "Where are you now? We tried the number to that hotel in St. Moritz and the clerk didn't know who you were."

"I'm in Juhatu, a small island near Monaco. It's a long story, but I'm coming home in two days."

"You thought by calling me at work, I'd be too busy to press you for details but you're out of luck. What the hell is going on?" Joe demanded.

"I told you I needed to get away from work. I needed a vacation."

"I heard you when you said that, but I don't believe you. I didn't want to say anything in front of Mom and Dad, but I know you're lying. Either tell me what's going on or I'll fly to Jubumba or wherever the hell you are and find out for myself."

"Joe, there's no conspiracy or covert plot. I just wanted to enjoy a little time by myself," Abbie lied through her teeth.

"Is that why your passport's still at home?"

Abbie rolled her eyes in exasperation. Joe was a lawyer but always considered himself a detective, even when they were children. She should have known he wouldn't simply accept her strange explanation.

"You searched my apartment?" She pretended indignation.

"Damn right I did," Joe said firmly. "My sister calls me from across the world with some strange story about an impulsive vacation when she's never done an impulsive thing in her life. What kind of big brother would I be if I didn't look into your story? And Adam was tearing your place apart with me."

"I should have you both arrested for trespassing," she muttered.

"Too bad you're not here to do just that," Joe responded cheerfully. "Are you going to tell me what's going on? Because I'm going to tell you what I think. Chris told us you had dinner with some man named Davis who worked at your building. I think he sweet-talked you into going to some tropical paradise then left and stiffed you with the bill. If that is the case, Adam and I have already vowed to hunt the worthless weasel down, rip out his lungs, and tie them around his neck."

Abbie laughed at her brother's defense of her and how far from the truth he was. "Thanks for the thought, Joe, but you couldn't be more wrong."

"I know that Davis character is involved. I swear, Abbie, if he's hurt you in any way, I'll kill him."

"I am perfectly capable of taking care of myself. Don't treat me like a child."

Joe sighed the same sound Abbie had heard often over the years. "We'll discuss this when you get home, which better be in forty-eight hours or I'm on the next flight to this place. Understand?"

"Yes, Joe," Abbie said rolling her eyes.

"Are you sure everything's fine?" he asked seriously. "You don't sound well, sis. Do you want me to fly out just for the hell of it? We could go drinking, eat all day long, swim. We could have fun. I bet I could even talk Adam into taking a few days. Just the three of us."

Tears filled her eyes at how sweet her brothers were. "I'm ready to come home. When I get there, I'll tell you and Adam all my adventures."

"It's a deal. I love you, sis. Take care of yourself." Abbie hung up the phone before she bawled and worried Joe even more.

She wiped away her tears just as she heard the door knob of the patio door jiggle. Her breath stuck in her throat as she imagined Kevin Munji and his men bursting into her room to take her hostage. Abbie searched the room for a weapon and finally grabbed a pillow from the bed. She stood to the side of the patio doors and held her breath.

The patio door slowly opened and a man stepped into the room, shadowed by the night. Abbie screamed and swung her pillow at him. She recognized Davis's familiar grunt as the pillow whacked him squarely on the back. He turned to her and laughed, which made her angry because she wanted to laugh herself.

"What are you doing?"

"I thought you were—What are you doing? How'd you even get in here?"

"One of my cousins would stay in this room when he visited every summer. We started sneaking out and going to the bars in town when we were fifteen. The stones on the walls make excellent foot holds."

"You could fall and break your neck."

"You thought I was a burglar, didn't you?" Davis guessed then glanced at the pillow she held defensively against her chest. "What did you possibly expect to do with that?"

"This." Abbie swung the pillow at his head and Davis easily avoided the blow. He wrapped his arms around her, trapping her own arms at her side, and fell onto the bed. Abbie stared into his eyes as he hovered over her and she knew she was powerless to resist him.

"What do you think you're doing?" she demanded as he slowly unbuttoned her pajama top with one hand while the other hand held her arms above her head.

"Did you really think I would leave you alone while you're under my roof, in the room next door to mine?"

He nipped her lips and Abbie moaned in pleasure. Her arms went completely slack as his mouth traveled to her neck. She felt his tongue travel down the column then move over her chest and between her breasts. Her pajama top hung open at her sides, revealing her breasts, and Davis suckled at a nipple. His hand released her and she immediately buried her fingers in his hair, pulling his head closer to her breast.

"I don't want you to do this," she murmured as his wicked tongue traveled to the other breast.

"Tell me that again in thirty seconds and I'll stop," he said, the warm breath from his mouth cooling the wetness on her breast. One of his hands trailed down her stomach to reach inside the pajama shorts. Abbie nearly burst as he touched her sensitive center.

She managed to grab his hand and she felt the tremors race through his suddenly still body. She saw the frightened look in his eyes and immediately kissed him before he thought she wanted him to stop. Davis grinned and kissed her again, swirling his tongue in her mouth, touching every sensitive spot. His hands gently massaged her breasts, squeezing them and molding them into his hands.

"What about protection?" Abbie finally uttered her question before she forgot how to speak.

Davis grinned and pulled a condom package from his pants' pocket. He captured her lips in a blinding kiss then whispered, "I aim to please."

Abbie ran her hands over his shoulders and began to unbutton his shirt. "You certainly were sure of yourself," she murmured.

Davis didn't respond as his mouth was too busy running down her stomach and lower. Abbie didn't think any more as his tongue and hands pushed her over the edge and she lost herself in his world of love.

SIXTEEN

Slivers of morning sunlight spread across the bed, waking Davis. He groaned as he glanced at his watch. He would have to run to his room if he wanted to avoid any of the servants and the gossip that would invariably follow if someone saw him leave Abbie's room this early in the morning. Hiram had told him the palace guard was already filled with rumors of his feelings toward Abbie after their swim. Davis didn't know whom he was protecting, himself or Sophia or Abbie. He definitely knew Sophia played no part in his decision, but he certainly didn't want her to hurt Abbie in any way with her particularly vicious tongue.

Davis glanced at Abbie as he slid from the bed. Even asleep, she seduced him. His hands moved, as if with a mind of their own, and slowly stroked her hair. She smiled and snuggled deeper under the covers. Davis smiled and lightly kissed her forehead. He didn't want her to leave and that admission made him leave the room before he woke her up to make love again. Even after two hours of lovemaking last night, Davis was more than ready to have her again.

Instead of climbing the wall like a love struck teenager, Davis slipped on his clothes and walked out of the room. Fortunately, he didn't see anyone in the hallway and slipped into his room, closing the door. Davis turned and looked directly at his father. With a disappointed expression on his face, Henry sat on the couch in his pajamas and robe.

Davis sighed then rubbed his face. "Good morning, Father."

"Where have you been, Davis?" Henry's voice was low and dangerous.

"I'm twenty-eight years old. Where I spend the night is not your concern or business."

"Don't you dare get snide with me," Henry warned, rising to his feet. "You were with that American woman, weren't you?"

"I am tired, Father. You can resume yelling at me in a few hours." He sat on the couch and placed his feet on the end table. He *was* tired. He didn't sleep at all the night before with Abbie constantly nibbling on his ear.

"Where else could you be except with her? Wasn't that picture in the newspaper enough embarrassment, without someone reporting you sneaking from her room? We know American women have no morals or ethics, but I expect more from the future king of Juhatu."

"Morals?" Davis couldn't resist the bitter laugh that escaped his throat. "The wife you hand-picked for me has tried every trick in the book to seduce me before the all-important wedding night. I can't even begin to tell you how many times I shuttled her out of this room unclothed in the middle of the night. I left for America partly to get away from her."

Confusion crossed Henry's face. "I thought you approved of Sophia."

"Does it matter?"

"It matters a great deal. There were four other ladies you could have chosen from—"

Davis jumped to his feet angrily. "Four other women on a pre-approved, pre-selected list. That summarizes my whole life. Everything is weeded out and presented to me for my royal choice. The thought alone makes me laugh. You and mother wanted me to marry Sophia and that's who I picked."

"Davis—"

"I came back, didn't I? No one knew where I was when I escaped from Kevin Munji, but I came back. Isn't that enough?"

All the fight left Henry's face and he sat on a chair. "What's wrong with you, son? Why are you so unhappy?"

Davis shook his head, annoyed with himself for yelling at his father. "I don't know."

"You don't have to get married right away. It's true no Beriyia male has been unmarried on his twenty-ninth birthday but that doesn't matter."

"Everything matters in this family," Davis said tiredly. "I can't break tradition."

"It would be wrong, Davis."

"I know."

"I'll tell Lowell to cancel your appointments for today. Maybe you just need to relax. You have been through a difficult experience these past few months. Living on your own in America, being kidnapped, maybe you're feeling the effects of that."

"I'm fine. In a few days, I'll be back to my old submissive, bland self."

"You're not bland or submissive, Davis," Henry protested. "What has this woman done to you?"

Davis laughed, knowing he sounded like a crazy person. "I wish I knew. It's like I feel her inside me. Even when she's nowhere to be seen, I can taste her lips and feel her hair on my arm. She makes me feel like a man. Not a prince but a real man, who's not ashamed to have these needs inside of him, the need to have another human being hold him." Davis turned from his father and stared out the window at the ocean view that usually calmed him, but now only made him think of Abbie. "She's in my heart, and I don't know how to get her out."

"You must know you can never marry her," Henry said softly. "You are pledged to Sophia and Juhatu law says—"

"I know what the law says," Davis interrupted firmly then reined in his emotions before his father sent him to the palace doctor. "I'm fine, Father. I have a meeting with the arts council in an hour. I must prepare."

Henry stood, obviously still shocked by his son's admission. "I understand. Is there anything I can do for you?"

Davis smiled at his father. "You've done enough." Henry seemed uncertain what to do next then simply walked out of the room.

Davis walked into his private bathroom and once more tried to erase the image of Abbie from his mind.

Abbie was bored out of her mind. She wanted to go to town and window shop but she heard one of the servants say Davis had gone to town. Abbie certainly didn't want to run into him after last night or this morning. Once more, he had left her alone in bed, without even a goodbye kiss. She refused to allow him to hurt her any more. The next time he crawled into her window she would push him out of it.

Abbie wandered the palace from one room to the next, conversing with the servants who seemed to know everything about Juhatu history. They regaled her with stories of Davis's ancestors and their courage and intelligence. Abbie could almost see where Davis got his own personality from. She wished she could meet his parents but judging from their reaction at the dinner table, Abbie had the distinct impression that they didn't approve of her. Not that she blamed them.

She finally wandered into the gym and was awed by the massive structure. There were floor mats spread throughout the room, along with various weight machines, bicycles, treadmills. It would have rivaled the most advanced health club in America. She noticed the gleaming fencing equipment hung on one wall and immediately walked to it.

Abbie had taken fencing lessons in college, at first as a class for an extra unit then because she loved the sport. After graduating, she barely had time to exercise every day much less register for fencing lessons but she did miss them very much, no matter how much fun her brothers had made of her. Abbie picked up a foil, the lightest weight of the weapons, and sliced the air. She smiled from the familiar sound of steel running through air then picked out a white mask and vest.

She lunged and advanced on her pretend partner, who surprisingly resembled the beautiful Lady Sophia. Abbie hadn't said more than three words to the woman and hated her with a passion.

"You fence?" came a male voice.

Abbie whirled around to find a man dressed in the all-white outfit of a fencer prepared for a match. The protective mask covered his face. "I try," she replied.

"My partner had a pressing family engagement. Maybe you could fill in for him."

"I'd love to."

The man lifted his helmet and Abbie gritted her teeth as King Henry stared back at her. "I don't believe we've met. I'm Henry, Davis's father."

"Your Majesty." She quickly took off the mask. "I didn't know it was you."

Henry smiled and picked a foil from the wall. "Then that means we shall not fence?"

Abbie met the challenge in his eyes and she smiled. "I would never dream of letting Your Majesty down."

Henry closed his mask and walked to the strip and said, "Then *en garde.*"

Abbie prayed for strength and replaced her mask. She ran to stand across from him on the strip and the two began. The high-pitched clash of steel immediately made Abbie smile and forget her opponent's identity.

Abbie could tell Henry was a superb fencer. He was quick, athletic, and intelligent, like his son. She was also proud of herself for holding her own as her lessons came back to her with ease. The longer they fenced, the more comfortable she felt with King Henry. He encouraged her attacks, gently critiqued her stance and posture, and praised her good moves.

"You do well, Abbie," Henry said after an hour, as she nearly pressed the blunted tip of the foil into his chest for the second time.

"I took lessons in college."

"Why did you stop?"

"No time, and my brothers told me black people don't fence." Abbie immediately realized her mistake and allowed her guard to slip. Henry placed the blunted tip of his sword at her neck. "I'm sorry, Your Majesty. In America, things are different."

Henry laughed through his mask and his gasps for air. "Of course, they are. I just don't understand why everything is based on color in your country. A man's color is not as important as his brain, his honor, his duty."

"I would agree with you if I didn't live in America." He took off his mask and Abbie followed suit. Sweat gleamed on his face and Abbie could feel the sweat bead on her forehead.

"We shall break?" Henry asked, motioning toward the tables on the terrace outside the gym. "The staff brings me lunch here every Sunday. I would be most honored if you would join me."

"I don't want to intrude—"

"The woman who saved my son's life could never intrude."

Abbie felt her face grow more hot as she followed him into the cool air outside. A slight man dressed in a dark suit was setting a plate of sandwiches on the table and a pitcher of water.

"Another plate and glass, Jean," Henry said to the young man who quickly scurried away. He held out a chair for Abbie who nervously sat down. She didn't know how to talk with a king. She didn't know how to eat in front of a king.

"Don't be nervous, Abbie. I am only a man and I must eat too."

Abbie laughed as he sat next to her. "How do you and your son do it? Read my mind like that."

"Years of practice and training. We must be able to look at a person and immediately tell who they are, what they will do when pressed."

"Forgive me for saying so but someone got through the system. I've been thinking about the kidnapping and how it happened after the palace found out Davis was in America. There has to be a leak somewhere."

Henry nodded, his pleasant smile gone. "I have concluded the same." Jean reappeared with an extra plate of sandwiches and a glass. He poured their water then disappeared, leaving the two with the gentle cool breeze and the colorful, lush view of the garden across the emerald green lawn.

"What's being done to locate Kevin Munji?"

Henry looked at her with one raised eyebrow and Abbie realized she had broken another unspoken rule. Henry suddenly smiled. "Many things, Abbie. You do not have to worry about your safety. This is the safest place you could be."

"I'm not worried about me. What would Kevin want with me? I'm worried about Davis. He gets these ideas and does things that aren't necessarily safe."

Henry rolled his eyes in exasperation, the universal sign of a frustrated father. "Believe me, I know."

"I talked with Kevin Munji and he's obsessed with Davis. The longer Kevin is out there, the more I worry about Davis."

"Davis will be safe if he follows the rules of the palace guard. They were embarrassed and frightened when he disappeared without a trace. Two months and no one knew where he was. They won't allow anything to happen again."

"If you say so," Abbie said unconvinced.

"You must be a very strong woman to stare down Kevin Munji."

"I really had no choice in the matter. He decided I was going to have dinner with him and then he started ranting. I just sat there."

"I read my son's debriefing. From his description of the events, I wouldn't think just sitting, as you phrase it, is something you do well."

Abbie didn't withhold her laughter when she saw Henry's smile. "Davis did become very frustrated with me."

"And enamored."

Abbie stared at the king open-mouthed. "Excuse me?"

"Do you love my son, Abbie?"

"I . . . excuse me, Your Majesty, but I don't think that's any of your business."

Henry's warm smile never left his face. "Anything that interferes with the smooth operation of my kingdom is my business. Believe it or not, you have."

"My feelings for Davis are my own," Abbie said carefully, meeting the older man's eyes. "We shared a unique experience that will probably affect us both for the rest of our lives. I suspect because of that I have feelings for Davis. He's come to mean a lot to me, but I would never do anything to jeopardize Juhatu or Davis's position here.

And neither would he. Whatever feelings Davis imagines for me are nothing compared to what he feels for the throne and the traditions of this country. Does that answer your question?"

Henry placed a hand on her arm. "The last thing on earth I meant to do was offend you."

"I just want to go home," she said, as tears filled her eyes. "I don't belong here."

"Is that why you didn't come to dinner that night?" he asked, with an understanding smile.

"I apologize, Your Majesty. I never thought about how impolite it would seem. I just needed to get away from the palace."

"I know how intimidating all this—the palace, the guards, my wife—seems, but you should have been at dinner." His gentle censure made more tears fall. She could have handled the king screaming, but not his soft and almost loving tone. "When you're a part of the royal family, you're not allowed to 'get away' like others. We must attend dinners and banquets. We must smile for the cameras. We must lower our voices when we want to yell. No matter how unfair it is, we're held to a higher standard. No more missed dinners, Abbie."

Abbie nodded in understanding, not certain why he took the time to explain the breach in protocol to her. Henry wiped a fallen tear from her cheek then smiled at her.

"At one point in my life, I wished for a daughter. I hope she would have been as sweet and passionate as you."

Abbie smiled through her tears then used the napkin to wipe them away. "I'm so sorry. I normally don't cry. When I was younger, my brothers would beat me up if they saw me crying."

"Well, your brothers aren't here." Henry pulled her into his arms and Abbie cried on his solid chest.

An hour later after finishing their lunch and laughing over Abbie's childhood and Henry's embarrassing moments with international royalty, Abbie and Henry walked arm in arm into the palace. They entered the lounge to find Lissette and Sophia sitting at a small table. Abbie immediately stopped in her tracks until Henry placed a discreet hand on the small of her back and propelled her farther into the room.

"Your Majesty," Sophia greeted brightly then barely managed to hide a sneer as she glared at Abbie. "Abigail."

"Good afternoon, Sophia, Your Majesty," Abbie greeted.

"Abbie gave me quite a work-out fencing," Henry said pointedly in English. "It was the most fun I've had fencing in years."

"That's lovely, dear," Lissette responded in English then patted the empty chair next to her. "Abbie, please join us for afternoon tea."

"I'm sweaty and—"

"I insist," Lissette interrupted with a smile of steel.

"When the Queen insists, you don't have a choice," Henry said while holding out the chair for her. Abbie glared at him then sat in the chair with as much grace as she could manage with a sweaty shirt sticking to her back and rumpled slacks. "I have a meeting in an hour. Good day, ladies." He gently nudged Abbie in encouragement then walked from the room.

"Am I to understand that you fence, Abigail?" Sophia asked sweetly.

"I took lessons in college."

"How interesting," Sophia said as she stirred her tea. "But, then I guess women are different in the United States. You all have a different set of morals in the colonies, don't you?"

"Is the United States still considered the colonies to

some people? That's such a quaint attitude," Abbie replied sweetly.

"Ladies," Lissette said lightly.

"I apologize, Your Majesty," Abbie said sincerely. "I'm just anxious to return home and it's made me irritable."

"And where exactly is home for you, Abigail?" Sophia asked.

"Los Angeles."

"I've been there a few times," Lissette said. "I found it overcrowded, smoggy, and too loud. How do you ever manage to live there?"

"I agree, Your Majesty. The people all look fake. There's either fake hair color, fake breasts, or fake attitudes. Here, in Europe, we see through all those things in an instant," Sophia said cheerfully then smiled sweetly as she asked, "One sugar lump or two, Abigail?"

Abbie swallowed the ball in her throat as Lissette smiled proudly at Sophia. She hadn't imagined it. Queen Lissette didn't like her. Abbie imagined the queen probably knew about the night she spent with Davis and thought she was a woman with no morals. Abbie almost couldn't blame either woman for hating her.

"One lump, Sophia. Thank you."

"Abigail, what exactly do you do at *Los Angeles Fashion Magazine*?"

"How did you know where I work?"

Lissette laughed, obviously amused by her question. "What kind of fools do you take us for, Abigail? Before anyone enters the palace, especially an overnight guest, there is a thorough background check. I probably know more about you than your parents do."

Abbie bit her lower lip to attempt for once in her life not to say exactly what was on her mind. "I'm an assistant editor. I do a little bit of everything. I edit articles, find new contributors to the magazines, help find photographers and models. Sometimes, I help the accountant with our records. We're a small magazine, so everyone helps where they're needed."

"So, you like money?" Sophia asked bluntly. Abbie clenched the napkin in her lap and looked to the queen to come to her defense.

Lissette smiled, without a hint of warmth in her eyes. "Excuse Sophia, dear, we just don't get many non-titled women in this house. Not that there's anything wrong with that. You are American, after all."

Abbie nodded for no apparent reason, concentrating on the vase arrangement on a nearby table to refrain from crying. "I've never before felt like I should apologize for being American," she finally said in a quiet voice, staring at the queen. Lissette met her eyes briefly then quickly looked away.

"We all have our faults that we can't change," Sophia said sweetly then handed the cup of tea to Abbie. Abbie reached for the cup and the next thing she knew, hot tea spilled all over her white pants. Abbie flinched in pain at the scalding liquid and jumped from her seat as Sophia profusely apologized.

"I'm so sorry, Abigail," Sophia cried, as a tear actually glistened in one eye. Abbie glared at her as she used a napkin to try to wipe the liquid from her now damp pants.

"Are you all right, Abigail?" Lissette asked truly concerned.

"I need to go change," Abbie muttered, throwing the wet napkin on the table.

"I am so clumsy," Sophia said dramatically. "I truly apologize. You must send me the bill for those pants. They couldn't have cost more than thirty dollars, right?"

"Actually, I wouldn't know how much they cost since Davis bought them for me," Abbie said, looking the woman squarely in the eye. Sophia's eyes narrowed and her chest heaved with quiet indignation.

"In that case, Sophia, I'm sure Davis doesn't want your money," Lissette said quickly.

"I need to change. If you'll both excuse me." Abbie walked from the room, as fast as possible without running. She leaned against the wall at the top of the stairs. She couldn't believe she had allowed Sophia to grate her nerves. Abbie took a deep breath then ran toward her room.

SEVENTEEN

Davis sat in his office in the palace, half listening to Lowell read an economic analysis but mostly staring out the window. He wanted to find Abbie and run off the cliff again. Except this time he didn't plan on swimming to shore. He wanted to find a deserted island and make love every night for the next year. Somehow, he still didn't think that would rid him of his insane urge to have Abbie around him, every hour of every day.

Davis twirled a pen in his fingers then noticed the quiet in the room. He glanced at Lowell, who stared at him expectantly.

"I also have a full calendar that I must attend to, Prince Davis. If you'd rather stare out the window, we can try this later."

"I'm sorry, Lowell," Davis said. "What were you saying? I need to go to Paris to talk to the president about modifications to the trade agreement."

"That particular item I said about half an hour ago," Lowell said with barely restrained irritation. "Something is obviously on your mind."

"Tell Michel to arrange my flight and accommodations for Paris for next week."

"I spoke with your father this morning and he's very concerned about you."

"I am fine, Lowell." Davis saw a whirl of movement on

the ground below and Davis glanced out the window to see Abbie walk across the hallway windows that faced his office window. She wore a white terry-cloth robe and Davis knew she wore a bathing suit underneath since she walked toward the Olympic-size pool in the back of the palace. He smiled to himself as he felt the sudden desire to swim, along with the adolescent fantasy of seeing Abbie in a bathing suit. "Actually, I do have a headache. Could you have Michel reschedule my two o'clock appointment with Monsieur Richald?"

"I'll inform him on my way out the door." It took Lowell several seconds to gather his papers and briefcase in his arms. He stood and Davis hurriedly escorted him out. Davis opened the door and Lowell said, without looking at him, "Have a good swim, Your Highness."

Davis opened his mouth to speak then just laughed. "Thanks, Lowell."

"Just be careful. Remember, she leaves tomorrow for home. And her home is not yours." Davis didn't smile as Lowell walked from the room.

Davis found her sitting in the Jacuzzi, her eyes closed, as the bubbles soared around her shoulders. He didn't know what was wrong but something was. He could tell from the tight lines around her mouth and the flush on her cheeks. Davis immediately pulled a lounge chair next to the Jacuzzi and sat in it. Abbie opened her eyes at the sound of the chair legs scraping the deck. Water splashed onto his shoes as she sat up and glared at him.

"What are you doing?"

"I wanted to see you in your bathing suit," Davis replied truthfully.

Abbie shook her head but he could see a small smile tug on her lips. "Well, you saw, now you can leave."

"After seeing you in a bathing suit, do you really think I could leave?"

She stopped smiling and stood from the Jacuzzi. For a

brief second, Davis watched the water sluice off her gorgeous body and the almost sinful blue bikini. His pants instantly became uncomfortably tight. He was partially grateful when she wrapped the robe around herself and quickly tied the knot.

"I just wanted to swim, Davis. Can I, at least, do that in peace?" She sat in the deck chair next to his with a tired sigh.

Davis pulled his chair next to hers. "What's wrong?"

"Nothing that won't change as soon as I go home."

He tried not to react to the panic that filled his heart when he thought of her leaving him, although he unconsciously gripped the arm rests. "Did someone hurt you? Did someone say something to hurt you?"

"Why, Davis? What are you doing to do? Are you going to ride to the rescue and defend my honor?"

"Yes."

"Why do I doubt that?" she said dryly. "You sneak from my bed in the middle of the night because you're too ashamed to be with me in front of your people. Why should I believe that you'd do anything to help me?"

"That's not true, Abbie," Davis protested. "I'm not ashamed to be with you."

"Whatever, Davis." She stood but he quickly jumped to his feet and grabbed her arm.

"I'm sick of you walking away from me when we're having a conversation. Something obviously upset you. Tell me what or who it was, and I'll take care of it."

"And I'm sick of you manhandling me," Abbie screamed, yanking her arm from his grip. Davis was completely confused when tears brimmed in her eyes. "At least, be man enough about it and admit you're only using me for sex. If you would just admit that, I think I could feel a little better about myself, because then I could hate you without any guilt."

"Hate me?" Davis tried to understand her rambling.

He knew he wouldn't be able to when she was in this mood but he did know that he had to tell her the confusing feelings in his heart. He had to tell her that he loved her. "I don't want you to hate me, Abbie, and what we have is not just sex."

"Stop lying to me."

"I'm not. In fact, I think—"

"Don't you dare say it," she choked out through the tears streaming down her face. She wiped the tears away with the sleeve of her robe. "I hope you're happy now that you made me cry."

"I didn't want to make you cry. Abbie, let's start this entire conversation over, please."

"If you care anything about me, you won't touch me, and you'll never contact me again."

"Abbie, I haven't understood one word in this entire conversation. What did you do today?" Davis could handle her anger but he couldn't handle her tears and the sadness.

"I just saw the truth and how foolish I've been. It's like I met you and every brain cell in my head disappeared."

"Abbie, wait—"

"Good-bye, Davis." She ran into the palace, slamming the door behind her. Davis fell back into the chair, completely confused and hurt.

Abbie stormed into her room. The tears streamed down her face and her hands shook as she moved to the telephone. She couldn't wait until the next morning. She didn't care if she had to fly to Belgium then to Russia to arrive home, as long as she could leave this island and Davis. Abbie picked up the telephone just as there was a knock on the door.

Abbie slammed the phone down and crossed the room

to open the door. Edward walked into the room, with an apologetic smile.

"Edward," she muttered then raked a hand through her hair. "Can you take me to the airport?"

"The airport? I came to invite you to tour our downtown."

"I'm leaving."

"The flight for New York doesn't leave until tomorrow morning. The only flight still available is the one to Monaco."

"Could I catch a flight home from Monaco?"

"Not directly. A flight leaves for France every two hours. Are you sure you want to leave right now? You'll only be—"

"I can't stay on this island one more second." Abbie felt more tears threatening to spill over. "Please, Edward."

"I'll have to inform Prince Davis—"

"No," Abbie said louder than she intended. "At least, not until my plane is gone. I . . . I need to get home. It's a family emergency."

"I need to make a few phone calls and arrange for the U.S. State Department to have your travel documents in Monaco. I can have the car ready in twenty minutes."

Abbie smiled and impulsively threw her arms around his neck. "Thank you, Edward." Edward blushed then quickly walked from the room.

Abbie ran to the telephone and dialed her older brother's telephone number. She knew Joe would wire her money without too many intrusive questions while Adam would have interrogated her until she broke down and told him everything.

"Hello," came her brother's groggy voice. Abbie groaned as she glanced at the clock. She forgot it was 4:30 in the morning in Los Angeles. Joe was not a pleasant person to wake up in the morning.

"Joe, it's Abbie. I need your help."

"Abbie," Joe murmured confused. She heard the bed sheets shift as he probably moved to turn on the lamp on his night table. "Abbie, what's wrong? Are you okay?"

"I need money, Joe."

"How much?"

"Enough to get back home. I'll pay you back as soon as I get home."

"You know I don't care about the money," Joe said. "Are you okay, Abbie?"

"No questions, Joe, that's why I called you and not Mom and Dad or Adam. Just please wire it as soon as possible and don't tell them."

"How about I meet you at Heathrow airport?"

Abbie rolled her eyes and wiped tears away. "That doesn't make sense. You'll take an eight-hour flight to meet me then turn back around to take an eight-hour flight back home? Just wire the money."

"Okay, Abbie."

Abbie sighed with relief and sank into the couch. "Thank you."

"I love you, sis. You know I'd do anything for you," Joe responded. Abbie didn't answer because as much as she loved her brother, she wanted to hear those words from someone else.

Half-an-hour later, Abbie followed Edward to the rear entrance of the palace where the car waited. A driver already sat behind the wheel with the engine idling. Abbie took one last look at the palace and silently said goodbye to Davis before she sat in the backseat. Edward slid in next to her, closing the car door. The driver started the car and slowly drove from the palace grounds. Abbie refused to turn and look or cry but she was losing both battles.

"You'll be okay, Abbie," Edward said, patting her knee.

Abbie smiled at him. "I know."

"He's not worth it."

"Who?"

Edward laughed, his hand remaining on her right knee. "Prince Davis. I saw you two arguing at the swimming pool. I know how you feel about him."

Abbie grabbed his hand and pointedly moved it to his own knee. "I appreciate your help, Edward, but if this car ride is going to wind up being a psychiatric evaluation then I'll walk the rest of the way."

"I apologize, Abbie," Edward said.

The car suddenly stopped and Abbie looked out the windows for any signs of the airport. They were in the middle of the forest, which she thought was on the way to the airport, but she distinctly knew the town was in the opposite direction.

"Why are we stopping?" she asked, feeling a tingle of fear in the pit of her spine.

The car door suddenly opened and Kevin Munji slid into the car on the opposite side of her. Abbie immediately tried to climb out the door before he closed it but Edward roughly grabbed her hair and pulled her back inside. Abbie screamed as she felt each individual strand almost being pulled from her head. Kevin slammed the door and the car continued down the road.

"Hello, Abigail," Kevin said with a grin.

"What do you want?" Abbie demanded then winced as Edward abruptly released his hold on her hair.

"What do you think I want?" Kevin asked with the same maniacal smile that haunted her nightmares. "I want Davis. And the only way I get to him is through you. Too bad you'll be killed in the process."

"If you hurt Davis—"

"Why do you still defend him?" Kevin asked, truly confused. "You're a bright, intelligent woman and because you refuse to see the Stone Prince for exactly what he is, you will die. Think about that, Abbie."

Abbie turned to Edward, hoping to plead with him. His stony expression didn't give her much hope. "Edward, you have to know this is wrong."

"What the Beriyias have done to Kevin and this country is wrong," Edward retorted.

"You know the Beriyias had nothing to do with Kevin's mother's death."

"Be quiet, Abbie," Kevin snapped.

"Edward—"

"Abbie, don't make me knock you unconscious." Kevin's voice was surprisingly neutral, which made Abbie realize he was serious.

Abbie stared straight ahead, refusing to look at either man.

EIGHTEEN

Davis stood at the window in his office, once more unseeing. He twirled the pen in his fingers, trying to think of where Abbie could have gone. He sat in her room for two hours, after he got his thoughts together, and she still hadn't arrived. He finally sent Hiram and several of the guards to search downtown for her. Davis didn't care who knew he was searching for her or why. He was worried. Kevin Munji was still loose. Davis knew that wasn't the real reason why he was worried. He worried because he figured he may never see Abbie again and she would never know how he felt about her. That he loved her.

Davis turned as the door opened. Hiram limped into the office with the help of a cane. Davis didn't like the expression on his face. "We can't find her, Your Highness."

Davis threw the pen across the room in a burst of anger. Hiram didn't flinch. "Monboit is not a big city. She is here. Why haven't your men found her?"

"We searched everywhere downtown, Your Highness," Hiram responded calmly. "I didn't say we searched all Juhatu but she is not downtown."

Davis tried to calm down but he couldn't. He slammed his fists on the desk. "I want that woman found, Hiram!" All the fight left him and he sank into his chair. "What if Kevin has her?"

"We don't know that, but I can tell you what we do know." Davis nodded and Hiram continued, "Two hours ago, from the telephone in her room, she called a Joseph Barnes in Pasadena, California. We assume he is a family member."

"Her older brother," Davis interjected.

"She must have asked him for money because there is five thousand dollars waiting at the wire office downtown in her name."

"She hasn't picked it up?"

"Not yet," Hiram said, shaking his head. "There was also a reservation in Abbie's name for the 5:00 flight to Monaco."

"She was going to leave?"

"She's missed the 5:00 flight to Monaco, but there is still a 7:00 flight she could possibly plan to take."

"Kevin has her," Davis sighed, tears filling his eyes. He bit his lower lip to restrain the tears but it didn't work. "I swear to you, Hiram, if he hurts her in any way, I'll kill him with my bare hands."

"There's no need to worry until we know for certain, Your Highness."

Davis turned the chair to stare at the setting sun. He imagined Abbie alone with Kevin. The thought made him want howl at the moon, to scour every inch of the island until he found her or Kevin.

"I just can't help but think if I had never seen her, never talked to her, she'd be home perfectly safe in her apartment in Los Angeles. But, because I'm selfish and arrogant that bastard has her. This is all my fault."

"What's your fault, Davis?" Henry stood in the doorway with Lowell standing beside him.

Davis wanted to run to his father like he did when he was a child and tell him to make everything better. Instead, he remained in his seat and clenched his hands into fists.

"Nothing, Your Highness." Hiram replied.

"Abbie is missing," Davis told his father.

Henry immediately was concerned. "What do you mean?"

"We can't find her anywhere. Her brother wired money to her and she hasn't picked it up. She also didn't arrive for her plane reservation to Monaco," Hiram explained.

"She was going to leave without saying good-bye?" Henry looked more crushed than Davis felt.

"We don't know that for certain," Hiram said tiredly.

"I agree with Hiram. We're drawing conclusions from illogical assumptions," Lowell, the voice of reason, said. "For all we know, Abbie took another flight, received money from a different source. She is a capable woman, as Prince Davis knows better than any of us. Until it's proven differently, I don't think we should worry."

"I'm still calling the chief of police," Henry said, reaching for the telephone on the desk just as it rang.

Davis quickly picked up the telephone, his heart rapidly pounding against his chest. "Abbie?"

"Are you missing something, Davis?" Davis's blood chilled as he recognized Kevin's voice on the other end of the telephone.

"Kevin, don't make things worse. Return Abbie to the palace." Davis saw Hiram immediately grab a cellular phone from his suit jacket pocket and dial a number.

"Worse for whom, Davis?"

"What do you want?"

"I want you to suffer like I have. I want you to know what it's like to lose someone you love, someone who can't be replaced no matter how hard you try to forget and move on with your life."

Davis nearly broke the phone receiver in half as the anger and helpless frustration raced through his body. "Anything you want, Kevin, I will give it to you." Davis ignored Hiram and Lowell wildly waving their arms for him to stop. "Do you hear me? Everything I own, everything I am is yours, if you just put Abbie on a flight to America. Do you have any idea how much I'm worth?"

Kevin laughed bitterly. "You rich people are all the same. You think money solves everything. I want my parents back."

"Abbie had nothing to do with their deaths." Davis wiped his eyes as a new idea formed in his head. "How about an exchange, Kevin? Me for her?"

"Your Highness," Hiram scolded loudly as Lowell gasped in shock.

"Nice try to keep me on the phone long enough. Too bad it won't work. Say good-bye to Abbie, Davis, make it sweet and touching for all those listening ears."

"Davis?" It was Abbie.

Davis's heart tore into a million pieces as he heard the tremor of fear in Abbie's voice. "Abbie, are you okay—"

Kevin was immediately on the phone. "She's so beautiful, Davis. It's such a waste." The phone line went dead and Davis jumped to his feet and threw the telephone across the room. The phone shattered.

Hiram's cellular phone rang and he immediately answered it. He said into the phone, "I understand, Laurence." Hiram placed the phone back in his jacket pocket. "He wasn't on the phone long enough. We couldn't get a trace."

"Are you insane, Davis?" Henry demanded angrily. "I know you have feelings for this girl but to offer yourself in exchange for her? You have lost your mind."

"I owe that woman my life, and I would give everything I own and more to return her safely to her home," Davis exploded. A tense silence hung in the room.

"We have time to find her, Your Highness. Kevin won't kill her right away," Hiram said quietly.

"He'll want to use her against you. He craves the power she gives him over you," Lowell confirmed.

Davis raked a hand over his eyes, still glaring at his

father. He abruptly turned on his heel and stared out the window. "We have to find her."

"We will." Hiram left the room with Lowell close on his heels.

Davis felt his father standing behind him. "It's getting dark. I wonder where she is. If she has a comfortable place to sleep, if she's warm or scared."

Henry placed a hand on his shoulder and Davis turned into his father's arms. "We'll find her, Davis."

"I love her, Dad."

"I know, son. I know."

For a few seconds, Davis felt everything would turn out fine with the world, then the door opened. He jumped from his father's arms as Lissette walked into the room. She looked surprised by Davis's tears.

"There's such a commotion in the palace, guards running every which way, the servants in disarray. What's happening?"

"Kevin Munji has kidnapped Abbie," Henry said quietly, his hand still on Davis's back.

Lissette placed a hand over her mouth. "That poor girl. What does he want?"

"Nothing," Davis said, choking on the unshed tears. "He just wants to torture me."

"What are we going to do?"

"We're going to tear this island apart until we find her," Davis said firmly. He didn't feel pain anymore, only anger and the desire for revenge. He straightened his tie then met his father's eyes. "When we find him, he's mine.

Henry nodded in understanding.

Davis felt a small sense of accomplishment as various members of the local police and the palace guard assembled in the conference room in the palace. Search parties had been organized and sent out two hours ago. The first reports were discouraging, but at least Davis knew they were doing something. He would've been out there himself if the entire guard hadn't protested the idea and made him promise to stay within the palace.

"We're going to find her, Your Highness," Edward approached Davis as Davis stood on the balcony of the conference room, out of the way of the officers.

"I hope so," Davis replied absently, watching the beehive of activity inside the room.

"It's frightening that an insane lunatic like Kevin Munji could get to her on our own grounds. As captain of the palace guard, I feel responsible. We're here to prevent this exact scenario.

Davis turned his full attention to Edward. "How did you know she was taken on the grounds?"

"That's the theory we came up with," Edward said, shrugging. "Hiram told us not to tell you because it would upset you more."

"Hiram's always looking out for me," Davis said, watching Edward's every move in the darkness of the balcony.

"Get some rest, Your Highness. It will probably be a long night." Edward turned to leave but Davis grabbed his arm and swung him toward the rail. Edward reached for his gun but Davis snatched it from the holster and shoved it under the man's chin. Davis pushed him half off the railing. The only thing that separated Edward from a twenty-five-foot fall to the ground was Davis's hand holding his shirt.

"Where is she, Edward?" Davis demanded through clenched teeth.

"You're obviously tired, Your Highness—"

"I don't buy your act any more," Davis interrupted, digging the gun into Edward's skin. "Hiram has never kept anything from me and he never would. And no one has any idea where or how Abbie was taken. Tell me what you know or you will die."

"You can't kill me," Edward winced. "You're the prince."

"Choose your death, Edward. Head first over this rail or a bullet in your brain."

"Your Highness, what are you doing?" Hiram demanded, running to the rail as fast as his cane would allow. All the men in the room ran to the balcony and froze in shock.

Henry pushed through the crowd and grabbed his son's arm. "Davis, put the gun down."

Davis ignored them all as he stared into Edward's eyes. "You have ten seconds, Edward. How much did he pay you? Is it worth your life?"

"I don't know where he has her," Edward pleaded.

"Your Highness, stop this," Hiram demanded.

"Of course you know, Edward. You'd have to know so you could steer us in the wrong direction. You're wasting Abbie's time."

"He'll have killed her by now," Edward cried, his eyes darting between the ground below and Davis.

"Do you know something, Edward?" Henry asked gently.

Davis pushed him a few inches farther over the rail and Hiram reached for Edward but yielded when Davis shot him a hard glare. He looked back at Edward. "Start talking, Edward."

"He's at the cliffs, the old Munji burial grounds. There's a caretaker's house with a cellar."

Davis released his shirt and Edward began to fall over the railing but Hiram grabbed him. Davis turned to the police officers assembled in front of him. "You heard the man. Let's go." The men ran back into the room, grabbing weapons and maps.

Henry grabbed Davis's arm as he tried to follow the men. "We follow at a safe distance, Davis."

"If that was Mother?"

"Abbie is not the queen or your wife," Henry said gently.

"You'll only get in the way," Hiram said as two police officers handcuffed Edward and led him back into the Palace. "The officers will be so busy trying to protect you, they'll make mistakes."

Davis swallowed the bitterness in his mouth and nodded. "Fine. We'll follow at a safe distance."

"Excuse me, Your Highness," Lowell said from the doorway of the balcony.

"What?" Davis bit out, initially not realizing that Lowell spoke in English. He whirled around to see a tall man with caramel brown skin, brown eyes, black curls and Abbie's straight nose standing next to Lowell. Davis knew without a doubt that this was one of her brothers.

"May I present Mr. Adam Barnes, Abigail's brother," Lowell introduced.

Davis stepped forward, offering his hand, which Adam only stared at. He scanned the faces of the men around him then asked bluntly, "Where's my sister?"

Davis slowly brought his hand to his side and stared blankly at the man. Henry quickly stepped forward. "I'm Henry, a friend of your sister's. I'm afraid she's been kidnapped."

The color drained from Adam's face and he looked blankly at the men for a moment. "What? Kidnapped?"

"It's a rather long, complicated story that we'll be happy to tell you in the car," Henry said smoothly. "We have discovered her location and we have launched a rescue operation."

"Fine," Adam said confused. Henry and Lowell walked out of the room. Davis tried to walk past Adam but he grabbed Davis's shirt. Davis stopped an advancing Hiram with the discreet flick of his hand. "I don't care who the hell you are. If anything has happened to my sister, I'll kill you."

"And I wouldn't blame you," Davis responded sincerely

then said coldly, "You can threaten me more or we can go see if she's safe."

Adam reluctantly released Davis's shirt and mockingly bowed for him to walk first. Davis sighed and walked from the room with Adam close behind.

NINETEEN

Abbie frantically searched the small, cramped room for a weapon, a door pick, anything to escape, which was hard to do in the dark confines. There were no windows, no knob on her side of the door, and the walls were stone and thick. She didn't know how long Kevin had held her or if it was night or day. She didn't know if they were alone or if his men were above. Abbie cursed herself for not seeing through Edward. Her only thought was to escape and warn Davis about Edward before he tried to hurt Davis. Abbie would not allow anyone to hurt Davis, least of all a coward like Edward.

The door at the top of the stairs opened and Kevin filled the doorway. The light from above spilled onto the stairs, and Abbie saw the spaces between the old, wooden stairs. She quickly moved underneath the stairs, crouching in the darkness. She prayed for strength and courage as her legs shook at her idea to escape.

"Abbie, I have dinner," Kevin called temptingly. She heard him pump a chamber in the gun he always carried around her. "Abbie, I know you're down here. There's no use hiding. It's over. Davis is dead. I killed him. I told you I would. Come out so you can see his finger. I took it as a souvenir."

She remained silent, even though tears ran down her cheeks. She refused to believe Kevin had killed Davis. She would know in her heart if anything had happened to Davis. It had to be a trick by Kevin to make her come out of hiding. She moved further into the shadows as Kevin walked down a few steps until he stood right in front of her face. She placed her hands on the step, preparing to grab his ankles and run for her life.

"Abbie! Don't make me find you," Kevin warned. The light from the top of the stairs suddenly went out followed by a loud series of booms. Kevin must have heard them too because he suddenly became very still. He abruptly turned to leave and Abbie grabbed his ankles and pulled. Kevin screamed in surprise as his gun flew in one direction and he rolled down the remaining steps.

Abbie ran from her hiding place, jumping over a dazed Kevin, and took the stairs two at a time. She could see the interior of a house through the door. Just as her hand reached the door, she felt a tug on her ankle and she fell to the steps, her chin hitting the first step hard. Abbie tasted blood and looked over her shoulder to see Kevin holding on to her right ankle. Blood trickled from his nose and the look in his eyes was so demented that Abbie knew he was going to kill her.

She screamed and kicked at his face. She landed a solid kick to his face. He howled in pain and his grip on her ankle loosened. Abbie jumped to her feet and ran into the house. It was small and all the lights were off. She bumped into furniture as she raced to what she hoped and prayed was the front door.

"Abbie!" Kevin thundered. She screamed as the loud sound of a gun exploded in the house and she felt a sharp pain in her right arm. Abbie fell to the ground, her ears ringing from the shot and the searing pain in her arm. She saw the blood from the wound soak the sleeve of her blouse and she placed her other hand on the wound, wincing from the pain of the contact. She gasped as Kevin stood over her, the gun pointed directly at her face. "At least, you'll be getting what you want. The chance to be with your boyfriend forever."

The door suddenly flew open. Abbie screamed in fear as a man dressed in all black with a light coming from the top of his head crouched in the doorway. Kevin raised his gun to the man but fell with two bullets in his forehead before he could scream.

The man in all black crouched over her and asked in French-accented English, "Are you okay, Miss Barnes?"

At his soft words her internal dam broke and Abbie began to cry. The man placed a hand on her arm, applying pressure as she continued to sob. She heard him speak into a radio but she couldn't make out his words or hear him through her own tears.

Paramedics suddenly appeared by her side, cutting off her shirt. Then Abbie thought she was hallucinating when her brother took the hand of her uninjured arm.

"Adam?" she whispered, as a black cloud threatened to overtake her.

"Don't talk, sis. You're going to be fine," Adam said, squeezing her hand.

"It's really you?"

"It's me. Your big, meddling brother." He smoothed her hair from her forehead as the medics continued working on her arm. She felt the sting of a needle and winced. "Here I came thinking we'd get drunk and lie on the beach. You had something more exciting planned for me."

Abbie laughed for her brother's sake then asked, "Is Davis okay?"

"Don't worry about him. Concentrate on you."

She tried to squeeze his hand as hard as possible and managed to open her eyes wider. "Kevin said . . . he said Davis was dead."

"He's not dead, Abbie. He's very much alive and well, at least until I see him again."

Abbie tried to shake her head but her body wasn't co-operating with her. She knew it was the effects from the shot the paramedics gave her. "Don't hurt him, Adam. I love him."

Abbie couldn't control the heaviness in her eyes as the paramedics transferred her to a stretcher. Her brother continued to hold her hand as they wheeled her out of the house. She saw the whirling red lights of the ambulance reflected against the blackness of the sky, the flash of white lights, and her brother's face before she slipped into unconsciousness. The only person she wanted to see was Davis.

Davis raked a hand through his hair as the paramedics wheeled a stretcher from the house. He couldn't see her but he could tell from Adam's concerned expression and the way he hovered over the person that it was Abbie. As soon as the police had taken care of Kevin's three guards, Adam had jumped the barricade and was the third man into the house. When Davis heard the gun shots he tried to follow him but Hiram tackled him to the ground to stop him.

Davis's right shoulder still hurt from the impact of hitting the ground with Hiram's weight on top of him. Davis didn't care about his shoulder. He knew Abbie was hurt and he had to see her. He started across the barricade but his father placed a restraining hand on his arm.

"The press, Davis," Henry reminded him.

Davis looked at the crowd of reporters that stood farther from the house, snapping pictures and talking to the video cameras. All of their cameras were directed at the ambulance and Abbie.

"I have to go to her."

"You can see her in the hospital. You're announcing your engagement to Lady Sophia in three months. If anyone takes a picture of you with Abbie, they'll know who you really want to be with."

Adam climbed into the ambulance and the paramedic closed the door then ran to the front of the ambulance. Davis watched, frustrated and helpless, as the ambulance drove through the traffic toward the downtown hospital.

"Hiram, go with her," Davis said.

"My job is with you—"

"Hiram, go with her. Make sure she leaves Juhatu and safely returns to America. There's no telling who else is connected with Edward or Kevin."

Hiram nodded and turned toward his car. Davis felt the lights of the camera turn to him and he quickly walked toward his own car.

Henry fell into step besides him. "The pain will become less with time—"

"I'm going to Paris in the morning for my meeting with the president. I'll see you in a week." Davis waited until a guard opened the car door then sat and slammed the door shut. Only when he was alone did he sigh with relief that Abbie was alive. He tried to pretend that knowledge would get him through the rest of his life.

Davis waited impatiently at the open front door as attendants carried his luggage to the waiting car. He turned up the collar of his coat as rain drops sprinkled the earth. The night had once been clear but suddenly buckets of rain began to fall. Davis thought it perfectly matched his mood. He didn't have to leave for Paris tonight. He should've been at the hospital, but if he went to the hospital he would never leave Abbie's side and he owed his country more than that. Davis tried to think of one good reason why he shouldn't grab Abbie and live by her side forever but he couldn't. Only the words *duty* and *respon-*

sibility kept flashing in his head, words he'd been hypnotized with since birth.

"Everything's ready, Your Highness," the attendant said, motioning to the car.

"Thank you." Davis had just started for the car when he heard Sophia's voice. He turned and tried not to groan as she ran through the front door and stood under the protection of the porch.

"Davis, are you leaving again? You just returned from your last trip."

"Some things can't be avoided."

"Well, I wish you would have stopped by and said good-bye."

Davis forced a smile and placed a kiss on her forehead. He quickly stepped into the rain because he knew she wouldn't dare wet her expensive clothes to reach for him. He was right because she only stepped farther into the house. "Good-bye, Sophia. I will return in a week."

"And within three months we'll announce our engagement to the world?"

"Nothing's changed," Davis said. "Our families made vows to each other when we were born, and we are pledged to each other. Both of our families will benefit from this union."

Sophia simply stared at him. "I heard about your friend on television. I hope she's all right."

"Dr. Gibbon assures me she is."

"Do you love her, Davis?"

Davis peered through the pouring rain at the guard holding open the car door. He finally looked back at Sophia. "She will not interfere with our engagement or marriage."

Sophia smiled and stepped into the rain for a brief second to kiss his lips. "Have a safe trip." Davis quickly turned and moved into the car. The guard, Paulo, slid into the backseat with him, closing the door. Both men shook the drops of water from their clothes.

"To the airport," Paulo told the driver.

"First, the hospital," Davis said before he lost his courage.

"Your Highness?" Paulo stared at him confused.

"To the hospital," Davis repeated then leaned back in his seat. He had to see Abbie one more time, to see for himself that she was well.

Davis walked through the empty hallway of the hospital, his heels pounding on the linoleum floor. Paulo and two other security guards trailed behind him. Abbie had been placed in a recently completed wing of the hospital to keep away the press and prying eyes. Hiram had personally hand-picked the guards and nurses.

Davis stopped in front of her room and nodded in greeting to the two guards who sat on either side of the door. He took a deep breath then opened the door and walked inside. Hiram sat in a chair in the corner of the room and immediately stood when he saw Davis. Davis glanced at him then stared at Abbie.

She was asleep. He moved to the side of her bed and placed his hand on her soft cheek, memorizing the feel, the texture. Her hair fanned around her and her full lips were pursed in a frown of pain. Her right arm was encased in a white plaster cast that jutted awkwardly from her body. Davis was embarrassed as tears filled his eyes. He had never felt such an overwhelming flood of emotions for one person as he felt for Abbie. He knew he would never feel this again.

"Dr. Gibbon said the bullet grazed a major artery and broke a bone but there was no permanent damage. She'll have to wear a cast a few weeks," Hiram told him in a soft voice.

"Was she awake when you saw her?"

"Yes. She's fine, Davis." Davis met Hiram's eyes over

the bed, noticing the use of his first name. He had told Hiram many times over the years to drop the titles but Hiram always refused. "She was in a little pain, but the doctor gave her a shot for that. She's going to be fine."

"This is all my fault."

"It's not your fault or her fault or, God bless him, even Kevin's fault."

"If I had never met her—"

"Then you'd never know what it's like to truly and deeply love someone else and neither would she."

Davis smiled at Hiram then brushed the hair from Abbie's face. Light from the hallway spilled into the room as the door opened. Davis turned as Adam walked into the room and judging from his expression he wasn't pleased with his sister's new visitor. Adam set the cup of coffee he held on the table.

"I accepted the tree over there because he's here to protect my sister but you have no reason to be here," Adam said then held the door open. "I want you out of this room."

"Excuse me, Mr. Barnes, but you have no idea who this is," Hiram began but Davis held up his hand to stop him.

"You'll be happy to know that I'm leaving town right now." Davis took one last look at Abbie then walked from the room. Adam followed him, taking the time to quietly close the door. Davis gritted his teeth in annoyance. The only reason he didn't have the man thrown off his island was because he was Abbie's brother.

"I still have to talk to you," Adam began. "How dare you place my sister in this position? While she's laying in a hospital, you're gallivanting on your royal horse somewhere else. You could at least have the courtesy to stay around and be here when she opens her eyes."

"I'm confused, Mr. Barnes. Do you want me to stay away from your sister or be here with her?" Davis asked, deliberately sounding snide.

Adam took a step closer to Davis but a pleasant expression remained on his face for the attentive guards standing a few feet away. "I could snap your neck before your guards even took one step to save you."

"But you won't because you're a law enforcement officer."

"I won't because, at the moment, my sister thinks she cares about you. Believe me, she won't suffer from that disease for long."

"I have to catch my flight. Is there some other way you would like to insult me before I leave?"

Adam shook his head in disbelief. "You don't care anything about her, do you? I can't believe my sister is in a hospital with a bullet in her arm over a man like you."

Davis wanted to leave Adam Barnes with that opinion but he couldn't. Some deep part of him wanted the man to understand him. "If I could trade places with her, I would in a second. If I could take her pain and make it mine, I would without question. But, I can't. There's nothing I can do. Your sister told me she never wanted to see me again. She was going to leave this island, leave me, without saying good-bye. I'm just respecting her wishes."

"I don't know exactly what happened between you two and I'm not sure I want to know but I do know if you want a chance with her, you shouldn't leave."

Davis smiled and offered his hand once more. Adam shook it but Davis could see the reluctance on his face. "Take care of her. And don't tell her I came by to see her." He quickly moved down the hallway before he confessed his true feelings to Abbie's brother.

TWENTY

Abbie cursed to herself as the shirt she tried to fold with one hand fell off the hospital bed and onto the ground. She already couldn't wait for the cast to come off and she had only had it on for nine days. Nine long, excruciating days. The only reason she didn't give up and lay back in bed was because the doctor was finally allowing her to fly home. Abbie couldn't wait to be home in Los Angeles. Her family couldn't wait. Every day when her parents called, she had to beg and plead with them not to fly to Juhatu. Having Adam around to badger her about her foolishness was enough.

The door opened and Abbie's heart skipped a beat. She smiled at Hiram, trying not to betray her true feelings. Every time the door opened, she prayed it was Davis to see her. And every time she was disappointed. Many nights Abbie had cried herself to sleep after her brother had turned off the lights.

"I bought some magazines for you to take on the flight," Hiram said, handing her a stack of magazines.

Abbie smiled and hugged him as much as she could with one arm and a heavy cast. Over the past nine days, Hiram had become her friend, like a third brother. He and Adam had become good friends, leaving her in the hospital when Hiram was off duty while they went to bars and parties. Abbie always enjoyed the stories Adam and

Hiram would tell her about their experiences with Juhatu night life.

"Thanks, Hiram. I'm going to miss you."

"I'm going to miss you too," Hiram said with difficulty then quickly cleared his throat as the king and queen walked into the room.

Henry had visited her as much as his busy schedule allowed over the last week while Lissette had kept her distance. Abbie was almost glad she didn't have to try and impress the queen while she lay in a hospital bed. At least now she felt like a human being, with regular clothes and combed hair.

"You're leaving us, Abbie?" Henry said, disappointed, as he held his hands out to her.

"I have to return home at some point, Your Majesty." She embraced him, smelling the familiar scent of Davis. She pulled away from him before tears threatened to render her speechless.

"Lucky for America," he replied, while patting her cheek.

"Is your bag ready?" Hiram asked as he closed it. "I will put it in the car. We are ready to leave whenever you are." He nodded to the king and queen then left the room.

"I'm going to miss this room," Abbie said brightly.

"I know you may not want to for a while, but please keep in touch with me," Henry said softly. "I would very much like to hear from you."

"I will, Your Majesty."

"You promise?"

"Cross my heart and hope to die."

Henry frowned and he shook his head. "Don't ever hope for that."

Abbie laughed and took his hands. "It's an American saying, Your Majesty, nothing more." Henry grinned and hugged her once more then glanced at his wife.

Lissette didn't look at him as she said, "Henry, I would like to talk to Abigail alone. If you'll excuse us."

Henry winked at Abbie then left the room. Abbie didn't look at Lissette as she slipped one arm into her jacket. She frowned as she stared at the other useless sleeve, then she took the jacket off. Finally, she couldn't bear the silence any more and looked at Lissette, who studied her.

"Well, I guess this is good-bye," Abbie said with as much politeness as she could muster.

"I was like Lady Sophia when I was younger," Lissette said. "I guess that's why I like her so much. I wasn't as shallow or as beautiful but I was in love with a prince who couldn't have cared less if I lived or died."

"I never meant to come between Lady Sophia and Davis. I couldn't have even if I had wanted to. To Davis, I was just someone to pass the time with. He's marrying Sophia."

"My husband tells me that you love my son and my son loves you."

"No—"

"Listen to me. He's engaged to Sophia. That was arranged years before when they were first born. He's never questioned that fate until you."

"I didn't mean to—"

"In our kingdom, an official engagement cannot be broken, and a Beriyia has never broken an official engagement. In three months, their engagement shall become official."

"I would never ask Davis to break his engagement to Lady Sophia nor would I expect him to for me."

"Did you ever hear the story of Davis's great-great-great grandfather, Maurice?" Lissette didn't wait for Abbie to answer. "The woman he loved, Daphne, was pledged to another man. Before their official engagement was announced to court, Maurice challenged the other man to a duel to the death for the hand of Daphne. The other man accepted, Daphne's father agreed to abide by the winner, and the duel took place."

Abbie was confused why Lissette would tell her this story but also fascinated. "What happened? Did Maurice win?"

"He lost an arm but he won. He and Daphne were married and they lived happily ever after."

Abbie smiled in spite of her sadness. "That's a wonderful story."

Lissette abruptly hugged Abbie, pressing Abbie's head to her shoulder. Abbie was stunned for a moment then embraced the woman. "We can learn a lot from our ancestors, Abbie." She released her as tears shone in her eyes. "Take care of yourself. I hope I see you again." The queen walked from the room, leaving a trail of expensive perfume.

Abbie barely had time to examine the conversation before her brother walked into the room. He whistled softly, "Royalty sure is beautiful, huh?"

"What?"

"Queen Lissette is a knock-out."

"Right." She zipped her purse and forced a smile for her brother. "Are you ready?"

"Are you?" Abbie nodded but Adam remained doubtful. "I think we should track that bastard down in Paris and make him face you."

"Adam, leave it alone."

"I don't like seeing you this way."

"I was shot nine days ago; I'm not in the best of moods."

"You've been living with these people for too long," Adam muttered. "Are you sure about this, Abbie? I don't want you to regret anything."

"I thought you didn't like him."

"I don't but . . . but, you do."

Abbie laughed and hugged her brother. "Are you actually conceding that I have a mind of my own and I can make my own decisions?"

"You're such a brat," he teased, playfully tousling her hair. "Let's go home before I start sprouting French and wearing Speedos." Adam walked out the room with a shudder.

Abbie laughed at her brother then glanced out the hospital window where the top of the palace was barely visible through the trees. She touched the glass, wishing she touched Davis's face, then grabbed her purse and walked from the room.

Davis sat in his office in the palace and watched the airplane become a small dot in the blue horizon. He didn't know if that was Abbie's plane but he liked to think it was, as he waved good-bye. It was as if his body could feel her departure from the area. The entire room seemed to deflate.

Davis sighed then looked at the paperwork on his desk. There was a knock on the door and Lowell walked inside the room. He seemed surprised to see Davis sitting at the desk.

"Your Highness, when did you return from Paris?"

"This morning. I told Michel not to inform anyone."

"You missed Abbie's departure from the hospital," Lowell sputtered. "You could probably still manage to catch her at the airport—"

"Please arrange a meeting with my father to discuss my meeting with the French president," Davis interrupted, while shuffling the papers on his desk. "Also, make certain the Minister of Finance is there. I think the president and I may have stumbled upon a very profitable exchange for both countries."

"Did you hear me, Your Highness? Abbie is still in

Juhatu. You could still talk to her and clear up any . . . misunderstandings."

Davis pretended to read the papers on his desk, although all the words blurred into Abbie's face in front of him. "Lowell, you are not my therapist nor my doctor. You are the official advisor to my father, not me. Considering your duties, please arrange a meeting with King Henry to discuss my trip to Paris."

Lowell's entire body stiffened. Davis knew he had hurt the older man's feelings. Lowell took his job very seriously and Davis knew he had no right or cause to imply otherwise.

Lowell finally cleared his throat and opened the omnipresent black folder. "The king could meet with you at 2:30 tomorrow in his office."

"Thank you, Lowell." Lowell didn't move and Davis forced himself to look at him, hoping the heaviness in his heart wasn't visible on his face. "Is there anything else?"

"No, Your Highness." Davis heard the bite in Lowell's voice. Lowell sharply turned and left the room, firmly closing the door.

Davis pushed the papers aside and turned in the seat to stare out the window. He sat in his office until the sun went down.

TWENTY-ONE

"Abbie, peel the sweet potatoes," Karin Barnes ordered as she set a full bowl in front of Abbie.

Abbie automatically took the knife from the table and commenced the task. She had been running on auto-pilot for three months, ever since she left Juhatu. She thought she would become better. She thought she wouldn't still think of Davis every day, of his smile, his laugh, his aftershave. And every time Abbie thought she was almost over him, she would see a tree or smell his aftershave on another man, and every vivid memory would rush back to her.

She tried to move on with her life. Her arm still ached at times but the cast was off and she had almost her full range of motion back. She had even gone on two dates since returning home, and she had returned to her job, but she still felt there was a large piece of her missing since she had flown from the gorgeous paradise, Juhatu. Then when Abbie finally felt like she could at least function normally she had gone to the doctor earlier that morning.

The doctor told her the one piece of news Abbie prayed she wouldn't hear. She was pregnant. Abbie's mind still hadn't cleared since she left the doctor's office two hours ago. And the last place she wanted to be was at her parents' house. But, since her disappearance three months ago, her family went slightly insane if she didn't arrive when she said she would. And Abbie knew if she missed their dinner, her entire family would track her down.

"Okay, Abbie, what's wrong?" Karin said tiredly, sitting across the kitchen table from her.

Abbie stared at her mother, surprised. "What makes you think anything's wrong?"

Her mother gracefully brushed black hair from her beautiful brown eyes. If Karin had been in her daughter's position, Abbie knew her mother would've charmed Lissette and intimidated Sophia without even breaking a sweat. Abbie knew if she was more like her mother, she wouldn't be in this predicament. Her mother would've run when Davis told her and none of it would have happened.

"I know my daughter, and I know something's wrong," Karin said. "You've done everything I've asked to make dinner, without once going to the door and yelling for Adam and Joe to come in here and help."

"I feel helpful today," Abbie dismissed lamely.

"Ever since you returned from Juhatu, you've been listless and sad. I know you went through a horrible ordeal with that awful Kevin Munji person chasing you but did something else happen that you haven't told us? Were you hurt in any way, with scars we can't see?"

"I'm fine, Mom. I'm still trying to catch up with my projects from three months ago."

Karin smoothed Abbie's hair from her eyes. "Look at me, honey." Abbie stopped peeling the potatoes and met her mother's eyes. Immediately, tears filled her eyes. Karin sighed and took Abbie in her arms.

"Don't tell Dad, Mom. Please."

"What am I not supposed to tell your father?"

"I'm pregnant."

Karin's hand stilled on Abbie's shoulders as her mouth dropped open in shock. "What?"

"I'm three months pregnant." A loud crash followed her statement and they both turned to see her father standing in the doorway. Pieces of a cup lay shattered on the ground at his feet. Joe and Adam ran into the kitchen from the living room, at the sound of the glass breaking.

"What happened?" Adam asked, concerned.

"You're what?" Floyd Barnes whispered, staring at Abbie.

Abbie and her mother stood and Abbie forced herself not to hide behind her mother's skirts, like she would when she was a child. Although her father had relaxed in his later years, his infamous temper still made her quake in her shoes.

"Daddy, calm down," Abbie warned, seeing the anger swirl in his coffee-brown eyes.

"Who is it?" Floyd demanded angrily. "What is the name of the jerk who did this to you? I'll kill him."

"It's Davis, isn't it?" Adam muttered.

"Who's Davis?" Joe asked, his eyebrows crunched together in anger.

"That prince from Juhatu," Adam answered then glared at Abbie. "You slept with him?"

"I didn't say Davis was the father." Abbie tried to stare the three men down but quickly looked at her shoes as they all glared at her.

"So, all we have to do is fly to this Juhatu place and kill him," Joe said simply then reached for the telephone. "I'll get our tickets right now."

"Good idea, Joe," Floyd complimented seriously.

"Will you three stop behaving like children," Karin said exasperated. "Joe, hang up the phone." Joe reluctantly complied as Karin turned to Abbie with a soft smile. "My baby is going to have a baby and the only thing that matters is what she wants."

"Well, what do you want, Abbie?" Adam asked impatiently. "Please tell us that you want us to kill him."

"She can't have a baby without a father." Floyd dismissed the idea of murder.

"A lot of women do," Joe said, shrugging. "Haven't you heard the latest statistics about single mothers?"

"No daughter of mine is going to be a single parent," Floyd muttered.

"Will you all shut up for two seconds?" Abbie said loudly. The three men looked at her surprised. "I know I've made a lot of mistakes these past few months and I haven't been exactly honest with you all. I haven't been honest with myself. What I'm trying to say is . . . my biggest mistake was leaving Davis without telling him how I feel."

"What are you saying, Abbie?" Joe asked, confused.

"She's saying she wants to go back to Juhatu," Floyd answered quietly.

"Is that true?" Adam asked in disbelief. "You can do so much better, sis."

"Than a prince?" Karin asked, laughing.

"I love Davis. I loved him before I knew who he was or what he was and I'll love him for the rest of my life. If he doesn't love me then I'll learn to deal with it but I have to tell him how I feel."

"He's marrying another woman, Abbie. That should be some indication of how he feels," Adam responded dryly.

"His family wants him to marry her. His country expects him to marry her. He doesn't love her."

"I don't want anyone to hurt you. I don't care who he is," Floyd said, taking her hand.

"I have to do this," Abbie said, silently pleading with her father.

Floyd suddenly smiled and nodded. "Looks like the Barnes family is going to Juhatu."

Abbie felt the sudden horror at the thought of her family running free in Juhatu. "What did you say? The Barnes family?"

"You didn't think I'd allow my pregnant daughter to trot across the globe without her family, did you?" Floyd asked with a secret smile.

Her brothers laughed with the anticipation of her embarrassment and followed their father into the living room to make the plane and hotel reservations. Abbie turned to her mother, who stared at her with a sympathetic expression on her face.

"Mom, stop this before it goes any further," Abbie pleaded, grabbing her arm.

"I can't believe my baby is pregnant," Karin cried as she wrapped her arms around Abbie. Abbie rolled her eyes in exasperation and gasped for air as her mother's arms tightened around her.

Davis stood at the window in his sitting room, staring at the stars. That's all he ever seemed to do besides work. He watched the stars, hoping Abbie was safe and being loved. Davis had picked up the phone too many times to call her and confess his love for her, regardless of whether she wanted to hear it or not. Then he remembered her face when she told him not to speak to her. He remembered his promise to marry Sophia. And he remembered the life ahead of him, full of rules and traditions that would drive Abbie crazy. Davis wanted her to be free. He wanted her to never be ashamed or embarrassed of who she was.

Davis stared at the check in his hands. He would've denied it if anyone asked him but he couldn't bear to throw away Abbie's check. A week after she returned home, she sent him a personal check for the price of her clothes and whatever imagined expenses she thought she owed him. There was no letter or personal note with the check, just an envelope addressed to him and the check inside. Davis had already spent hours staring at her neat handwriting.

His parents walked into the room and Davis quickly stuffed the check into the pocket of his tuxedo jacket. His parents practically glittered in their evening clothes, in preparation for his engagement party. Davis knew he should've been excited or apprehensive as more than two hundred people from around the world and Juhatu gathered in the palace's ballroom. But Davis wasn't excited or nervous. He felt nothing and that's what frightened him the most.

"Mother, you look beautiful," Davis said, kissing her offered cheek.

"And you're not ready," Lissette admonished, eyeing his untied tuxedo tie. She tied it with the practiced ease of a woman who did it often. "The guests are already arriving."

"Sophia is looking for you," Henry said, standing at the window. "She wants to walk in together, in case she forgot to tell anyone on earth about your engagement." Davis glanced at his father as he heard the coldness in his voice. Over the last three months, Davis had noticed his father's pointed disinterest and dislike for Sophia. The harder Sophia tried for him to like her, the more Henry ignored her. Davis would have found it amusing if he cared about anything in life any more.

"Let me look at you," Lissette covered the silence in the room as she brushed imaginary lint off the front of Davis's black tuxedo. "You are a dashing young man."

"Mother, are you becoming sentimental on me?"

"Don't be ridiculous," Lissette responded with a huff of indignation. "We don't want to be too late. I promised Sophia we'd call her before we walked into the ballroom."

"We're going to be presenting a united front with that

girl for the rest of our lives, must we deal with her before then?" Henry suddenly pouted. Davis wanted to laugh at his father's stubborn expression. Henry wasn't a patient man and he obviously found Sophia not worthy of his time.

"Darling, I wish you would try to be nice to Lady Sophia," Lissette said, patting his arm.

"She's so insufferable. I can't believe she'll be part of this family in another four months," Henry muttered then straightened his jacket. "I'm going downstairs. You two can deal with her." He stalked from the room, not sparing a glance at Davis.

"He's just in a bad mood," Lissette dismissed.

"I hear that's going around."

Lissette smiled briefly then caressed his cheek. "Davis . . . you don't have to marry Lady Sophia. There will be embarrassment and hasty explanations but your happiness is more important to me. Your father has become short on patience with you and Sophia because he thought for certain you would have called off the wedding by now."

"I will marry Sophia." Davis noticed his mother's crestfallen expression and was placed in the unfamiliar position of trying to comfort her. "It really won't be that horrible, Mother. Sophia and I will probably never be in the same place for more than a month. We'll have a child immediately then have probably nothing to do with each other."

"That's such a sad existence."

"How can I be sad when we're one of the richest families in the world?"

"Wealth, money, things mean nothing unless you have someone to share them with."

"You are becoming sentimental, Mother."

"Stop taking this so lightheartedly, Davis. We're talking

about the rest of your life, a life that I want you to enjoy, to embrace, to live. I know Abbie—"

"Please don't mention her name," Davis interrupted, turning to the dresser to check his reflection in the mirror. "We should get Sophia before she starts to worry."

"You haven't allowed anyone to mention her name in three months."

"Mother, I can't talk about her. I'm pledged to Sophia and I won't let down this country or you and Father." Davis opened the door and looked expectantly at his mother. "We have a long night ahead of us. There's no use looking to the past."

"You still have two hours to call it off, Davis," Lissette reminded him softly as she walked from the room.

Davis stared after his mother, completely confused. His entire life his parents drilled into him his duties and responsibilities. They made him accept Sophia, invited her to their home, looked after her and now they practically begged him not to marry her. The only woman Davis wanted to marry lived in Los Angeles and she didn't want to marry him.

Davis pulled the check from his pocket and looked at Abbie's writing once more. He tore the check into little pieces and dropped them in the trash can. It was time for him to move on with his life. He took a deep breath and walked from the room.

"This is beautiful," Karin exclaimed as the five stepped from the taxi in front of the palace gates.

Abbie stared at the lit palace with mixed emotions. She thought she would never see the place again, smell the unique ocean air of Juhatu. She realized she felt home. She loved the United States but Davis was here and wherever he was, was where she wanted to be.

"It looks like a party's going on," Adam said as beautifully dressed men and women stood on the second-floor balcony.

"I don't want to dance, I just want to face that miserable coward," Floyd muttered.

Abbie grabbed her father's arm. "You will not embarrass me, Dad. Davis is a good man and I love him."

"You talk to him first, and if things don't go according to plan then I'll talk to him," Floyd threatened.

"Let's just get this over with," Joe murmured, yawning. "We just flew for fifteen hours. I could use a bed."

The family walked toward the front door of the palace and were immediately stopped by armed guards. The guards looked over their casual clothing with disgust.

"You have stumbled to the wrong place," one guard said in English. "The Seville gardens are three miles down the other road."

"How'd he know we were American?" Floyd asked, annoyed.

"I would like to see Prince Davis," Abbie said firmly.

The two guards looked at each other and murmured in French, both expressing looks of incredulity at American behavior. The same guard said dryly, "The prince cannot be disturbed tonight. Maybe tomorrow you can call his assistant and make an appointment."

"I don't think you heard me. I would like to see Prince Davis."

"And he is busy, announcing his engagement to the Lady Sophia," the guard sneered.

Abbie felt her entire world crash to the ground and she glanced at her mother. She could feel her father and brothers tense, as if preparing for a fight.

"Engagement?" Abbie repeated.

"I thought you spoke English. Engagement."

Abbie refused to cry any more over Davis and especially in front of the pompous guard. Even though she had known the engagement was a possibility, the reality made her entire world explode with pain. "Let's go back to the hotel," she told her family. She reflexively placed a hand on her stomach to protect her baby from her own pain. She already loved her baby, which she just now realized. She didn't want her baby to have a father who would be ashamed of him or her.

"We aren't leaving until this young man takes responsibility for his actions," Floyd said stubbornly, crossing his arms over his chest.

"I completely agree, Dad," Joe said. "We'll sue him for every penny he's worth if he refuses to acknowledge Abbie or the baby."

"You won't do anything because I won't allow it," Abbie said, poking her brother in the chest. Joe looked at her, surprised, since she rarely stood up to him. "I don't need anyone in my baby's life who doesn't want to be there. And if legal action is what it takes to make Davis care for him then forget it."

"Abbie, as your attorney—"

"As my brother, let it go," Abbie interrupted then turned to her father. "I'm leaving, Dad. If you have some testosterone thing you need to do then fine, just know your pregnant daughter is going back to the hotel."

"I thought you came here to tell this man you love him," Karin suddenly said.

"He's getting married, Mom," Abbie protested.

"And what does that change?" Karin questioned. "You're not asking him to leave his fiancée, you're telling him how you feel. Besides, from what you said, he doesn't love this woman anyway. He just feels obligated to be with her."

Abbie ignored her brothers, her father, and the two guards who were transfixed by the exchange. "What if he doesn't love me, Mom? What if he looks at me and turns away? I don't think I could handle that."

Karin smiled at Abbie. "You can handle anything, Abbie."

"Abbie?" Abbie turned at the sound of her name. Wearing a black tuxedo, almost as if he were born in it, Lowell, looking bewildered, stood in the doorway. "Abbie, what are you doing here?"

Abbie glanced at her mother who nodded her encouragement. She proudly met Lowell's eyes. "I want to see Davis. I need to talk to him."

"You are aware that this celebration is to announce his engagement to Lady Sophia?"

"I'm aware of that," Abbie said, without flinching.

To her surprise, Lowell beamed at her. "I thought so. Follow me."

"I need to go to the gym," Abbie said.

Lowell gave her a strange look but nodded. "Anything you wish, Abbie." Abbie shot the guard a haughty look then walked between them into the palace. Her family followed, causing stares from the numerous richly dressed guests in the foyer.

TWENTY-TWO

Davis stood on the vaulted platform behind his father's throne and watched the multitude of elegantly dressed people twirl around the platform. He glanced at his watch and his throat constricted and he realized there were only fifteen minutes until his father announced to the world that Davis would marry Sophia. Davis watched couple after happy couple twirl around the dance floor. He had never noticed how many happily married couples there were. Husbands holding their wives, wives staring at their husbands with such love. He watched Sir Francois dance by with his wife, Angelique. Despite all their arguments and differences, the two looked completely in love with each other.

Sophia grabbed his arm, forcing him to meet her excited eyes. "Aren't you excited, Davis?" She practically bubbled from the strapless gold dress she wore. "In only a few minutes, everyone will recognize us as an engaged couple."

Davis stared at her and tried to imagine spending the rest of his life with her. Spending the rest of his days on earth, wishing she were Abbie. Davis suddenly realized how selfish that would be, how unfair to Sophia, who despite her numerous faults deserved someone who would treasure her as much as she believed she should be. "Sophia, we need to talk."

"Afterwards, Davis," she promised with a large smile.

"No, now," Davis said firmly as his father stepped toward the microphone in front of the platform.

"It'll have to wait," Sophia dismissed as she watched his father, with anticipation twinkling in her large hazel eyes.

Davis groaned in frustration then quickly grabbed his father's arm even as the orchestra abruptly stopped playing. "Father, don't," Davis whispered in his father's ear.

Henry looked at him. "What's wrong, son?"

Davis noticed the majority of the guests had turned to the platform as the music stopped. Davis shot the crowd a bright smile then turned his back to them and said in a low voice to his father, "I can't marry that woman."

Henry's eyes bulged and he quickly placed a hand over the microphone. "Explain yourself, Davis Beriyia."

Lissette quickly joined their conference as Sophia watched them with wide eyes. The entire crowd hushed as the three stood near the microphone, talking in hushed tones to one another.

"What's going on?" Lissette asked, with her trademark, polished smile shining for the interested crowd.

"Davis said he can't marry Sophia," Henry hissed, glaring at Davis.

"Why didn't you say this upstairs?" Lissette said through clenched teeth.

"What are you going to do?" Davis asked his father.

"Me?" Henry exclaimed, his eyes wide with shock. "Why do I have to do anything? This is your mess, you clean it up. And I recommend not telling Sophia within ten miles of anyone else."

"I request an audience with the king," came a loud voice from the middle of the guests.

Davis recognized the female voice, the American-accented, mispronounced French words. His heart momentarily stopped beating as he turned to the crowd.

Abbie made her way through the various guests, wearing black pants and a black shirt, and carrying a large medieval sword that he recognized from the display in the gym. She looked beautiful and fierce, like the day in Natillas when she saved him from Tazeh, when she practically dared Tazeh to continue to hurt him. She looked like his warrior queen, who would give him proud sons and proud daughters.

For that exact reason, Davis didn't know whether to run to her or hide. He noticed Adam and two other men and a woman trailed behind her, fortunately with no weapons. When Davis met the cold eyes of the older man who he assumed was Abbie's father, he decided the idea of hiding certainly had its merits.

A few of the palace guards, with frantic looks on their faces, started toward Abbie but Hiram stepped onto the stage and held up his hand. The men stopped and looked at one another in confusion, along with the guests.

"Abbie," Davis's whisper resounded like a cannon in the quiet ballroom.

"I don't remember addressing an invitation to you," Sophia snarled, moving to stand next to Davis.

"She is my guest," Countess Jana Van de Owtis announced from the rear of the room. Davis grinned at Countess Jana as Sophia glared at her.

"I request an audience with the king," Abbie repeated, walking to stand directly in front of the platform.

"What is it, Abbie?" Henry asked confused.

"I challenge the Lady Sophia to a duel for the hand of Prince Davis." A loud din resounded through the ballroom, followed by light sprinkles of laughter and applause. Davis almost laughed himself until he saw the completely serious look in Abbie's eyes. He recognized that look. He almost felt sorry for Sophia.

"Bravo," came Sir Francois's voice from the back of the room.

"Excuse me," Sophia said angrily. "Who do you think you are? I don't know how the women are in America but in Juhatu we leave the fighting to the men."

"Will you sanctify and enforce the results of this duel, Your Majesty?" Abbie only looked at Henry, completely ignoring Davis and the ranting Sophia.

Davis looked at his father and saw his mother nudge the king in his arm. Henry sputtered, "Yes, Abbie. Why not?"

Abbie grinned and Davis felt like his entire life was now worth living. Somehow, Abbie found out about his ancestor, Maurice Beriyia, and the only legal method, in hundreds of years of arranged marriages in Juhatu, to break an engagement.

Henry looked at his son and asked loudly, "That is, if it's all right with you?"

Davis glanced at the rage written across Sophia's face then at the love on Abbie's. If Davis even thought for a second Sophia would harm Abbie, he wouldn't agree to anything. However, what little Davis did know about the Lady Sophia, he knew Sophia would rather run naked through the ballroom then risk breaking a nail by doing any physical activity. Since the possibility of anyone hurting Abbie was not a concern, Davis allowed himself to enjoy the moment.

He looked at Abbie who finally met his eyes. He smiled at the light twinkling in hers. "It depends," Davis said to his father but looked directly at Abbie. "If the challenger loves the prince or not."

"Davis," Sophia screamed, grabbing his arm. Davis didn't look at her. All three hundred guests in the ballroom stared at Abbie, breathlessly anticipating her answer.

"The challenger loves the prince more than she thought it was possible to love another human being," Abbie replied softly, tears forming in her eyes. "The challenger would do anything for him, including make a fool of herself in front of two hundred people. The challenger would live in a strange land for the prince and accept his home as her own. The challenger loves the prince very much."

Davis grinned and walked down the few steps of the stage to stand in front of Abbie. "Then the prince has no objection to the duel," he said softly, meeting her eyes.

"Davis," Sophia screamed louder.

Abbie pointed the sword at Sophia, her face completely serious. She assumed the fighting stance of an expert swordsman, causing murmurs of approval from several men in the crowd. *"En garde,* Sophia."

"I'd think twice about accepting that challenge if I were you," Henry advised Sophia, with a twinkle in his eyes. "I've sparred with the young woman and she's quite good."

Sophia's father, Lord Zidane, stepped to the front of the room, with a helpless expression on his face. Davis did feel sympathy for him. Sophia blamed every misfortune in her life on her father. He accepted the blame then retreated to the family library, to bury himself in his books and brandy. Lord Zidane hesitantly spoke up, causing the entire room in one mass group to shift their attention to him, "Excuse me . . . Your Majesty, please, what is the meaning of this? Can this young woman do this?"

Lissette nodded and answered soberly, "If a challenger comes forth before the announcement of the marriage to court and the king accepts the challenge on behalf of the prince or princess then it must be honored."

Sophia sputtered in outrage then looked to Lissette for help. "This is ridiculous. Davis and I have been pledged to each other since birth."

"Then fight for him, Lady Sophia," Lissette replied simply.

"You people are crazy," Sophia declared through clenched teeth.

Henry's eyes turned hard as he looked at Sophia. "Watch yourself, young lady, and remember who you are and who we are."

Her cheeks burned with anger but Sophia muttered, "Forgive me, Your Majesty." She turned and ran from the room, slamming the door behind her.

Davis didn't see everyone in the room or Abbie's family inch closer to her. He only knew Abbie stood in front of him, the woman his soul cried for, his body cried for, his heart cried for each and every moment he breathed. Without saying a word, he took the sword from her hand and pulled her to him. Their lips met as applause burst throughout the room.

"There's supposed to be music at an engagement party," Henry called into the microphone. The orchestra immediately began to play and slowly the crowd began to dance, laughing and gossiping about the events that had transpired.

Abbie couldn't stop grinning as she stared at Davis. She stroked his face, making absolutely certain this wasn't a dream, that Davis was really with her, holding her like she wanted. She loved Davis and he loved her. She knew that now. All she had to do was look in his eyes and she could feel his love. Davis handed the sword to Hiram, who had no doubt swooped across the room for that purpose, then led Abbie from the ballroom onto the secluded balcony, through the open French doors.

Abbie pulled away from him, keeping her arms around his neck, unable to release him. She caressed his beautiful face in the dimly lit shadows of the balcony as Davis smiled down at her.

"You are the most insane, unorthodox, beautiful woman I've ever known," Davis whispered.

"And don't forget it," she said then glanced back at the ballroom. "I'll have to apologize to Sophia for the rest of my life and I still wouldn't blame her if she didn't forgive me."

"I have a feeling Sophia will be fine." Davis pointed to the balcony across from theirs where Laurence Metrioste, a young member of the palace guard, comforted a distraught Sophia. "Laurence loves her. He has from the beginning."

"Will she give him a chance?" Abbie asked concerned.

Davis laughed at some remembered conversation and shook his head. "You won't have to worry about Sophia, Abbie."

Abbie nodded, turning to him. She took a deep breath then blurted out, "I've missed you, Davis."

"I've been miserable without you," he admitted, which made her heart soar. "I finally realized around the second week after you left that I just can't bear to be without you. I'm not a complete person. I'm not me unless I have you near."

Abbie rained kisses over his face, like she had dreamed about doing every night for the last three months. She abruptly pulled from him and demanded, "What would you have done if I hadn't come here? Would you have married her?"

Davis placed his hand on her face and said softly, "I couldn't spend my life with anyone else but you. I would've come to you. I would've forced you to give us another chance . . . although probably not in as dramatic a fashion as you."

Abbie laughed, her face still flushed from the embarrassing scene in the ballroom. She still couldn't believe she had the strength to lift the heavy sword or to proclaim her love for Davis in front of half the royalty of Europe. "I do have a certain flair, don't I?"

Davis didn't smile but traced her lips as he said softly, "Be my wife, Abigail Barnes."

"I won't make a very good princess."

Davis laughed, looking at the night sky. "I know, Abbie. I'm going to warn my parents as soon as possible."

"And my family is not exactly royal material either."

"Good. Two royal parents are enough."

Abbie wrapped her arms tighter around his neck, loving him more with each second. "In fact, I've already done my first non-traditional break against custom."

"The sword was a little unnecessary," Davis teased.

"Make this my second break against custom."

Davis studied her face and said, "I don't understand."

"I'm pregnant, Davis." She waited for a reaction, for him to be disappointed. Davis looked at her, uncomprehending for several seconds, then he suddenly grinned and lifted her in his arms, twirling her around the balcony. Abbie laughed, spreading her arms wide, believing she could fly through the air, as long as she was with Davis.

"Pregnant?" Davis exclaimed, finally setting her down. "I'm going to be a father? We're going to have a baby?"

"You're not upset?"

"Upset? I'm ecstatic, I'm happy, I'm . . . I love you, Abbie." He pulled her close to him, his lips inches from hers. "I can't wait to share my life with you. With you, your family, my family, and the family that we'll create together, my beautiful princess."

"I can't wait either, Your Highness."

Abbie snuggled in the shelter of his arms. The one place filled with love and warmth, the one place that was meant only for her, forever.

More Sizzling Romance from
Candice Poarch